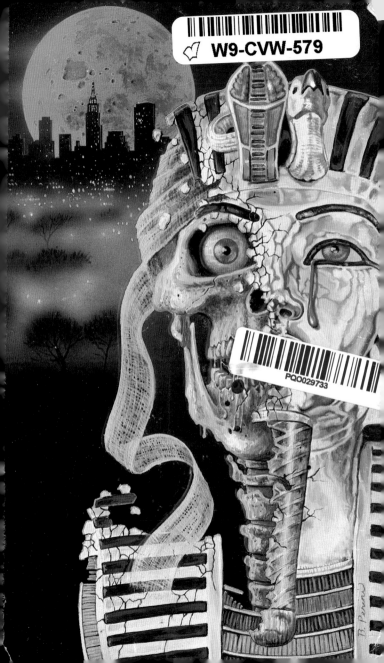

IN THE TOMB OF THE PHAROAH

Swiftly the eclipse moved towards its completion; the priest trembled as he saw the thin sliver of light that still shone in the sky.

Too late. Too late.
Unless. Unless he took the spirit of Menket into himself.

Hurriedly, his hands shaking, he felt for his jugular, digging his fingers in his throat to find the pulse.

He fell to his knees, head back as he watched the eclipse through the rough-edged shaft.

"Now, Isis, spread your wings!" he gasped, and plunged the knife in his throat, twisting it deeper in an agony of desperation.

OBELISK

EHREN M. EHLY

LEISURE BOOKS   NEW YORK CITY

A LEISURE BOOK

Published by

Dorchester Publishing Co., Inc.
6 East 39th Street
New York, NY 10016

Printed in the United States of America

OBELISK

PROLOGUE

Slowly the time drew near.

The aged priest stood quietly in the shadowy darkness of Menket's tomb, ignoring the terrified naked slave kneeling at his feet.

A shaft, cut 20 paces up through rock and shale to the surface, gave him a clear view of the moon in the sky above.

Now, he thought.

He began to chant the spell, carefully intoning the words that would bring a new life to his lord.

"O Osiris, he who is resurrected from the dead. Release the Ka-spirit of Menket, that he may live again, to be nourished by flesh and bone, and drink the eternal waters of the Nile."

His hand tightened on the sacrificial flint knife in anticipation. His stroke must be sure, the young slave's death swift and clean.

"O Isis, extend your wings to fan the Ka-spirit of Menket. Guide him to this new temple made for his shadow, that he may live again, and drink the eternal waters of the Nile."

He could smell the slave's fear. The hot, pungent stink filled the tomb, and he curled his nostrils in disgust, angry at the distraction.

Nothing must interfere with the correct incantation of the spell.

If all went well, *and it must*, at the precise moment of the eclipse, Menket would live again in the flesh of this insignificant youth groveling in the dust. And the youth would gain the high honor of being the shell that housed the new Pharaoh.

For Menket *would* be Pharaoh — of that, the old one was sure. Death had claimed the young prince, but now Menket would cheat Death, and live forever.

The old one stared up at the moon again, half-hidden now by the swift hand of Nut, goddess of the sky, and waited tensely for the total eclipse.

"Come, Menket," he whispered. "Come, Lord, to your earthly house, and like the buried seed of Osiris, sprout and live once more."

He raised his hand, the blade clutched in readiness. With his other hand, he grasped a handful of the slave's coarse hair and pulled back the head, revealing the taut neck that waited for the knife.

"Now, Isis, spread your wings."

With a sudden hoarse scream, the boy jerked back, rolling on the dusty floor, kicking out in terror as the old priest's hand swung down.

"Spawn of Seth!" cursed the priest, powerless to stop the boy's frantic attempt to escape up the shaft.

Swiftly the eclipse moved towards its completion; the priest trembled as he saw the thin sliver of light that still shone in the sky.

Too late. Too late.

Unless. Unless he took the spirit of Menket into himself.

Hurriedly, his hands shaking, he felt for his jugular, digging his fingers in his throat to find the pulse.

He fell to his knees, head back as he watched the eclipse through the rough-edged shaft.

"Now, Isis, spread your wings!" he gasped, and plunged the knife in his throat, twisting it deeper in an agony of desperation.

His lips moved wordlessly as he lay on his back, watching through glazed eyes the distant fragment of sky. High above him, Nut slowly removed her hand from the silver orb.

The moment had passed.

Too late, he thought in anguish, feeling his life ebb away in a widening circle on the dusty floor.

Too late.

ONE

Steve Harrison looked like a quarterback. He had played that position in college, and had also done some boxing, which caused the girls to notice him.

He kept his sandy hair cut short, and his gray eyes had a glint to them—not a cold glint by any means, but as though they meant business.

At first he had liked Egypt, liked his job as an assistant at the Cairo Museum, even if it didn't pay much.

But now he needed money. Fast.

It had been a stroke of luck to find someone he knew over here. But if Bill Evans didn't agree to go along with what he wanted, he'd have to call the whole deal off.

That meant he'd have to find the money someplace else. Unfortunately, there was no place else.

Not here. Not in Cairo. Except in drugs, and he wasn't fool enough to try that.

He shifted restlessly against the soft cushions on the couch, feeling uncomfortable in the overwhelmingly plush apartment.

"C'mon, Bill. What d'you say?" Steve kept his voice quiet. No point in seeming too eager.

Bill Evans, U.S. Cultural Attaché in Cairo, leaned against the balcony's iron rail and surveyed the dusty street below.

"Would you look at this place? Shit City. God, I can't wait to leave!" Bill said.

"You haven't answered my question," Steve said, lighting another cigarette, and slowly drawing the smoke deep into his lungs. "So what do you think? Will you do it?"

"You shouldn't smoke so much," Bill said. "I don't remember you smoking that much at school."

"Goddamnit, Bill. If you won't do it, I know plenty of people who will!" Steve sat hunched forward, staring intently at the short dapper man on the balcony.

"Is that right? Who, for instance?" Bill Evans came back into the room, and helped himself to one of the cigarettes in the box on the table. "No, Steve. There's no one else you can trust, and you know it."

"You'll do it then?"

"Sure, why not? How much will I get?" Steve relaxed, laughing cynically. "How did you ever get to be Cultural Attaché?''

"Quit the bullshit. How much?" Bill asked.

"I figure your end should be a couple of thou."

"Like hell! I'm the one taking all the risk. Do you know what they could do to me if they found out?"

"No one's going to find out," Steve said. "They're not going to search the diplomatic pouch even if they suspect something. And why should they suspect anything? The tomb hasn't even been opened yet. Not officially, anyway." Steve ground out his cigarette in the ashtray on the table, and stood up slowly, stretching his broad frame. "I've got to go. There's a meeting at the museum in ten minutes." He paused at the door, his hand on the knob. "I'm counting on you, Bill."

He walked down the four flights of stairs to the ground floor. No use trying to take the elevator, he thought, remembering the fitful ride on the way up. It was probably ready to break down, like everything else in this poverty-stricken country, he thought.

He felt edgy, excited. This was his chance to get out from under Caldwell's thumb. The son-of-a-bitch loan shark had kept him dangling for too long. Once he had Bill's help, he could call it quits.

He had been a fool to go to someone with underworld connections for a loan, he knew, but he had been in a hole, and

Caldwell had made it seem so easy. But somehow he couldn't get past the interest payments, and Caldwell's bookkeeper was better at multiplying than a pair of rabbits.

When the job offer came from his old professor at Fullerton, he grabbed it. Egypt. Christ, it was the other side of the world.

But not far enough. He should have known that he couldn't escape.

In the end, Caldwell had come up with the answer to his problem: All Steve had to do was ship something to him; something rare, something priceless.

And something very illegal.

He stepped out onto the sidewalk, eyes crinkling in the glaring sun, and a passing Egyptian woman glanced at him quickly, then looked away.

The Cairo Museum sat like an aging dowager on the opposite side of Sharia el Tahrir Square. He walked toward it, crossing over to the sidewalk behind the Nile Hilton. Too bad he didn't have time for a drink, he thought. The cool, dark bar inside the hotel would provide the next best thing to confidence.

But he knew he had better not keep Peterson waiting. He had to be the professor's fair-haired boy, just in case the shit hit the fan when the tomb was officially opened.

The air was dry and hot: the burnished sky shimmered like a searing lid on the city. The noise and smells were overpowering, as the blaring horns blended with stale carbon monoxide and fresh camel dung. A fine gritty dust settled on everything, rising up in clouds as the traffic surged around the busy square.

Damn sand, he thought irritably, the air was thick with it. It must be time for Khamsin weather.

He headed for the museum, ignoring the ragged street urchins who grabbed at his sleeve, peddling necklaces and fake scarabs. Two beggars tagged along with him, whining for the traditional *baksheesh*, but he knew that if he gave them any money, he'd never get rid of them.

Airbrakes squealing, an air-conditioned charter bus pulled up alongside him, disgorging a gaggle of slightly bewildered tourists, and the street Arabs deserted him for the riper prey.

As a middle-aged American woman frantically clutched her handbag to her chest, Steve smiled grimly. Tourists were like lambs being led to slaughter, he thought; they would never know what hit them.

Pushing past the museum guides who clustered around the entrance, he ran quickly up the steps and into the cool, shadowy interior.

"Ah, Steve," Professor Peterson said a few minutes later. "Come in and meet Mr. Farid. This is my assistant, Steve Harrison."

The swarthy Egyptian stood up and proffered his hand. "Welcome, Mr. Harrison. It seems we have quite a discovery before us." He indicated one of the two wooden chairs in front of his desk. "Please make yourself comfortable."

The professor sat back in a well-worn leather easy chair, and beamed at Steve. Despite the heat, the older man managed to look cool, his white hair combed neatly. His clear blue eyes contrasted with ruddy cheeks.

"Mr. Farid is expediting the actual opening of the tomb," Peterson said. "He wants us to start tomorrow."

Tomorrow! Damn, he hadn't thought that permission would be granted this soon. "I expected a delay of a few weeks," he said. He had counted on it, hoping that the Ministry of Antiquities would delay the go-ahead until he had time to get what he wanted. "No offense, Mr. Farid," he added hastily. "But you know how long authorization can take here."

"Yes," the Egyptian said, his dark eyes cold. Sudden anger stiffened his small frame, and to cover his resentment, he toyed with the ivory paper knife on his desk. "I am very familiar with delays of one kind or another," he said.

"Mr. Harrison didn't mean—" The professor's face seemed to get even redder, and he ran an agitated hand through his thick white hair.

"It doesn't matter," Farid said, his full lips parted in a smile that didn't quite reach his eyes. "Your young friend still has much to learn about our ways." He replaced the paper knife neatly on the desk, and folded his slender hands in front of him. "In a couple of months the fast of Ramadan will be observed by your workers at the excavation. You won't get much done then. The Minister thought that it might be better to start right away."

"We're very grateful," the professor said. "Of course, this might not be a major discovery. But then again, it may well prove to be quite important. After all, according to the seal, Menket was a member of the Royal Family." He paused as a servant knocked once at the door and entered carrying a brass tray. Three small cups of Turkish coffee were handed round, then the servant left, closing the door behind him.

"At least it will provide more information on the Fifth Dynasty," Peterson said.

"So. It is agreed then. Tomorrow, *Insha Allah,* we break the seal and enter the tomb," the Egyptian said with a satisfied smile.

"The first living being to enter in over four thousand years," Peterson added. "Right, Steve?"

"Sure," Steve said. *But not if I get there first,* he thought grimly, raising the coffee cup to his lips.

TWO

He had to get to Bill Evans before he left his office at the American Embassy.

Pleading that he had to make arrangements for the early start the next day, Steve ran down the museum steps two at a time, his jacket slung carelessly over one shoulder.

Glancing at his watch, he saw that it was almost five, and a rush of adrenaline caused his heart to pump wildly. He had to get into the tomb tonight; he couldn't risk any delay. After tonight everything would be catalogued, which meant he would have to disappoint Caldwell.

It had to be tonight.

Dodging traffic across Sharia el Tahrir, he pushed past crowds of pedestrians strolling on the cracked and broken sidewalk, and turned into the district known as Garden City.

Sweat eased its way down his spine and under his arms as he crossed over to the U.S. Embassy entrance. Further along the sidewalk a helmeted Egyptian soldier stood in front of the heavy ornamental gates that guarded the embassy. Bringing his rifle to port arms, the soldier barked a question at Steve in Arabic. But Steve ignored him and turned into the side door by the consulate.

The red-headed U.S. Marine guard looked painfully self-conscious in his light-gray civilian suit. No dress blues for Egyptian duty, Steve thought. The Egyptians were very touchy about foreign military uniforms.

"Good afternoon, sir. May I help you?" the Marine asked.

Steve smiled at the "sir." The guard must be all of 20. "I want to see Mr. Evans in the U.S.I.S. building. Is he in?"

"Yes, sir. Would you step inside a moment, and sign the register? I'll just check with his office," he said.

Steve went into the guard room, every nerve tensed. If the kid didn't hurry with the call, Bill Evans might leave, and God only knew where he'd go. The U.S. Cultural Attaché had acquired a reputation for investigating the ancient arts, especially those associated with the most ancient of professions.

"He's sending his secretary down for you, sir."

"Thanks," Steve said, watching the

guard go back to the gate.

What does a kid like that think of Cairo?
he wondered impatiently. *Probably the
same as Bill Evans.*

A big German shepherd came from
behind the main building, ambled over
to the guard room, and lay down with a
grunt.

"Here, boy," the Marine called, and the
dog got up immediately, walking toward
the gate with his master.

The sound of quick footsteps coming
down the pathway alongside the consulate
building caught Steve's attention.

"Mr. Harrison?" The woman looked
cool and efficient. *Trust Bill to have a
good-looking blonde working for him,*
Steve thought. He nodded.

"Mr. Evans is going to a reception tonight at the Egyptian Ministry of Culture.
He said to tell you that he can only spare
you fifteen minutes at most."

The bastard, he thought angrily. *Always
jerking me around.*

He followed the blonde down the pathway, past the white chancery building,
watching her from behind as she walked.
Bill had certainly kept this one under
wraps.

They reached the smaller administration building next to the Marines' quarters,
and one of the two Marines coming down
the front steps of the Palm House gave a
low whistle as the woman went by.

"I wish they wouldn't do that," the blonde said.

I'll bet, thought Steve.

He caught up with the woman and walked beside her into the U.S. Information Service building.

"I've got something to check on in the library," she said. "Remember, only fifteen minutes."

He smiled his tight smile, eyes cold as ice chips, and she turned away.

"What the hell's going on?" Bill Evans asked angrily as Steve walked into his office. "I don't think we should be seen together until everything is taken care of. As far as I'm concerned, this could blow the whole deal."

"Shut up and listen," Steve said. "Something's come up. If we don't act quickly, there won't be any deal to blow." He took out a pack of cigarettes, shaking one out and lighting it nervously. "After tomorrow it will be too late."

The Cultural Attaché got up from behind his desk, and with an angry voice said, "I've been thinking. I can't risk my position here for a measly couple of thou. I had to bust my ass to get where I am today."

Steve gave a disgusted laugh. "Sure you did."

"What's that supposed to mean?"

"It means, asshole, that I know your uncle back in D.C. pulled every string he could reach to get you this job. So don't give me any of that crap about busting your ass. I don't buy it."

"Okay, okay." Evans sat down nervously. "What do you want me to do?"

"We're going to take care of everything tonight. First thing tomorrow they break the seal on the tomb, so it's got to be tonight."

"So what's the problem? Bring the stuff to me tomorrow, and I'll do the rest," Evans said.

"You're not listening to me," Steve said. "We've got to do this together. It's too late to get hold of the workman who is in on it."

"Now wait a minute, Steve! I don't know anything about this kind of thing," Evans protested.

"You don't have to. I'm the expert, remember? All I want you to do is wait by the shaft head, and help me back up when I'm through."

"Forget it. The deal's off," Evans said.

"Wrong. The deal is on. Or I might be tempted to repeat a story I heard about a certain nasty episode that happened last year. The one about the coke deal and the dead Greek?"

The Cultural Attaché's face turned a sickly shade of green. "My God, Steve. You wouldn't do that. I had nothing to do with his death. That would finish me as far as the Ambassador is concerned. The old man is hyper about anything that even smells of dealing," Evans said.

"So I've heard. A story like that could give the old guy hives. Might even cause an international incident. You know how these foreign diplomats love a juicy scandal," Steve said.

"You bastard," Evans said, holding his hands out in front of him. "Look how I'm shaking."

"Well, pull yourself together," Steve said coldly. "Because it's got to be tonight, and you're in, right up to your neck."

THREE

Funny how much clearer the air is once you get out of the city, Steve thought. He had borrowed the professor's old black Citroen. Any guards that might be around would recognize the car and wouldn't bother to investigate if they saw it parked in the vicinity of the tomb. The guards stayed close to the trailer after nightfall anyway. The old guy himself had probably gone to bed early, visions of scarabs dancing in his head, Steve thought.

Bill Evans sat hunched in the passenger seat. "Where are we now?" he asked gloomily.

Steve peered down the two-lane asphalt road. The pale moonlight dappled the sandy ridges on their left, making it difficult for him to distinguish the landmarks so familiar by day. "We're close to Memphis. Should be reaching the turnoff to Saqqara in a few minutes."

They rode in silence for a while, and Steve concentrated on driving. The old Citroen rode low to the ground, shaking roughly over every bump in the uneven blacktop. A thick, bushy stand of palm trees appeared on their right, restlessly moving in the faint desert breeze.

"Almost there," Steve muttered, jerking his head at the sign by the side of the road. "We turn off here."

He swung the car to the left, and Evans grunted irritably. "I hope this damn car makes it," he said. "I'd hate to have to walk back to Cairo."

"It'll make it," Steve said. "Just quit worrying. Save all that nervous energy for when we get there."

They both fell silent again, as they drove farther out into the desert.

"I've figured it out," Evans said slowly. "It's Caldwell, isn't it?"

"What the fuck are you talking about?" Steve glanced at him sharply. *Goddamn. How did he find out? It had to be a good guess.*

"Who are you trying to bullshit?" Evans asked smugly. "This is your old pal Bill, remember?" He laughed softly. "We've heard some complaints about him from the Egyptians. They think he's got more of their junk stashed away than the Cairo Museum."

"Take some advice from your old school pal and say nothing to anyone about Caldwell. Nothing, you hear? He has no sense of humor when it comes to the stuff he collects," Steve said.

"Who's laughing?"

"Just don't get cute," Steve said.

"You've got it all wrong. Why should I blow any whistles? Maybe we can up the ante a little, that's all," Evans said.

"Like how?"

"If he'll pay big bucks for one artifact, what would he pay for two? Or even ten? I can handle the shipping," Evans said.

Steve steered the car around a rock in the center of the road. "Christ! I knew I shouldn't have brought you into this. You always were a greedy bastard." His jaw tightened in anger. "If we take more than one piece, the Egyptians will know. There was a pattern to what the ancient priests put in with a mummy. One object missing might be a mistake, two or more would spell robbery. I don't want them to call the police in." He pulled off the narrow road onto a stretch of sand. "We're here."

They looked up at the largest step pyramid ever built, its uneven exterior clear in the pale moonlight.

"Come on, let's go." Steve climbed out of the car, and a pack of small desert dogs, beige coats gleaming in the moonlight, scattered silently. He opened the trunk and took out a coil of rope. "This way," he said, pointing to a rise.

"How far is it?" Evans asked.

"Not far enough. That's the trouble. I'd feel safer if it weren't so close to the road." Steve pointed out a trailer parked near the head of an excavation. Dim yellow light filtered through the windows. "That's the guard," he said. "We'd better be very careful now. Sound travels for miles out here."

The fine, powderlike sand dragged at their feet, treacherously hiding rough-edged rocks and half-buried slabs that constantly hampered their progress. A jutting ledge tripped Evans. He pitched forward with a muttered oath.

Steve dropped down silently beside him, as the trailer door opened, revealing the guard standing in a shaft of light.

"*Meen henaak?*" The guard's hoarse voice shouted the question out into the night. A reassuring murmur came from somewhere behind him in the trailer, and after a moment he turned back inside, shutting the door.

"There are two of them," Steve whispered. He got to his feet carefully, brushing the dust off the front of his pants. "Come on."

"Was he armed?"

"Yes."

"Two thou isn't enough, Steve," Evans

said. "Not for this. Using the diplomatic pouch for a little private enterprise is one thing. Shit, we all do it. But this is something else. I didn't think that I'd have to be a fucking hero."

"We'll talk about it later," Steve said.

"No. Not later, now," Evans said.

"How much do you want? And for Christsake be quick about it," Steve said.

"Half," Evans said.

Steve stared murderously at him a moment, not saying a word.

"Half, or no go," Evans said stubbornly.

Son of a bitch is blackmailing me, Steve thought, but there was nothing he could do about it now. "Let's just move it," he said. "We don't have all night."

They stumbled on, until suddenly Steve dropped to his knees by a pile of rocks. "What are you stopping here for?" Evans asked.

"This is it," Steve said. "Help me pull aside these rocks. The workman and his sons cleared most of the big ones away."

"I don't get it. Shouldn't there be a door or something?" Evans asked.

"There is. More than two hundred yards away. This is an ancient shaft that leads directly into the main burial chamber. I'll have to climb down."

Evans grinned at him, his teeth flashing in the moonlight. "I have to hand it to you, Steve. What a sweet deal. Everyone is waiting for the big opening tomorrow, and you get in the back way. How did you find out about this?"

"It's my business to find out, remember?" Steve said. "Anyway, I'm paying off the workman who discovered the shaft. It was pure luck, a once in a lifetime shot. The whole thing was covered over with twenty, thirty feet of sand. Maybe more. Sand moves all the time. A sandstorm blew most of it away one night, and he did a little nosing around. He figured out what the storm had uncovered. Knew that the next strong wind could cover it up again. So he marked it with some of these broken rocks." Steve dragged away a thick slab. "You'll have to come up with something for him too, now that you're an equal partner," he added bitterly.

"Why not?" Evans said. "I can afford that now."

They moved the rocks quickly, breathing hard as they worked, until the heavy block covering the shaft head was clear. Grunting with the effort, the two men shifted it away from the opening.

"I'm going down," Steve said. "The sides have rough-cut ledges to provide a foothold, so I guess I'll be able to climb down all right. You be ready with the rope when I want to get back up."

"Have you been inside yet?" Evans asked.

"No," Steve said, looking down into the darkness. They couldn't risk a light. Moonlight would have to do. But how had he known about the footholds? Steve wondered. He couldn't remember if the workman had told him about them, or not.

He paused, struck by an eerie sense of déjà vu.

"What's the matter?" Evans's hoarse whisper was an annoying intrusion of his thoughts.

"I don't know," Steve said. "Something. Maybe because it's so quiet. It must have been like this centuries ago."

"Like what?" Evans asked, annoyed. "Who gives a shit? Let's get it over with. This place gives me the creeps."

Steve ignored him. The desert stretched out serenely in the moonlight, almost like a stage setting. Only real.

Real . . . and ready. Waiting.

He shivered slightly.

"Come on, Steve. I don't want to stay here all night," Evans said. "What if that guy in the trailer decides to look around?" Evans stared at him, his face contorted with anger. "You bring me out here," he said. "And now you're fucking around looking at the moon. Christ. Let's get out of here now, if you're going to chicken out."

"Shut up," Steve said, "I'm thinking."

"Oh, great."

Steve knelt down by the shaft, peering inside. A chilling feeling of dread engulfed him.

At the bottom of the shaft, in the dark, the tomb waited.

He shivered again, almost wishing he could be somewhere else. Anywhere else.

"Ah, screw it," he said finally. He had to go down.

He sat on the edge of the shaft and eased his legs over the side. Moving carefully, he found a small, jagged ledge for the first foothold, and began a slow descent.

He looked up once and saw Evans's head outlined against the moonlit sky. Once his foot slipped, and a shower of small rocks cascaded downward, echoing noisily as they skittered across the unseen floor.

The air was stale, dry—tainted with the ancient dust of decay. And yet he thought he smelled a trace of incense, a light perfume. . . .

He came to the end of the shaft, and he lowered himself carefully to the ground, his muscles aching with the effort.

At first he could see nothing. Then his eyes grew accustomed to the gloom. Gradually, bit by bit, the glint of gold flashed in the moonlight that had filtered down.

Gold everywhere. Delicate statues of Isis and Nephtis lined one wall, their beauty evident despite the lack of light. A golden throne encrusted with malachite shone a mystical green.

Carved cedar chests inlaid with ebony and edged in gold promised to reveal more treasures when opened.

The stone sarcophagus stood near the far wall backed by a green, life-sized statue of Osiris, the god of vegetation and resurrection.

How had grave-robbers missed a windfall of this magnitude? Steve wondered. Nothing in any scribe's tally of this era had ever hinted of this kind of treasure.

The Egyptians would be delirious with joy. A discovery of this importance would help the faltering tourist trade, and provide an opportunity for favorable international news coverage.

The next question was why—why such an elaborate funeral chamber for a minor prince? Who was Menket? What had he done to rate all this? Steve wondered.

Straining to see in the gloom, he peered at the hieroglyphics on the walls of the burial chamber. They had remained bright and well-preserved through the centuries because of the bone-dry desert air.

Steve began to read the ancient symbols, slowly at first, dredging up all his knowledge. Then it grew easier, and at last he understood.

He had entered the burial chamber of a man who had been titled Master of All the Secrets, a powerful priest of *Hakau*, the magical arts of the underworld.

On the wall behind the sarcophagus a

cartouche enclosed the name *Menket*. And a message:

He has lived, and will live again.
Like the mystical jackal, flesh and bone
shall feed his spirit. Life-giving marrow
shall he eat.
And he shall live again to drink the eternal
waters of the Nile.

A scraping sound behind Steve heralded the arrival of Bill Evans. "Jesus Christ!" Evans said. "No wonder Caldwell hired you, you really know your stuff! Look at that!" He reached toward a small gold replica of a bull.

"Don't touch *anything*!" Steve said tensely. "For Christ's sake, why did you come down? We don't want your finger-prints showing up on anything."

"You're not going to leave all this, are you?"

"Caldwell only wants one thing. He knows that if anything else is missing," Steve said, "the Egyptians might suspect me."

"So what does he want?" Evans asked.

"He sure as hell doesn't want an investi-gation to stir things up," Steve said, mov-ing over to the sarcophagus. For some reason, the heavy lid had been left off, and there were no inner casings. The mummy lay wrapped in what must once have been fine linen. Blue lapis lazuli and red cornelian jewels adorned its throat and wrists. A layer of dust covered everything, and Steve hesitated, wondering why the sarcophagus had not been sealed.

"Something is wrong," he said, pausing a moment. Careful not to disturb the dust on the edge of the case, he reached into the sarcophagus, loosening the funerary scarab bracelet on the mummy's wrist.

"Hey, wait a minute! What about your fingerprints?" Evans asked.

"I'm not touching anything except this bracelet. Anyway, I'll be one of the first in here tomorrow, and who's to know if I get a little careless and forget to wear gloves." He held up the blue-and-gold lapis lazuli bracelet in the pale light from the shaft, admiring its intricate beauty. Then he slipped it on his wrist. "Let's go," he said.

"Forget it," Evans said. "I'm not walking away from all this. I say we take a couple more things. They won't miss 'em."

Suddenly, Steve could hardly see the other man's face. Darkness seemed to be swallowing everything. He looked up the shaft uncertainly. Above him an eclipse had started, its advance inexorable.

"Ah, shit!" he said. He'd forgotten about that. It would be pitch black in a few seconds. "Let's go, Bill," he whispered urgently. "We must go now, before we knock anything over."

"Goddamn it, Steve! Not without some of this stuff."

"Screw you, asshole!" Steve lunged at the other man furiously, his big hands clenched into fists. In the last shred of light, he sensed more than saw the flint knife in Evans's hand, a knife aimed at his throat, where his jugular throbbed.

As if in a dream, he lay on his back listening to Bill scramble back up the shaft. The frantic sounds grew fainter and fainter, and he heard a rushing in his ears.

Oh, God, I'm dying, was his very last thought, as the shadow blackened the face of the moon.

FOUR

Now Isis, spread your wings.

The whisper echoed in the chamber, swirling around and around, gaining life in the time-deadened stillness of the tomb, until at last it faded away.

I must be hallucinating, he thought.

He sat up slowly, and a wave of nausea hit him, bringing the hot, sour taste of bile to his mouth.

Easy does it, he thought. *Try to get up. Not dead yet.*

He felt light-headed, and the chamber suddenly spun around violently when he tried to stand. But he wasn't dead, not by a longshot.

Wait a minute. Got to rest. Getting up too fast.

With a trembling hand he reached up to feel the wound in his throat. Gingerly touching the deep cut, he felt pain, but only a trace of blood.

He stared unbelievingly at his dry hand. *How could that be?* he thought. *Why wasn't there a gush of sticky wetness draining away his life?*

The eclipse had ended, and pale light filled the tomb again. Slowly a laugh started to bubble deep in his chest.

I'm alive. Alive!

Luck. Pure, unadulterated, one-hundred percent luck, he thought. The best luck he'd ever had.

And the worst for Bill Evans.

Time to settle accounts, he thought, cold anger sitting like a stone in his gut.

Weakness still kept him from standing, and he dragged himself over to the sarcophagus, holding on to the smooth side for support. He leaned his head against the cold slab, wondering if he could rally enough strength to make the climb up the shaft.

Don't rush it. Still feel too weak.

He couldn't take too long. The workmen would be arriving early, and he couldn't risk being seen anywhere near the tomb, not with the blue-and-gold bracelet in his possession.

He looked at the bracelet again, turning it over on his wrist. God, it was beautiful. Caldwell would be pleased. If this didn't get him off the hook, nothing would. He was feeling better already. In just a few more minutes he would tackle the climb back up the shaft.

Suddenly an inexplicable thrill of fear washed over him. Someone, something was watching him from the darkness by the wall.

Watching. Waiting.

Waiting for what?

Cold sweat sheeted his body, and he shivered uncontrollably, clenching his teeth to stop them from chattering.

For Christsake, pull yourself together, he thought.

The tomb was eerie enough to drive anyone crazy, he thought. It was mystical, magical, in the pale moonlight.

Again, he felt a chilling sense of déjà vu.

I know this place. Oh, Christ, I know it.

He felt the sweat under his arms, cold and clammy, sticking to his shirt.

He stared at the opposite wall, shivering feverishly, his eyes not focusing.

Jesus. I even know what the hieroglyphics will reveal before I read them.

His heart pounded in his chest as the vivid colors on the wall blurred and wavered in the pale uneven light. He closed his eyes tightly, trying to shut out the familiar words.

Don't look. Don't look, he thought wildly.

He pressed the heels of his hands into his eyes, but it didn't help. Against the inside of his eyelids the ancient words still rippled like a crazy rainbow around the burial chamber.

Calm down. Take a few deep breaths. That's better. Easy does it.

The pictures faded. He opened his eyes.

Everything seemed to be out of sync, like a double-exposed negative. He took a few more deep breaths, and all at once everything cleared.

He felt an unexpected surge of strength rush like a hot tide through him. With an effort he pulled himself upright, still holding on to the open sarcophagus, and looked down at the mummy.

A shrill, high-pitched shriek of fear echoed through the silent chamber, shocking him with its strange intensity, until, flesh crawling, he realized that it tore from his own throat.

Oh God oh God. It's me in there!

His legs ached with the urge to run, to get out and put miles between himself and the thing with his own withered face that stared back at him sightlessly.

Half-crazed, he felt the binding constriction of the burial linen and smelled the sickly-sweet corruption of centuries all around him like an aura of decay.

Panic loosened his bowels, and half-falling, he staggered over to the shaft opening.

Chilling terror provided the fuel to climb up the shaft. To keep on going up. Up past the nausea that choked him. Past the

faintness that threatened to defeat him.
Past the ripped nails and bleeding hands
that clung desperately to the shallow
ledges. Up, up, to the surface far away
from the mocking darkness below.

Exhausted, he lay down near the lip of
the shaft, his face streaked with sweat and
covered with a film of sand.

A faint breeze came from the east, carrying with it the bittersweet scent of the Nile.
He raised his head, gulping in the
memory-laden air that freshened his
lungs.

Gradually strength returned, and he remembered.

Getting to his knees, he held out his
arms to embrace the midnight sky above
him, his gray eyes darkening to black in
the moonlight.

"Old one, I am truly here," he whispered in the ancient tongue.

Menket paused a moment, feeling the
intoxication of life course through his
veins, until a sudden ravening hunger
drove him to swiftly cross the uneven
stretch of sand towards the road.

The pale, brownish desert curs lurked
nearby, cringing back as he turned and
faced them.

*Like the mystical jackal, flesh and bone
shall feed his spirit.*

A red film covered his eyes as he felt the
terrible hunger within him, and suddenly a
dog lay dead from a single blow.

Whining softly, the pack crouched back listening to the man.

Listening as raging hands tore flesh away from carcass loosing a sudden spray of hot blood.

Listening to the crack, as bone after bone lay splintered to reveal the soft red marrow within.

FIVE

Bill Evans gulped from the glass he gripped with both shaking hands. How could he have been such a dumb bastard?

They'd find Harrison in the morning when they opened the tomb, and the investigation would lead straight to him.

Unless he could come up with an alibi.

Why in God's name had he taken that gold statue? Too late to worry about that, it was already on its way to Caldwell. Or anyway, it would be, once the diplomatic pouch left in the morning.

No one but the guard had seen him return to his office last night, and that dumb jarhead wouldn't think anything about it anyway.

He had returned the professor's Citroen to the street outside the old guy's apartment, but what about fingerprints?

If the Egyptian police handled it, Caldwell thought, he'd have a better chance—
especially if they found out about the
workman who had discovered the shaft.
They would want to wrap it up into a neat
package as soon as possible; maybe he
could drop a hint or two to help them
along. Tell them Harrison had revealed his
intention to rob the tomb together with
one of the natives.

Oh, he'd tried to talk him out of it, he'd
say. Oh, shit, yes. But Harrison wouldn't
listen. So he'd been quite prepared to go
to the police in the morning, but he'd
hoped that it wouldn't be necessary.

He finished his drink and poured another. Mustn't get drunk, he told himself.
Need a clear head. Have to think things
out.

He took another drink.

God, it was hot in here, he thought.
Air-conditioner never worked, nothing
ever worked in this godforsaken country.

He opened the wide glass doors that led
to the balcony. A cool breeze from the
river blew into the room, making the long
white curtains billow and furl like the sails
on a boat.

He turned sharply at a sound behind
him. "Who's there?"

The sound had come from the hallway,
near the front door.

Why hadn't he turned the lights on? he
thought. It was crazy to sit in the dark. But

he'd wanted it dark. Easier to think.

"Who's there, Goddamnit!" he said aloud.

A man moved out of the shadows toward him, and Evans staggered back, clutching wildly at the flapping curtains.

"Stay away, Steve! For God's sake, leave me alone!" The curtains billowed into the room, entangling him in their sinuous embrace. Muttering an obscenity, he tugged ineffectually at the silky cloth, dropping his half-empty glass to the floor at his feet. "I never wanted to be a part of the deal. You forced me into it. Threatened me. Didn't want to hurt you, Steve, but shit, all that stuff in the tomb—I lost my head," he said nervously. "You son of a bitch, I'm so fucking glad to see you're alive. You don't know what I've been through!"

Still holding on to the curtains, Evans swayed toward the other man. "Steve? Say something, damnit!" He stared into the shadowed eyes, and was stunned by what he saw.

His mouth slackened, trying to frame a question; he strained to understand. . . .

Menket raised his hand slowly toward Evans, the bracelet a band of blue fire in the moonlight. He took another step forward, and Evans jerked violently away, awkwardly catching his heel in the glass at his feet. Desperately hanging on to the curtains, Evans, half-drunk and wildly afraid, stumbled backwards against the balcony rail, his heart lurching as he heard the drapery tear under his weight.

For an instant the torn curtains spread like a pair of wings above him, then he fell over the rail, his scream echoing shrilly as he plummeted to the street below.

SIX

The scream rang in Steve's ears like a discordant alarm. Jolting awake, he saw the lights snap on in the building across the street. A scattering of voices raised the general alarm.

He peered around the room in confusion. What was he doing in Bill's apartment? He started to go out onto the balcony, but the voices in the street were louder now.

Whatever had happened, he'd be in deep shit if they thought he had anything to do with it.

He drew back into the room, stumbling over the coffee table. Why weren't the lights on? He sat down on the couch suddenly as his knees gave way. The horror of everything that had happened in the tomb came back.

He got up off the couch quickly, nausea

sending the sour contents of his stomach percolating up his throat. How could he have forgotten? He tried to remember how he'd made it back all the way from Memphis.

And why had Bill fallen over the balcony railing?

He swallowed hard, fighting the nausea. A sudden pounding on Evans's front door made him jump. *Christ. Bastards'll hang my ass. Gotta get out. Now.*

Stumbling into the dark kitchen, he felt his way to the back door.

Thank God there's a way out.

He jerked open the door, finding himself on the metal stairway that connected with all the back doors in the building.

At the bottom of the stairway, a tiled, communal courtyard was quiet. He paused, breathing hard. *Up? Or down?*

If he went down and tried to get out the front door, he'd walk right into the doorman, who was usually sleeping near the elevator.

Too late, anyway, he thought. Excited voices rose up from somewhere inside the main entryway.

It wouldn't be long now. Curious neighbors babbling in Arabic, local police, eyes watching him with a calculated cynicism and asking him loaded questions in a careful English.

The metal stairway led up to the roof. He knew what he'd find there. Servants' quarters: square stucco rooms, one after the other like cells in a monastery, each with its sleeping servant bundled up in musty bedclothes. But how long could he count on them staying asleep? If anyone saw him up on the roof, it would all be over. *Only guilty men run away,* he thought.

A light suddenly went on in a kitchen three floors down. No time to hesitate now, up was the only way out.

His feet scraped the first step, and the metallic sound reverberated around the four walls of the kitchen courtyard. He slipped off his loafers, wondering at the torn dusty socks on his feet. What the hell had he done? Run all the way back from Memphis?

No time to figure things out now. Unless he wanted to be hauled away to an Egyptian jail. He'd heard some pretty sickening stories about them, and he sure as hell didn't want to find out if they were true.

He raced quickly up the stairs, reaching the door to the roof in double-quick time. *So far so good, now comes the hard part,* he thought.

The door was partway open. He pushed it cautiously, then stepped quietly through the door onto the roof. Just about all the doors to the cell-like rooms were open to the warm night air. A cacophony of snores reassured him that most of the men on the roof were asleep. Most, but not all.

A charcoal brazier glowed in one doorway, and though Steve couldn't see the man inside, he knew that he had to be awake. An ear of corn roasted on the brazier, sending up red sparks into the night.

He had to reach the adjacent rooftop without being seen. Then go on to the next and the next—as far away as he could get in as short a time as possible.

He pressed back against the wall, feeling the peeling paint flake off on his hands. A low stucco wall fenced in the rooftop, built right up against the wall on the adjacent roof. If he could just make it across the short distance to the wall, he could get away.

His heart pounded, the adrenaline giving him the push to sprint like a runner out of the blocks. Behind him, a muffled shout of surprise egged him on.

He fell onto the second roof, scraping his knees. But it didn't matter. Nothing mattered now, except escape.

Muscles that he hadn't used since his years on the gridiron came into action. He vaulted over the next two walls without looking back. No one could catch him now.

The closely jammed apartment buildings ended at the intersection with a main street. He raced down the back stairs and out into the pre-dawn night. Cars parked along the sidewalk as well as on it, in the haphazard Egyptian manner, afforded him a shadowy escape.

The moon had faded long ago. At the other end of the street, a gathering crowd separated to let a wailing ambulance through.

Sweat made his wet shirt cling to his body. He stank, but it was not just sweat and fear. It was something else—something hot . . . and gamy.

Moving stealthily through the still-empty streets like a thief, Steve made for home.

He heard the phone ringing as soon as he put the key in the lock. Before he could reach it, it stopped.

Goddamn. Whoever had been trying to reach him would know that he'd been out all night. They might even wonder if he knew anything about Bill, he thought.

He stood for a moment, by the phone, wondering who it could have been. Suddenly it rang again.

"Yeah?" His voice sounded gruff, but that would seem all right this early.

"Mr. Harrison?" He didn't recognize the woman's voice at first. "Mr. Harrison? This is Barbara Weber. Mr. Evans's secretary." The last sentence ended on a stammer.

He remembered her now. The blonde with the walk.

"What time is it?" he asked, staring at his watch. This might be the alibi he would probably need.

"Almost four A.M." She began to cry. "Something terrible has happened. It's Bill. I mean, Mr. Evans."

Heard you the first time, Steve thought. "Try to calm down, Miss Weber. Where is he?"

"He's . . ." She gulped. Tried again. "He's *dead.*"

Don't say anything yet. Wait a second or two. Sound surprised. For Christsakes, sound surprised.

"What d'you mean dead?"

"I just can't believe he killed himself. He wouldn't do that." She sounded stubborn.

"What are you trying to tell me? That he was murdered?"

There was a long silence at the other end. "I don't know," she whispered.

"What happened?"

"He fell . . . fell off his balcony. The police called the embassy, and the security officer called me," she said.

"So it could have been an accident?" Steve asked.

"It could have been," she said after a long pause.

"I'm really sorry. What can I do to help?"

"Nothing. The embassy's taking care of it," she said. "You saw him last night," she added quickly. Too quickly.

What the hell was she trying to say? Steve wondered.

"So did you," he said. "So did half a

dozen other people for all I know. He didn't say too much about his private life. Maybe it was an accident. Maybe it wasn't. I only talked to him for a few minutes, then I went home. I've been here all evening." He tried to sound sincere, "I wish that I could help you feel better about it. I don't think that there is anything either of us can do right now."

He waited for her to say something, feeling edgy, wondering if Bill had said anything about having to go to the tomb. It would have been just like the jerk, he thought. He never could keep his mouth shut. If she knew about the diplomatic pouch, she'd be sure to blow the whistle on him.

"Miss Weber?"

"Yes." She sounded tired, defeated. Maybe she really *had* loved the creep. Or was she just giving up on a crazy hunch? he wondered.

"Miss Weber. Try and get some sleep. I'm sure that Bill appreciated everything you did for him. But you can't help him now, can you?"

"No. I just wish . . ." The words faded into silence.

She doesn't know a damn thing, he thought, with sudden conviction. Not a goddamn thing.

"You've had a bad shock," he said, forcing some sympathy into his voice. "It's always tough when someone you know dies." He paused meaningfully. "I'm in shock myself. We were at school together." That did it.

"Oh, I know," she said sympathetically. "He was so pleased to see you again." He heard her blow her nose. "I guess you're right. Nothing much I can do now. Well, good night, Mr. Harrison."

He hung up the phone, feeling better. Clean as a hound's tooth, he thought. They wouldn't be able to pin anything on him. Not the break-in at the tomb, nor the accident at Bill's apartment.

He went into the bedroom and began to undress. *Better throw these clothes away,* he thought. Pants and underwear came off first. Then his shirt. It rubbed against his throat as he pulled it over his head, and he winced in pain. Of course, he remembered. Bill had stabbed him in the throat.

He threw the shirt on the floor, frowning as he saw the blood spilled down the front. *Guess I must have bled, after all,* he thought, picking it up again. A strange, musky odor permeated the material. He brought it up to his nose to sniff it, and a sudden terrible memory flashed across his mind like a subliminal message, conjuring up a taste of something hot, metallic.

He dropped the shirt as if it were on fire.

I'm overtired, he thought. *That's all it is. Too much for one night. Too much excitement. Clean yourself up and get to bed.*

He put on his bathrobe and went into the kitchen. Leaning tiredly against the sink, he filled a glass with water and drank it down. *Is there anything that tastes as good?* he wondered. But as he put the glass back into the sink, an uneasy memory kept trying to push its way into his mind. Something about the desert.

What happened in the desert?

Forget it, he thought abruptly. *Whatever happened out there is over. No need to think about it again.*

Only—what really happened?

SEVEN

"Of course I understand, Steve," the professor said sympathetically. "I know that the Cultural Attaché was an old friend of yours." He shook his head in disbelief. "It doesn't seem possible. It must have been an accident. Why should he kill himself, a young man like that?"

"I don't know why. He never mentioned any problems to me," Steve said.

"Well, anyway, you go ahead and take a couple of days off. We aren't going to be able to open the tomb today after all." He sighed with resignation. "I suppose that I should be used to these delays. Mr. Farid is doing all he can." He stared anxiously at the younger man. "You look terrible. You're not coming down with dysentery, are you?"

"No. I'm just worn out."

"You'd better see a doctor, my boy. I don't like the look of your eyes. You seem a bit feverish to me," Peterson said.

"I'm going over to the Hilton. I've got an appointment with the doctor there, and perhaps he can do something about this cut." He touched the inch-long cut with his left hand, revealing the bracelet, and the professor looked at him sharply.

"I don't think I've ever seen you wear that before, Steve. Where did you get it?"

Oh, Christ. Why had he worn it? He hadn't been thinking straight. Hadn't been thinking, period.

"Just something from the Khan Khalili market. I bought it a couple of weeks ago," he said hastily. He covered it with his other hand, the lapis lazuli cool against his fingers, trying to hide its beauty.

"May I see it?"

"I'm late for the appointment already."

The professor looked at him uncertainly.

If he gets a close look at the bracelet, I'm sunk, Steve thought. "I really should leave now."

For a moment the professor seemed about to insist. "Oh, of course. Take care of that cut."

Steve felt the professor's uneasy eyes staring after him as he left the office.

Pausing at the museum gatekeeper's

hut, he asked for a drink, then drank down the contents of the earthern water jar by the door. The water ran down his chin as he gulped thirstily, relishing the slightly bitter taste of the Nile.

He wiped at his mouth with the back of his hand, giving a nod of thanks to the man squatting in the doorway. The Egyptian looked at him askance, obviously surprised at an American drinking anything but bottled water. But it had tasted wonderful, cool and refreshing, reminding him of . . .

Of what?

Whatever it was seemed to be just out of reach, like a half-forgotten dream. He tried to remember.

O Nile, I feel your strength, its life-giving power coursing through me.

He stopped abruptly in the street, and with a blast from its horn, a swerving taxi narrowly missed him.

What the hell is wrong with me? he thought. *Why in God's name did I drink that water? The only thing coursing through me right now is probably a bad case of dysentery.*

He walked toward the back entrance of the Nile Hilton, suddenly breaking into a cold sweat despite the 90-degree temperature.

The police guard sitting outside the hotel at a makeshift desk waved him on without a challenge.

He must recognize me, thought Steve. *Or else I look too ill to search. God knows, I feel like shit.*

Inside the hotel's back entrance, he passed the long glass case filled with chocolate confectionery and French pastry, fighting nausea with gritted teeth.

Whatever I've got, it's a killer, he thought as he rode up the elevator to the second floor. *I feel as though I never want to look at any food again in my whole life.* As he stepped out of the elevator, a violent jolt of vertigo knocked him off balance, and he hugged the wall to keep from falling down.

"Need any help?" The man stood looking at him uncertainly.

"No, I'll make it. I'm just going in to see the doctor." Steve motioned toward the open door.

"Smart move. Well, if you're sure you can manage." The man moved on down the corridor. Steve saw the sweat staining the back of his shirt.

The doctor's office had a kind of unkempt comfort.

"Don't mind the mess," said the doctor, catching Steve's expression. "We've been busy as hell today." With his accent, the doctor could have been mistaken for an American. He began to wash his hands. "Sit down. I'll be right with you." He turned around, drying his hands on a paper towel. "Where did you get that cut on your throat?"

"Shaving."

"Is that right? Well, don't tell me if you don't want to. But you've got a nasty stab wound there, and I should report it to the police."

"No! I don't want to have to talk to them about it. Anyway, it's nothing. Didn't even bleed much."

"That doesn't make sense." The doctor chose a swab and began to dab at the cut. "You should have had it stitched up. It's healing all right, but there is always the risk of infection. When did it happen?"

"Last night."

"That's impossible!" The doctor stared at him, perplexed. "The healing process is too far along." He took a thermometer out of its beaker, and stuck it under Steve's tongue. Going back to the counter, he wrote out a prescription, whistling softly between his teeth.

He came back and took the thermometer out of Steve's mouth. "Well, it's just what I expected. You shouldn't be walking around with a fever that high. I'll give you a shot for the infection, and you can pick up these pills at the pharmacy in the arcade. Call me tomorrow to let me know how you feel."

Steve rode the elevator down to the ground floor not looking at the other passengers. He hesitated a moment before getting off. Why did he feel that there was something he had to remember? Something lingering just at the edge of his consciousness, teasing him with elusive memories of things forgotten.

Suddenly he felt the raging thirst again, and he went into the men's restroom, heading for the sinks. Leaning over one of the shallow basins, he turned on the faucet and cupped his hand under the water, drinking greedily.

So cool. The slaves have dug a small canal beside the palace. Nefrenofret is laughing by the water, her black eyes filled with newfound love . . . .

"Is anything the matter?" The fat tourist stood zipping up his shorts, watching Steve anxiously.

"No. Nothing's wrong. Just the heat."

"Tell me about it." The tourist shook his head, grinning wryly. He left the restroom, noisily banging the door behind him.

Gripping the basin, Steve stood upright, staring at himself in the mirror.

My God, what's happening to me?

His appearance shocked him. The normally fair, ruddy complexion now seemed sallow, and his eyes stared feverishly, dark and shadowed.

Bending over the sink again, he splashed his face with the cool water, pulling at the roller towel to dry his hands and wipe his face.

Better get back to the apartment and lie down, he thought. *No use trying to walk, not feeling like this.* He could barely stand, let alone walk.

Outside, he hailed a cab, climbed in, and gave the driver his address without arguing about the fare. He closed his eyes, resting his head on the back of the seat.

God, his head hurt. Better not try to think. No use thinking, anyway. Nothing seemed to make sense. Maybe he was hallucinating.

What happened last night?

Don't think about it. Just a dream, a nightmare.

He opened his eyes, staring blankly out of the window. He forced himself to watch the traffic as it surged by.

No use. The ugly thoughts pushed into his mind like a crazy soundwave that he couldn't control.

Maybe that's it. Maybe I'm going crazy.

As he opened the door to his apartment, he saw the message waiting for him. He sat down on his bed and tore open the envelope, reading the scrawl inside.

So the Marines were holding a wake for Bill Evans. A cynical smile creased his dry lips as he considered the irony. The Cultural Attaché's opinion of the Marines had been unprintable.

He stretched out on his bed, willing himself to relax. Rolling over, he reached for the pack of cigarettes on the bedside table. Shaking out a cigarette, he started

to put it to his lips. A violent wave of
nausea sickened him as he smelled the
tobacco.

"Oh, shit." He got up slowly and went
into the kitchen. Taking a glass off the
drain board, he filled it with water from the
tap and drank it down.

Through the kitchen window muted
sounds of traffic from the street became a
backdrop for the high-pitched wail of the
muezzin calling the faithful to prayer.

He glanced at his watch.

Time for a shower, he thought tiredly.
Then he'd better make an appearance at
Bill's wake, like it or not.

He walked over to the bathroom, slowly
unbuttoning his shirt. He took off his shirt,
dropping it on the floor. He began to unzip
his pants, frowning as he tried to remember.

What the hell *had* happened last night?

He couldn't remember getting back to
town. Bill Evans had taken the car, for
some reason. But then what?

And there was something else. Something about a dog.

What had happened to the dog?

He finished undressing and stepped into
the shower stall. Easing his large frame
into the cramped space, he turned on the
cold faucet, letting the water wash his
tiredness away.

As he reached for the soap he saw the

bracelet, and remembered Caldwell.

Too late to call New York tonight. He'd better wait until morning. Give himself time to come up with an excuse for the delay.

With Bill dead, it wouldn't be easy. Unless he could think of someone else with access to the diplomatic pouch. Someone who could be bought.

He looked at the bracelet again. An unwelcome picture came to his mind—of the thin, cold hands of Caldwell holding the band of gold and lapis lazuli.

He felt a sudden flash of rage.

Screw Caldwell. Screw the money.

This is mine.

Night had fallen by the time he got dressed and left for the embassy. Except for a slight persistant queasiness in the pit of his stomach, he felt almost normal. Maybe he was getting over whatever it was that had made him so sick.

He recognized the Marine on duty at the gate, and after an exchange of a word or two, signed in and began to walk back to the Marines' quarters.

The night air felt warm, sultry. He took off his jacket and slung it over his shoulder.

Music drifted towards him from beyond the chancery building, and he could hear the distant sound of laughter.

Maybe the blonde secretary was there. He smiled cynically. The Marines would help her get over any grief she felt for Bill Evans.

He felt better already. Must have been a 24-hour virus. Sure. That was it. That, and the heat.

He smiled again, drawing in a deep breath of fragrant air. A trace of jasmine hung in the moonwashed night, stirring the dust of memory.

The creamy lotus floats on the water. Its essence scents the unguent that perfumes Nefrenofret's golden breasts. . . .

Suddenly, without warning, the air around him felt charged with an unnamed terror.

Jolting tremors racked him from head to foot, and he desperately strained every muscle, trying to get back to the gate before it was too late.

Something powerful wrenched him back, propelling him toward the dark shadows under the trees.

Something controlled him again.

Something . . . *inside.*

He turned his head frantically at the sound of sharp claws scraping the cement walkway beyond the bushes.

Then he knew.

Sickened, he felt the ravishing hunger overcome him, almost choking him with its violent need.

A red film came before his eyes. Shuddering, he waited in the shadows as the German shepherd loped towards him.

Strange lights that challenge the dark of night.

Strange metallic smells that mask the harshness of the desert air.

I am lost. Lost in the labyrinth of Time. And thieves have scattered our immortal relics as a child scatters a handful of sand.

Menket stood a moment listening to the quiet night sounds around him. A snatch of song ended in laughter. Beyond the embassy wall, someone whistled off key.

A rustle in the bushes made him turn fiercely. Nothing.

He stooped by the garden tap, and drank his fill. Carefully washing the blood off his hands and face, he dried them with a handful of leaves torn from the trees around him. Picking up his jacket from where he'd dropped it, he quickly put it on and buttoned it over his bloodsoaked shirt.

He moved away from the thing under the trees, raising his clenched fist to the sky above.

"O Isis, hear my words. I am the prince of Egypt, and her enemies are mine."

He waited behind the guard room, until the Marine inside bent over the desk, then slipped shadowlike into the night.

"Her enemies are mine," he repeated bitterly as he ran swiftly through the dimly lit streets, and his mouth spat out the hated name like a curse.

"*Caldwell!*"

In the darkness, further along the pathway behind the chancery building, a terrified man stood trembling, fear parching his open mouth.

"*Allahu Akbar,*" whispered Ahmed the cook, urgently trying to ward off evil. "God is great."

Without making a sound, he melted into the shadows, wanting only to get away, to escape the horror that his terrified eyes had witnessed.

"Here, boy! Here, boy!" The young Marine came down the steps in front of the Palm House, and stood a moment, staring into the darkness. "Goddamn dog," he said good-naturedly, turning back into the lighted doorway to rejoin the wake. "Son of a bitch never comes when you call him."

EIGHT

Steve Harrison lay spread-eagled on a narrow wedge of muddy land that sloped down to the water. Opening his eyes cautiously, he stared up at the sky full of stars.

Where the hell am I? he wondered.

He became aware of water lapping against the soles of his shoes, and raising his head up, squinted as he looked down to his feet.

The effort made him dizzy, and he lay his head down again gently, feeling sick.

He moved his arms slowly, bringing them up over his chest. His clothes were wet and clinging and smelled somewhat gamy. Despite the mildness of the night, he felt cold.

Leaning over on one elbow, he dug his

heels into the slippery mud, and sat up awkwardly. The movement made him cough, and a thick gout of brackish scum came into his mouth. It felt loose and slimy, and he spat it out quickly, trying not to swallow.

Some people never learn, he thought cynically. *I shouldn't have drunk so damn much. This has got to be the mother and father of all hangovers. My mouth feels like something crawled in it and died.*

The good old Marines must have thrown one hell of a wake. Too bad Bill had to miss it. The little creep would have had a ball, pissing everyone off because he wasn't dead.

Don't want to think about that. Don't want to think about that at all.

He stood up unsteadily, wiping his muddy hands on his jacket. *Christ, I'm soaked through. How did I get so wet?*

Further along the bank, a small group of fishermen squatted around a charcoal brazier, talking softly among themselves. Beyond them, Steve could see the old bridge spanning the river.

You dumb bastard, he told himself. *You went for a swim in the Nile. You could have drowned. As it is, you'll be lucky if you don't get a dose of hepatitis.*

What had he drunk at the wake? He couldn't remember anything about it. Not a thing. Zilch.

Hope to God I enjoyed it, he thought

glumly. *Because I sure am paying the price now.*

He took off his shoes to empty out the dribbles of dirty water, and stumbled, feet sinking into the oozing mud. Angry now, he pulled off his wet, dirt-clotted socks, and flung them far out into the river, watching as they swirled in twin eddies before disappearing downstream.

A breeze blew across the water, bringing with it the acrid smell of smoke from the other side of the river. He stood and stared at the black oily drifts and currents in the Nile, transfixed by the somehow familiar sight.

His lips seemed to want to mouth a name. A name that hovered out of reach of memory, leaving him feeling empty and alone.

He started as someone shouted down at him from the corniche that ran alongside the river.

"Bug off," Steve muttered irritably.

The man on the corniche leaned over the stone wall. "You want taxi?" he asked again.

A taxi. Yeah. That makes sense. Beats gaping at the river all night, and anyway, he couldn't walk home like this. Come to think of it, he couldn't do much of anything like this.

"Okay," he said. "I want taxi. You're damn right I want taxi." He coughed up some more scum, and spat it out into the water. This time it had a sweet, rotted taste, and he scrubbed his wet sleeve roughly against his lips to clear the taste away.

He put his shoes on again, and squelched up the river bank to the stone wall. May as well throw these shoes away. Seventy bucks shot to hell. Well, no one to blame but himself.

He dozed fitfully on the way back to his apartment, undisturbed by the blare of a Mick Jagger tape in the taxi's cassette. A dream teased him with something that he ought to remember. Something about a dog . . .

He jerked awake as the taxi pulled up outside his apartment building, and he staggered as he got out and paid the driver. The doorman came forward to help him, and the cab driver laughed harshly. "*Sakraan,*" said the driver.

Well, he knew what that meant. Drunk. But he didn't feel drunk. Only sick. Very, very sick. And if they didn't get out of the way fast, he'd puke all over them, just like the little girl in *The Exorcist*.

But they did—and he didn't. He made it up to his apartment, stomach contents intact.

Close call. He grinned. *Helluva close call. Bastards wouldn't have liked that, now would they?*

He unlocked his front door and walked through to the bathroom without turning on the light in the hallway. Better get out of these wet clothes. He snapped on the light in the bathroom, unbuttoned his jacket, and glanced in the mirror over the sink.

For a sickening moment he just stared, aghast.

Then he slowly removed his jacket and threw it into the corner of the room, never taking his eyes off his reflection.

I'm going to pass out, he thought shakily. *Where did all that blood come from? Is it mine?*

He looked down at his blood-drenched shirt, and rubbed a trembling hand over his chest.

Then he stared down at the palm of his hand.

Blood. And something else. Fine splinters of an ivory whiteness tinged with pink.

Bone.

His heart began to thump like a hammer in his chest as he gaped at his hand. A smear of pinkish jelly gleamed wetly in the light, and he reached into his pocket with his other hand to get his handkerchief. As he pulled out the sopping wet square of linen, something fell to the floor at his feet.

Something brown. Covered with fur, and softly, cunningly curled in on itself.

His knees hit the floor with a crash, and he threw back his head and screamed. An unearthly gut-wrenching scream that kept on coming until someone upstairs pounded on the ceiling.

When he finally stopped, he crouched down with his face turned sideways on the cool blue tile of the floor. He kept his eyes closed.

He didn't want to open them. Not yet.

Because then he'd see the thing on the floor by the toilet.

The soft, brown thing. The thing he'd recognized immediately and irrevocably as the German shepherd's ear.

Later, he tried to sleep.

First, though, he took a long hot shower. He scrubbed himself from head to foot, opening his mouth to let the hot water wash the sickly sweet taste away. Then when he'd rinsed off, he scrubbed himself again, until his skin felt raw.

It didn't help. He still felt dirty. Soiled.

He didn't think that he'd ever feel clean again. Not if he lived to be a hundred.

After the shower, he made himself pick up the dog's ear and wrap it up in his handkerchief, before throwing it in the trash. A great tiredness overcame him then. But he couldn't sleep.

He found a large saucepan in the kitchen cupboard, which he filled with water, carrying it into the bedroom and setting it on the floor by the bed. He drank the water down almost at once, and had to go fill the saucepan again.

He couldn't make any sense of it. How in God's name had it all happened?

Shadowy wisps of memory plagued him, tormenting him with moments that he almost remembered.

Almost, but not quite.

He punched up the pillow and rolled over onto his side, a sick hollow feeling deep in his gut.

Perhaps it would be better if he didn't remember, after all.

NINE

Staff Sergeant Randy Thomas of the U.S. Marines sat on the edge of the bed and put a shaking hand up to his throbbing head. His dark face twisted in pain.

Jesus H. Christ, what a party!

The good ol' boys back in Tulsa didn't have anything on the guys at the U.S. Embassy, Cairo. Bunch of fucking party animals. He started to grin, but his face hurt, so he gave up that idea, concentrating on trying to stand up instead.

Who would have thought that coming out to this godforsaken country would have been so much fun?

Certainly not this Oklahoma farm boy. If he hadn't been corralled by the recruiting sergeant way back in June of '82, he'd still be ankle deep in hog shit.

He stood up carefully, steadying himself

with one hand against the wall. *Oh, Mama, if you could see your pore boy now.* He bent over Corporal Brewster's bunk and shook him awake.

"Rise and shine, man," he said. "You got patrol today."

Brewster groaned and buried his head in the pillow.

A series of rumbling snores and the sounds of heavy breathing came out of the other rooms on the second floor of the Palm House. Wasted, every last one of 'em. And why not? He and Brewster were the only poor bastards with the early watch.

At least he had the gate. Brewster had to walk security patrol. No rest for the wicked.

Wincing with the effort, he turned his head and glanced at the window. The pale light of dawn filtered in past the shutters' wooden slats. The last drink had been poured at four A.M. Little more than an hour ago. Should have stayed up. Would've made more sense.

"Come on, Brewster. Hit the deck!"

Jeez. What a way to start the day.

Coffee. That's what he needed. Before anything else. *Move, feet,* he thought shakily. *Come on, Marine. Get your ass in gear.* He walked unsteadily over to the door and opened it, poking his head outside into the hallway. Around about now, Ahmed, the number-one cook, should be carrying a pot of coffee into the large dining room, otherwise known as the mess hall.

Feeling groggy, the young Marine went downstairs in his skivvies, a definite infraction of the rules. But what the hell, Master Sergeant Kramer would be out like a light until noon after all the booze he'd managed to put away.

Funny, he couldn't smell any coffee. Most mornings the rich aroma of the brew they cooked up in the kitchen was strong enough to wake the dead. Which was just about what Thomas felt like this early morn.

He padded into the mess hall, hoping to see the coffeepot on the small table by the door that led to the kitchen area. Thick white mugs, lined up in an upside-down formation, had been set out the night before. But no coffeepot.

Where the hell was Ahmed anyway? Little creep was supposed to have coffee ready and waiting for the guys on early watch.

Something was wrong here.

He pushed open the door to the kitchen area. Stairs led down to the kitchen scullery. There was no sign of the little runt. Fuck him, Thomas thought with disgust.

His head had started pounding now, banging away behind his eyes.

''Jesus,'' he muttered weakly.

He went back up to the second floor, head thumping with every step. *Christ, did you have to drink all that beer? Speaking of which, you'd better get your ass up to the head, or you'll be pee-ing in your skivvie drawers, for sure.*

He hurried into the bathroom, sighing with relief as the pungent urine streamed into the bowl.

Next, he swallowed two Bufferin tablets (extra-strength, you could bet your sweet ass), then stepped into the shower.

He showered quickly, then dressed in one of the four lightweight civilian suits that the State Department had provided him with. Then he went down to the mess hall again.

Son of a bitch. Still no goddamn coffee.

No way would he go out on the gate without it. He pushed open the door to the kitchen. The rich smell of eggs frying reached his nose. Surprised, he felt pleasantly hungry. Thank God he hadn't had as much to drink as the other guys, Brewster included. He'd heard Brewster stagger into the bathroom upstairs. The asshole had downed at least three boilermakers that he knew of.

"Hey!" Thomas yelled suddenly. "Where's the goddamn coffee?"

"Okay, okay. Only one, two minutes more." It didn't sound like Ahmed. Must be one of the other servants that worked down in the kitchen. The sergeant sat down at the long table in the mess.

A tall, thin Sudanese, his blue-black

skin glistening with sweat, hurried into the room carrying a tray.

"Not too late," he said reassuringly. "Ahmed very, very sick. He go home to his village. In nighttime. Before sun come up. I fix good breakfast." He began to unload the tray, clattering the dishes against the thick white cup and saucer.

"Keep it down to a dull roar," muttered the young Marine, clutching his head. "I had one hell of a time last night, and now I'm paying for it in spades."

"Too bad. Eat, then you feel better."

Thomas drank his coffee, strong and black, then tackled the eggs. The old guy was right. He did feel better, though he didn't think he'd be able to finish the huge plate of food in front of him.

The cook came back with a glass of freshly squeezed orange juice. The young Marine buttered a slice of toast.

"Where's Corporal Schmidt's dog?" he asked, biting into the toast. "He can have the rest of the eggs."

The black cook's face suddenly turned an ashen gray. He backed out of the room, holding the metal tray up across his chest like a shield. The Marine could hear the slap-slap of the man's leather slippers retreating into the nether regions of the building.

"What the fuck?" muttered Thomas. All his training told him that his first instinct had been right.

Something was very wrong. And even the slightest thing out of whack in the embassy compound had to be investigated immediately.

He got up from the table abruptly, knocking over the chair behind him. Leaving the building quickly, he scanned the area outside the Palm House with studied expertise.

It looked quiet enough. Still too early for anyone to be around the U.S.I.S. building. The chancery wouldn't be open for another three hours. Ditto the consulate. No changes that he could see in the bushy shrubbery along the path.

But the black cook had looked terrified. And Ahmed, a confirmed asshole, was missing.

He ran back inside the Palm House, picked up the phone in the hall, and dialed the gate.

The Marine on gate duty, Staff Sergeant Sutton, a big black from New Orleans, answered calmly enough. "Main gate. Sergeant Sutton speaking, sir."

"Yo," said Thomas. "Anything unusual going on?"

"Like what, man?"

"I dunno. Something's wrong. I better wake Kramer up."

"Suit yourself, man. Ain't nothing going on here. Kramer won't like being woken up."

Thomas thought a minute. The Marine

on security patrol would have reported anything out of the ordinary. Unless he was unable to. "Where's Reiner?" he asked quickly.

"Sergeant Reiner is on security patrol. He hasn't seen shit."

"Where is he?" insisted Thomas.

"Last time he called in he was in the chancery building." The big black Marine laughed softly. "The dumb shit likes to play around with the computers. The old man'll kill him if he messes them up."

Thomas hung up the phone, gnawing at his lower lip. Everything seemed to be A-OK on the surface, and Kramer would have his ass if he woke him for nothing. He could just hear the bitching if he disturbed him because one of the kitchen help had taken off.

But . . . something didn't sit right.

He glanced at his watch. Forty-five minutes before he had to relieve the man on the gate. He could hear Brewster still messing about upstairs. He would be down in a minute. But that might not be soon enough. Better take a look-see around the perimeter before sounding any alarm.

He left the Palm House, heading down the cement path that led towards the front of the embassy compound. He approached the side of the consulate building on the right. Everything looked secure.

A small stand of trees and bushes near

the building shielded the path from the massive iron gates up front. The security gate, with its Marine guard, was around the corner on the right, out of sight of the path.

Thomas came to an abrupt halt, his eyes fixed on the edge of the path. A thin, unmistakable smear of blood tinged the path's gray cement near the bushes. A man walking patrol at night would have missed it. But in the early sunlight, it stood out like a sore thumb.

Under the collar of his white buttoned-down shirt, the young Marine felt the hairs rise stiffly on his neck.

Moving swiftly, he stepped off the path, pushing back the thick bushes with both hands.

Someone had defaced a small portion of the freshly painted consulate wall with blood. Signs and drawings that the sergeant guessed were hieroglyphics blazed like a warning in the bright sunlight.

He took a step forward, alert for any possible movement behind the bushes.

His foot slipped in something wet. He looked down, knowing with a sickening feeling what it was he'd stepped in. Even though there wasn't much in the squelching mess, he knew he had found what was left of Corporal Schmidt's missing dog.

The men stood in a confused cluster around the bloody bundle of fur under the trees in the embassy compound.

"Any idea who could have done this?" asked the Security Officer. He was a small, nervous man with graying hair, and his normally pale face had a greenish cast this morning.

"Beats me," muttered one of the Marines. "Eugene's taking this hard. He loved that ol' dog."

"Doesn't look good for the men who had the watch last night," the Security Officer went on. He frowned, trying to figure it out. "The Administrative Chief was called in to the Ambassador's office before breakfast. Any of you guys have any trouble with the Egyptians lately? Maybe this is a grudge killing."

"Why don't you find out what that shit on the wall is?" muttered Corporal Stowalski, a big blond Polish kid from Detroit.

"Don't worry, we're working on it." The Security Officer's frown got a little deeper. "Professor Peterson, or his assistant, will be coming over to the embassy to decipher it this morning."

"Steve Harrison was here last night," one of the Marines said. "At least, he signed in on my watch."

The Security Officer looked up sharply. "What time did he leave?"

"I didn't sign him out," the guard answered.

"Who did?"

"Sutton worked the late shift," volunteered another Marine.

"He didn't go out on my shift," Sergeant Sutton countered.

"Anyone see him at the wake?"

"The only person I saw last night was Evans's secretary," said Corporal Stowalski. "I was trying my best to take her mind off things. That kept me kinda busy."

A few of the men laughed, relieved to break the tension.

"The Administrative Chief's ready to chew nails," said the Security Officer sternly. "This'll have to be reported to Washington."

"Sir, what have they got to do with it? We'll take care of this ourselves," said the big blond Pole belligerently.

"Wish it were that simple," sighed the Security Officer. "Okay. Get back to whatever you were doing. Corporal Stowalski, you stand watch here until Professor Peterson comes. I don't want anyone touching anything around here until he has seen it. If it's an outside job, we'll have to double the guard. If someone here did this . . ." He broke off, shaking his head. "Call me when Peterson arrives. And I want to know what time Harrison signed out last night. He might have seen something."

He walked back to his office in the chancery building, followed by two or three of the Marines going back to the Palm House.

"Think Harrison had anything to do with this?" one of the other Marines asked Sergeant Sutton.

"What, are you crazy? Man, d'you think Harrison would do any shit like that?" Sutton shook his head, perplexed. "Whoever killed that dog had to be out of his fucking mind."

TEN

"Everybody at the embassy is talking about it, Steve. No one knows what happened. Or even how it happened." Professor Peterson shook his head slowly, a baffled expression on his incongruously boyish features. "It must have been ghastly. One thing is sure, nothing human killed that dog."

The museum janitor came into the office to empty the ashtray on the desk, and Steve waited until he left before speaking.

"How do you know?" Steve asked. *Careful*, he thought to himself.

"My God, if you'd seen it, you wouldn't be asking me that!" The professor ran a hand distractedly through his white hair. "Even its bones had been cracked open. Crushed. And grotesque as it sounds, the marrow had been eaten. Bones sucked clean." He glanced at the younger man. "I shouldn't be telling you this. You still look pretty shaky."

"I'm all right. How do you know what it looked like? The . . . the dog, I mean."

"They called me in. Someone, God alone knows who, had dipped their finger in the blood and left a message on the consulate wall. It really stood out against the white paint."

"Who did it?" Steve spoke with an effort. "I mean, who could have done it?"

"Someone with a twisted sense of humor, I imagine. They don't have any suspects at the moment. The Administrative Chief is very upset. Looks bad for embassy security. One of the couriers suggested that I might be able to decipher it, so they sent for me."

"I don't understand. Why you?"

"Well, this is the peculiar part. The message had been written in hieroglyphics. Very well done, by the way."

"What did it say?" Steve felt faint again, lightheaded. The professor's face seemed blurred and undefined, like melting wax. *Oh, God,* he thought, *I'm going to vomit all over him.* He concentrated on swallowing the bitter saliva that filled his mouth, trying not to look away.

Professor Peterson warmed to his subject. "Roughly translated, it said that Seth dies to feed Osiris. An interesting concept. Part of the ancient incantation to ensure

the provision of nourishment for the resurrected dead. You remember that a sacri-
ficed animal was always equated with the
evil god, Seth. And, of course, the god of
vegetation, Osiris, had been resurrected
himself, and was therefore revered by the
ancient Egyptians in their search for im-
mortality.''

"Yes . . . I remember," Steve said quietly. Clouded images swam before his eyes.
Images that he strained to see more clear-
ly, closing his eyes to block out the distraction of the professor's presence.

"Steve! Steve!" The professor's voice
pulled him back sharply from the edge of
discovery. He had almost reached out and
touched something just beyond the limit
of his conscious memory. Something majestic. Something lost . . .

"Steve! Are you all right?" The older
man's voice intruded again, and this time
Steve opened his eyes with an effort.

"I'm sorry," he muttered. "I don't know
what's wrong with me."

"My guess is that you've been working
too hard. I've become a regular slave
driver," said the professor apologetically.
"You need a vacation, a change. That's
why I'm sending you back to New York for
a couple of weeks."

"I can't go now. Not before we open the
tomb."

"Don't worry about that, Steve. The authorization to open the tomb has been

delayed, as you know. Perhaps it's just as well. Gives us more time for preparation."

Steve looked down at his hands and wondered why they weren't shaking. Outwardly he managed to seem calm, the exact opposite of his real feelings.

There was something he had to ask. "Do you think I did it?"

There was a pause. "I'd be a liar if I didn't admit that the thought had crossed my mind," the professor finally said. "Not about the dog, you understand. I told you that nothing human could have done that kind of damage. No. No, I mean about the message." The professor smiled ruefully. "But I know that you couldn't have managed that. To tell the truth, I don't think that I could have either. Even if I'd been insane enough to try." He paused, a perplexed look crossing his face. "Whoever wrote that message is as familiar with hieroglyphics as if he used that form of writing every day of his life. It couldn't have been either of us, Steve."

"I went to the embassy last night."

"Yes. They told me that you were seen going in, but not leaving. And you didn't sign out."

"I must have been drunk."

"Could be." The professor looked at him quizzically. "They want to question you about that." He leaned forward, laying a hand on the younger man's arm. "But don't worry about that now. If it's at all possible, I'm going to book you on the early morning flight tomorrow." He sat back in his chair, holding up his hand to forestall any objections. "You'll be doing me a favor, actually. I want you to see Brenholt at the Metropolitan Museum in New York. Find out what he thinks about a small exhibition of our findings sometime in the future." He sighed deeply. "I say small, although I must confess that I'm hoping for something a bit more. Still, one must be realistic. After all, everything points to Menket being a minor prince, not a Pharaoh."

"Would the Egyptians go for an exhibition so soon after discovery?"

"Stranger things have happened. And don't forget, they want the exposure. Tourism is way down this year, and that's where the money is. They'll want to whet the appetite of anyone who might consider coming to Egypt to see the really big stuff." The professor looked at him kindly. "Didn't I hear something about a young lady in New York?"

"Yes. Sara." He'd missed her like hell, come to think of it. He'd never gone for the local talent. No comparison.

But what would Sara make of him now? How would he be able to explain the crazy half-veiled memories that threatened to tip him over into insanity?

The professor seemed to be waiting for him to add something.

"We planned on her coming out here in November," Steve said, remembering the excitement in Sara's eyes.

"Well, now." The professor positively beamed. "I'm sure she'd like to see you sooner than that. That's almost four months away."

"Yes." It would work out, after all. Maybe when he got back to New York everything would be clearer. Sara could recommend a doctor. She'd mentioned seeing one in her last letter.

He could talk to Caldwell while he was in New York. Wrap this whole thing up and put it behind him. He must have been out of his mind to think that he could keep the scarab bracelet for himself. It had been a close enough call when the professor saw it the day before.

The bracelet had been bad luck from the very beginning. The sooner he got it to Caldwell, the better. He hadn't liked robbing the tomb, and he sure as hell wouldn't do it again.

In a way, Sara had been the reason for this deal from the very start. He'd been a jerk to think that money would impress her, but he hadn't been thinking straight.

Well, it was almost over. The bracelet would be enough to pay off his debt, with a nice piece of change left over to play around with.

And now he wouldn't have to share with Bill Evans.

The two Egyptians squatted on a worn scrap of carpet just inside the mud brick house. The smaller of the two spoke rapidly in Arabic, and the whites of his eyes glistened in the flickering light from an oil lamp.

"Now we are accursed for all time, and it is you, my brother, who has brought this misfortune upon us." He wiped the cold sweat off his face with the flat of his hand, and shivered slightly, despite the closeness of the room.

The older, heavier-set man drew his thick brows together in a knotted frown. "Tell me what you saw."

"One thousand times have I told you, may God bear witness."

"Tell me again."

"What will it signify?" said the smaller man." I saw him in the moonlight, may God defend me. The Americans were drunk, and I went out to urinate in their garden. It was there that I saw him. He spoke in the ancient tongue, then cracked the skull of the dog as you would crack an egg."

"The American?"

"The American. And yet, not he. Why did you disturb the spirits of Saqqara? You could have worked in the embassy kitchen, like me."

"Our father and his father before him dug into the tombs," said the older man. "I am always careful to show respect for the ancient ones. But the foreigners are greedy for what lies buried."

"Then let them be cursed, the children of dogs."

"With God's permission. Where is the American now?"

"They say he flies to New York," the smaller man replied. "Perhaps some thief there may kill him."

"They may shoot and shoot, but he will not die."

"Then, brother, we are lost," said the smaller man fatalistically.

ELEVEN

The shapely flight attendant on the British Airways DC-10 had pale blonde hair pulled back into a tight knot. The severe style stretched her delicately pink cheeks into an almost Oriental tilt, accentuating her large blue eyes.

She came up the aisle confidently, carefully checking the passengers' seat belts, and Steve put out a shaking hand as she went by.

"Would you get me some water, please?" His lips felt dry again. Dry as the desert, cracked and sore.

"I'm sorry, sir. You'll have to wait a moment. As soon as we take off, I'll bring you some." She smiled brightly. "Please fasten your seat belt."

"What time do we get to London?"

"Should be landing at Heathrow at thirteen hundred." She moved on down the aisle, and he closed his eyes, trying to sleep. It was time to take more of the Egyptian doctor's pills. But what good were they for his condition? Nothing had changed. Sometimes he felt as though he was losing touch with reality, fading away, only to be jolted back into the nightmare that his life had become.

The powerful jet engines released their force, and he felt the lurching rise that meant the plane was airborne.

"Menket, do you feel the wind? The wind-god Shu has cooled the hand of Re." Nefrenofret smiles happily in the autumn breeze, her black hair gleaming with auburn light in the mellow sun's rays. "Come, let us bathe, and I will anoint your head with oil."

He jerked awake as the flight attendant touched his arm.

"I've brought you some water, sir."

"Thanks." He gulped it down thirstily, and she raised her pale, undefined eyebrows.

"You really were thirsty, weren't you? Would you like some more?"

"No, I can get it, thanks." He looked up at the seat-belt sign ahead. The light was off. "I need to stretch my legs."

He got up clumsily and walked toward the toilets at the back, bumping into the seats as he went by.

The door on the toilet snapped shut

behind him, and he turned the water on, bending over and bathing his face.

Someone pounded on the door, but he ignored the interruption, sucking up some of the water in his cupped hands.

At least he felt better than he had the night before. Or was it just that he had become accustomed to feeling only half alive?

Drying off his face with a paper towel, he noticed the bracelet. The center section had been fashioned into a large scarab, unusually curved to fit around his wrist.

No. Menket's wrist. For God's sake, get that right, or you'll end up in the funny farm.

Anyway, no one at the airport had challenged him about it. Probably thought he got it in the Khan Khalili, just one of the thousands of brilliant fakes sold each year. Caldwell would be pleased.

The pounding at the door started up again, and a faint smile creased his face. Poor bastard probably had the trots.

"Just a minute," he said loudly. He leaned toward the mirror over the sink, touching his face with an exploring hand.

Dry, he thought. *Bone dry. Perhaps I am dehydrated.* His yellowish skin seemed stretched over the skull. Feverish eyes stared back out of shadowed sockets.

God Almighty, he thought with amazement. *I look like shit.*

He opened the door at last, and a

middle-aged woman glared at him, irritably muttering something unintelligible.

"Sorry," he murmured contritely. He pushed past her and made his way back to his seat.

The flight attendants had begun to serve drinks, but he asked for water again, unable to face anything stronger.

When the meal carts came trundling down the aisle, he felt now-familiar nausea wrench at his stomach. He got up hurriedly and made for the toilets.

Kneeling on the floor in the cramped space, he pushed his head down close to the toilet bowl. The previous occupant hadn't bothered to flush after use, and the sour ammonia stink of urine rose from the toilet-paper-clogged bowl. He began to heave uncontrollably, great wrenching heaves that left him watery-eyed and weak. But nothing came up. Nothing, except a thin, yellow, blood-streaked string of bile that hung from his open mouth.

Still he heaved, until finally he rested his clammy face on the cold, stainless-steel edge of the toilet bowl.

Got to get up, he thought tiredly. *Nothing in my stomach to vomit up.* He closed his eyes, catching his breath, and a sly voice in his head whispered harshly:

What about the dog at the embassy?

As if in a dream he licked his dry lips, tasting again the velvety marrow, still warm, and soaked with blood.

He stood up and opened the door.

Pushing past a young girl standing in the aisle, he muttered apologetically as he stumbled on her foot. He sat down in his seat, lay back his head, and closed his eyes.

What the fuck's wrong with me? he thought. *I must be losing my mind. And I don't know why.*

Sleep came, bringing merciful oblivion at last.

London lay below, enshrouded in a drizzle of rain.

"Mild precipitation," the captain said over the speaker.

"Couldn't he just say light rain?" The elderly man in the seat next to Steve's chuckled softly. "It's getting so that everyone has to use two-dollar words."

Steve smiled back with an effort, the skin on his face drawn tight. He didn't feel like talking to anyone.

Especially now.

His heart beat with erratic fury. Thank God he knew the city well enough to get around in.

All he had was a one-day layover, and there was something he had to do. Soon.

Soon.

TWELVE

How long till dark?

He'd counted on a few hours' wait. But now it was past nine P.M. and still light outside. He sat in the chair in his room at the Fleming's Hotel on Half Moon Street, staring at his twitching hands.

They seemed to have a life of their own, twitching, clenching, unclenching. *Ready.*

Couldn't wait much longer. The raging need within him had started its inexorable rise, whetting his appetite for something unspeakably horrible. He didn't know what would happen if he couldn't control it until dark.

The dog hadn't been enough. He could face what he'd done to the dog now because, God help him, he had to do it again. Had to have more, soon.

He licked his dry lips, shuddering.

He shifted impatiently in the chair. His bladder felt uncomfortably full, and why not? Shit, he'd drunk enough water to drown in.

He headed for the bathroom, unzipping his pants. Standing over the open toilet, he felt a sense of panic, noticing the deep reddish color that filled the bowl, staining the white porcelain.

Had he picked up a goddamn bladder infection as well? He hadn't noticed any other symptoms. But why should he? he thought cynically. With everything else that had happened lately, a bit of blood was nothing. At least it was his own.

He flushed the toilet, watching the orangy-red swirl away down the pipe, to be replaced by clear blue water.

I'm going to hell in a basket, he thought desperately. Both physically and mentally.

How long till dark?

He glanced out the window. Through the lace curtains, dusk softened the outlines of the houses across the street.

Wouldn't be long now, he promised himself. Just a little while longer. He took the raincoat off the hook in the closet.

Stealing it on the plane had been a stroke of genius. How had he managed to become so cunning?

The buttons were thick and round. Real tortoise shell, on first-class gabardine. English buttons on an English raincoat. That ought to throw the police off the trail.

His hands froze in the act of buttoning up the coat. What police, for Christsake? He hadn't done anything yet. Not here, anyway.

Oh, but you will, said a sly voice inside his head. *Oh, yes. Oh, yes, you will. Just a matter of time.*

He left the hotel quickly, his collar turned up to cover the lower part of his face. The young woman at the front desk didn't even give him a second look. He felt a fleeting sense of relief. The fewer people that saw him, the better.

Outside on the sidewalk, he hesitated a moment, then began to walk rapidly up the street toward the turnoff to Shepherd's Market. His heart raced with the urgency of the moment. Most of the stores that made up the old market had closed earlier. The narrow streets looked dark and empty.

The hunger was a ravening beast in the pit of his stomach now. He had to find something. Or . . . or . . .

He couldn't say a word. It clung to his mouth like a morsel of rotting gristle caught between his teeth.

Say it. Say it. For Christsake, spit it out.

"Gotta find something. Or *someone.*" The word wrenched itself out of his mind, like a grisly secret exposed for all time.

As if to escape the terrifying truth that hounded him, he hurried up White Horse Lane towards Piccadilly Street. At the end of the dark shadowy lane, the lights of Piccadilly Street glittered. Across the busy street, the seclusion of Green Park beckoned.

"Hello, love. Need some company?" The seductive voice came out of the shadows along the brick wall halfway up the lane.

The woman came towards him, narrow shoulders slouched, swinging a purse. He caught a whiff of cheap perfume, and the overwhelmingly familiar nausea filled his mouth with bile.

She put a hand on his arm, lipsticked mouth half open to reveal a yellow-coated tongue. Her breath smelled of stale cigarettes.

Suddenly he felt the urge to rip the tongue out, mouth to mouth, to taste, to tear—

"No! No! I can't," he muttered desperately, straining against the sinister presence within him. "Oh God oh God! Don't make me!"

"Buggar off then!" shrilled the woman, heading for the bright lights at the end of the lane.

He watched her go, her skinny hips rotating in an unsuccessful attempt at seduction.

The trembling in his hands was worse now. It couldn't be put off much longer.

He knew what he should have done. Why

had he let her go? Gutless. He craved the blood, the flesh. God, how he needed it. His whole body felt on fire, racked with great roiling shudders that made his ribs feel as though they would snap apart like dry sticks.

The lights of Piccadilly Street seemed blurred and wavy, a dangerous no-man's-land to be navigated before the shadowy darkness of Green Park could be reached.

Panting with the desperation of a wounded animal, he darted across the crowded street, long raincoat flapping around his legs.

Bulky London taxis sounded their horns in an orchestration of anger. A red double-decker bus swerved away clumsily, belching black smoke.

He reached the other side of the street, and raced into the park.

Quiet. Dim lights along the path, but dark among the bushes.

Safe. Hidden.

He crouched down, lungs heaving, pounding heart drunk on adrenaline.

Ready for the kill.

Bertie pushed his bike slowly through Green Park, the kickstand dragging on the ground.

He liked being alone at night. It felt peaceful.

People were always on at him. He

couldn't go anywhere without people saying, Bertie, do this, Bertie, do that, why did
you do it, Bertie, you're stupid, Bertie,
you'll never amount to anything.

It made his head ache sometimes, and
then he did bad things.

He knew that he was slow for 17, but he
was always willing. Everybody said so.
They had to give him that.

The trees are talking to me, he thought,
turning to look at the shadows near the
path.

"What did you say?" he asked, simple
expectation in his eyes. He smiled trust-
ingly as the hand came towards him out of
the shadows. He liked the pretty bracelet,
all blue and gold and shiny.

Then he saw the eyes.

He turned, panic-stricken. His foot
caught in the chain, and he stumbled
desperately over his bike, a thin, high-
pitched scream frothing his mouth as the
first crushing blow fell.

Detective Inspector Ian Potter rolled
over heavily in bed and turned off the
alarm. Six A.M. He didn't really need to get
up so early, but old habits died hard.

He knew all about the joke that used to
be passed around at New Scotland Yard,
the one that said you could set your watch
by the Inspector. That at 9:05 A.M. any
morning, rain or shine, you could look out

the window and see him coming down the street, his walk slow and deliberate, rather like his character.

Well, he wouldn't be going to work much longer.

Lots of rest, the doctor had said. Take some time off, have a little fun for a change.

Easier said than done, the Inspector thought bleakly. Still, doctor's orders. So, unless anything came up, he'd told them that he wouldn't be in to work today.

He shuffled his feet into his old wool slippers, wondering what he'd do with himself if they made him retire. He went over to the window and stared out at the early morning. He was a big, unwieldy-looking man, and people considered him plain, almost ugly, until they noticed the intelligence in his calm brown eyes.

Funny, him having a bad heart. He'd always been so strong. Molly used to tease him about it. She used to say that he was like a big brown bear. He sighed as he thought about Molly. What would she think of her brown bear now? Not much use for a policeman with a bad ticker these days.

The Inspector tried not to think about his heart as he took a bracing cold shower. Then he lathered up his face and began to shave. He took his time shaving because he wanted to make it last as long as possible. That way, he wouldn't be finished with breakfast until almost nine o'clock. Well, eight-thirty, anyway.

Had to get through the day somehow.

He combed his sparse brown hair carefully, making sure the parting was straight. Then he went into the kitchen, and made himself a cup of tea.

As his breakfast kippers cooked slowly, he scanned the front page of the newspaper. A paragraph about an odd occurrence at the American Embassy in Cairo caught his eye. Something about a dog. He frowned as he read the details.

The jarring ring of the telephone interrupted at that moment. The Inspector maneuvered his bulky frame into the foyer of his modest bungelow and picked up the receiver.

"Morning, sir," said the cheerful young voice at the other end of the line. "Sorry I had to call so early, but I thought that you might want to be in on this. Have you had breakfast yet?"

"No." The Inspector looked regretfully into the kitchen, where the two kippers sat steaming in a pan.

"Well, it's just as well. You won't want to have eaten after you see the mess in Green Park. Nasty, very nasty."

"Murder, is it?" asked the Inspector.

"Hard to say, sir. Could be some kind of wild-animal attack. Funny thing, though. No sign of any animal at all, except the usual domestic pets. Can't say that I see any of them involved in this." There was a pause. "Large bones and skull crushed. Contents removed and presumed eaten."

"Contents? What are you talking about, Sergeant?"

"Marrow and brain eaten by someone or something."

The Inspector prided himself on the possession of an iron stomach. But now he didn't fancy the kippers quite as much.

He'd seen it all, in his time.

Right from the very first day, green as grass, pounding a beat, the Inspector had learned about the unspeakable side of human nature. The dirty, secret side.

Timid-looking bookkeepers, nine-to-fivers all their lives, predictable as the day is long, except for one little weakness. Murder. It always seemed to come to that.

Quiet little men, hardly noticeable in the crowd. White hands and ink-stained fingers, burying bodies in the cellar. And not just the occasional one. God, no. Once they started, it was as though they couldn't stop.

And the women he'd arrested in his time. God Almighty.

Well, you know what they said: deadlier than the male, when all was said and done. Knock off a husband or two with a cup of tea that contained a trifle more than darjeeling and never blink an eye.

But none of them, not even the worst of

them, were anything like this.

Detective Inspector Ian Potter took out a neatly folded handkerchief and dabbed at his forehead. *Almost glad that it isn't my case.*

Must be getting old, he thought ruefully. *Time was, I could take in a nasty mess like this without batting an eye.*

Perhaps it was because of the lad's mother. Hysterical, naturally. Who could blame her, poor soul? It would be a long time before he forgot her howling screams.

They hadn't let her see the body. How could they? Still, she'd probably insist on viewing the remains before it was all over.

Funny about the bones. The Inspector frowned, deep in thought.

Seemed like he'd read about something that bore a remarkable similarity to this murder only recently.

Couldn't have, though. Papers would have had a field day. He could see it now, headlines as tall as houses.

"Cannibal Killer on Rampage."

No, this was a first.

Still, something about it rang a bell.

THIRTEEN

"Did you hear about the guy in the park? Freaked me out, man." The shaggy-haired youth in a dirty windbreaker and brand-new red high-topped Reeboks fastened his seat belt and glanced at Steve in the seat beside him. "Did you hear about it?"

"No." Perhaps if he pretended to be asleep, the kid would leave him alone.

"It was gruesome, man. I mean, really sick, you know?"

Steve looked away from the kid. He needed all his concentration to fight the waves of nausea that he knew would hit him as soon as they brought out the food.

With any luck the kid would watch the movie, read a book, get high, anything except talk all the way to New York.

He needed time to think. He'd see a

doctor just as soon as he took care of the business with Caldwell. But what exactly could he tell a doctor? That he, Steve Harrison, former football player and average all-round guy, who could eat three McDLTs at a single sitting, had suddenly developed murkier tastes? That his penchant for Miller Light had been replaced by a yen for something thicker, hotter, blood-red?

One thing was sure, he couldn't plead innocence any more.

Before the British Airways plane had landed at Heathrow, he had known what it was he had to do. Not only known. *Planned* for it.

In the confused rush to get off the plane, he'd managed to steal a raincoat from one of the overhead lockers. And after . . .

After it was over, he'd run across Piccadilly Street, away from the park, ripping off the purloined raincoat, now soaked with the simpleton's blood.

The police must have found it by now. But he didn't have to worry about that. Not a thing on it to lead them to him. He'd be in New York in just a few hours.

Long gone.

But what about the next time?

Because there would be a next time. And a time after that, and God knows how many other times, until they caught him and killed him or locked him up forever.

He closed his eyes with fatigue. It was

like the time he'd been ill in school. He'd shit in his pants, and had felt like dying from shame, until the nurse told him that she knew he couldn't help it. That his illness had made him lose control.

He still remembered the helpless feeling as his body disgraced him before his friends. They'd made vulgar jokes about it in a touchingly clumsy attempt to cheer him up—to show they understood and didn't blame him.

Well, he wouldn't get that kind of sympathetic understanding now.

No. This was a different sickness, evil and pernicious, draining away the last vestiges of conscious will.

Unforeseen urges had taken over, luring him down dark and powerful avenues that he could only half see, half remember. And always, always, the shadowy form of the other one. The one he recognized at last.

Menket.

Menket smothering him, ready to exert an evil, suffocating control for longer and longer periods, until at last he wouldn't be Steve Harrison any more.

Not ever.

Sara met him at Kennedy.

He could see her standing on tiptoe, a small, intense young woman, straining to find him among the stream of disembarking passengers.

She had cut her dark hair short, and the new style left her neck and ears exposed, giving her an air of vulnerability. Her brown eyes lit up when she saw him, and she grinned crookedly with unabashed delight.

It had been her grin that had attracted him to Sara in the first place. Everything about her seemed sharp and city-wise, until she let loose with that grin. Then it was like a warm light escaping through the crack of an almost-closed door.

Steve felt immediately that he had to know the warmth of that light up close or feel the lack of it forever.

He shouldered through the crowd toward her, ignoring the angry exclamations of the people he pushed aside. He dropped his carry-on bag to the floor, lifting her up in his arms and kissing her hungrily.

"Oh, God, it's good to see you," he muttered, holding her tightly against him.

"I've missed you too, Steve."

"Yeah, but you just don't know . . ." He broke off to kiss her again.

"Oh, I think I can guess." She pulled back slightly, smiling up at him. "Have you got everything?"

"Yeah." They began to walk towards the exit. "Didn't you have to work today?"

"No. I managed to get the whole day off. How are you feeling?"

"Okay. No, not okay. I feel like shit."

"Your boss told me. Guess what? He called me at work." She threw back her head, laughing unselfconsciously. "You can imagine the stir *that* created. Long distance from Cairo. My God!"

"What did he say?"

"That you feel like shit. He phrased it differently of course, but it's the same thing in the long run." She stopped suddenly, and turned towards him. "Wait a minute, let me have a look at you." Her eyes searched his face worriedly, a slight frown creasing her forehead. "He's right. What happened to you, Steve? The professor said something about dysentery." She took his arm and began to pull him toward the double exit doors. "Come on, let's go home. Then we'd better find you a doctor."

A doctor. What could a doctor do for him now?

How could he explain that he couldn't eat to save his soul? Hated the very smell of food.

Except . . .

No, he couldn't see a doctor.

"Forget it," he said abruptly.

"Forget it? No way, Steve. You look terrible. I'd send you to *my* doctor—except that he's an obstetrician." She glanced at him quickly, as if to see his reaction to her words, but he didn't catch the meaning of what she'd said.

He felt thirsty again—an all-encompassing thirst that seemed to burn down his throat to his stomach, unquenchable, never-ending. Even his skin felt seared and dry.

They began to pass a drinking fountain, and he pulled his arm away from her hand, bending over to drink. He couldn't seem to slake the thirst that burned like a fire out of control.

"My God, Steve! What did you have for lunch?"

He ignored her question, gulping at the cool, thin stream of water, until his stomach felt uncomfortably distended. He could feel the water sloshing about inside, and he stopped drinking.

But the burning thirst remained. He wiped at his mouth with the back of his hand, wanting to drink again, knowing full well that he'd vomit if he did.

"Come on," said Sara again. "Let's get a cab and go home." She smiled at him. A slow, sweet, smile full of promise and anticipation. "God, how I've missed you, Steve."

Home. How in hell would he manage things there? His mind tried to block out the thought of food. But people did eat, didn't they? Would Sara accept his aversion to the smell of anything cooking? Thank God she wasn't that crazy about cooking anyway.

She'd understand for a day or two, but then what? He couldn't keep ducking meals without her getting suspicious.

Another thing. What would he do when the raging need overcame him?

In the cab he leaned back, resting his head against the cool vinyl. He looked out of the window as Queens sped by, and wondered if he should have stayed in Cairo.

The ride to Manhattan seemed interminable, the impressive skyline a tantalizing mirage on the horizon.

For a crazy, distorted moment, the distant buildings blurred and meshed together, until he thought he saw majestic pyramids up ahead.

Nausea again. Nausea, and a sudden panicky wave of confusion at the sight of traffic zooming by.

Don't take over now, he pleaded silently. *I'll do anything you want, later.*

But for God's sake, not now . . .

"Steve! What's the matter?"

He shook his head absently, dragging his eyes away from the confusing scene outside the taxi. "Nothing. Just thinking of things. I've got to make a phone call."

"Can't it wait? You just got off the plane."

"No, it can't wait." He had to talk to Caldwell, get rid of the bracelet, settle accounts.

Maybe the bracelet was the cause of all this.

Maybe there was a curse attached to it,

to everything in the tomb. The ancient Egyptians were always leaving curses for those who came to rob the tombs. He should have thought about that. But all he'd thought about was money. That, and how to be rid of Caldwell.

Perhaps he felt guilty about stealing the bracelet. He licked his dry lips nervously. Perhaps his guilt was doing a number on his head. Punishing him subconsciously.

But what about the other thing? The killings.

Could he have read the account of the murder in the paper, and somehow imagined that he had done it himself?

He couldn't remember any of it in detail. Only the heady, intoxicating feeling of power, of life, afterwards.

But while it was happening, he'd felt detached. Almost like being an onlooker, an innocent bystander, until it was over.

None of it was his doing. He would have prevented all of it, if he could. It sickened him.

Funny about the blood, though. He could still taste it.

Hot and coppery. Smooth and salty.

And infinitely, infinitely stimulating.

He glanced out of the window. "How much farther is it?" he asked impatiently.

"What are you talking about? You know where I live." She stared at him in surprise. "We're almost there."

The cab turned into West 80th, pulling

up with a squeal of brakes at Sara's address.

"I guess I just lost my bearings for a moment," he said. "Don't worry about it." He got out of the cab and paid off the driver.

"You haven't been gone that long," she said quietly.

"I'm tired, that's all." A note of irritability crept into his voice. "Look, what d'you expect? I've been traveling for two days. Give me a break."

She stared at him for a long moment. "Something's very wrong, isn't it? Why don't you tell me and get it over with."

"Ah, shit, I don't need this." He made an impatient gesture with his hand, as if he could brush everything away. "Frankly, I don't want to stand out here and discuss it now. Let me put my bag away, then I'm going for a walk."

"Just like that?" She looked angry, hurt.

"Just like that."

He didn't feel like trying to explain anything yet. Anyway, how could he? He didn't understand it himself.

Sara went up the steps at the front of her apartment house and opened the glass security door with her key.

"In case you've forgotten, I live at the end of the corridor."

He followed her in silently, setting his bag down just inside her apartment door.

"Look, I'm sorry, Sara. I need some

time to myself. I'll probably be back later tonight. I just don't feel like talking.''

''I understand.'' She wouldn't look at him.

''No you don't.'' He made a helpless gesture. ''All I know is that I've got to be alone for awhile.''

He bent down to kiss her, but she turned away, and his lips brushed her cheek.

He could feel her staring after him as he left the apartment, and the salty touch of moisture on his lips told him that she was crying.

FOURTEEN

He used to like Columbus Avenue.

When he first came east from the lotus-land known as Southern California, he'd loved everything about Manhattan. The excitement, the people. Even the pace.

It made you stretch, he'd thought. Reach out for a taste of a life he'd only read about.

E.B. White had called it the city that is a goal, and that's how Steve had felt about it.

Until now.

Now everything hurt. The crowds, the noise, the restaurants were all too much for his senses to deal with.

Especially the restaurants.

He left Sara's apartment and walked to the corner of West 80th and Columbus. A cab swerved towards the curb, the driver

looking for a fare, and Steve watched dispassionately as a girl in tights climbed
in.

Still too early for streetlights, and just a
hint in the air of a summer storm soon to
come. Smells of food cooking drifted out
from the restaurants along the avenue,
stirring up the queasy feeling that rarely
left him now.

Nothing would ever be the same for him
again. He knew that with certainty.

He headed south toward Lincoln Center,
keeping an eye out for a public phone.

Fortune-tellers sat on the sidewalks
reading palms and Tarot cards.

*How would you like to read my palm?
Guess what you'd see there.*

He laughed bitterly to himself, and a
passing couple glanced at him, giggling as
they went by.

Why not? he thought. *I must look crazy,
possessed.*

If they only knew . . .

He came to an unoccupied public phone
and stopped short, fumbling in his pocket
for change. Among the Egyptian coins he
found a quarter. Time to make that call to
Caldwell. Get rid of the bracelet.

He could use the money right now. Sara
might throw him out, and hotels cost an
arm and a leg in this town.

Not that he'd blame her if she did throw
him out. Anyway, it might not be safe for
him to stay with her much longer. No

telling what might happen. He shivered slightly.

The coin dropped into the box, and he waited for the dial tone. Dialing with a shaky forefinger, he managed on the second try to get the number right. Goddamn Caldwell always made him feel uneasy, like trying to get close to a rattlesnake.

The phone at the other end rang and rang for what seemed to be an interminable time. The bastard liked to make people sweat. Got off on watching people sweat. And it worked every time. He was sweating now, wasn't he?

"C'mon, c'mon," he muttered nervously. "Hurry up and answer the goddamn phone." The hand holding the receiver grew slick and wet. He switched hands quickly, wiping away the sweat on his jacket.

"Yes?" The voice on the other end sounded cold and impersonal and slightly menacing. But it wasn't smooth enough to be Caldwell.

"Mr. Caldwell, please."

Silence.

"This is Steve Harrison. I want to speak to Mr. Caldwell."

"Wait." It sounded so final, he half expected to hear the click of disconnection. He switched hands again, shifted position, whistled nervously through clenched teeth.

A man in a dark suit, carrying a brief-case, came down the sidewalk and stopped near the phone booth. The man glanced at his watch, frowning slightly.

Steve ignored him. Let him wait.

Someone picked up the receiver at the other end.

"Mr. Harrison?" Caldwell. No one else had that peculiar drawn-out, flat-toned way of speaking.

"I've got something for you." Steve kept his voice low.

"What?"

"I don't want to talk about it over the phone." Steve glanced around. The man in the dark suit was still there. "Look. I can't stand here all night. Someone needs the phone. When do you want me to show you the item I got for you?"

"Which item is that, Mr. Harrison?"

"What are we doing? Playing games?" He cupped his other hand over the receiv-er. "You know what I'm talking about."

"Careful, Mr. Harrison." The voice held a threat.

What the hell did Caldwell mean? The cold son of a bitch was just jerking him around. "I went to a lot of trouble to get this out of the tomb. Do you want it, or not?"

"Another item, Mr. Harrison? My cup runneth over indeed."

"I don't understand." Steve looked

down. The edge of the bracelet showed under the sleeve of his shirt. "What do you mean, another one?"

"I have already received a rather nice statue of the goddess Isis, courtesy of a friend of yours. A Mr. Evans, I believe. But I'd be very happy to see what else you have for me." He paused, and Steve tried to make sense out of it all.

Bill must have taken something from the tomb, after all. The stupid bastard. That could prove to be disastrous. Professor Peterson would see at once that one of the goddesses was missing.

"Mr. Harrison." Caldwell again. Steve had almost forgotten the man at the other end, but now he'd better pay attention.

"Mr. Harrison. I have something for you too."

Of course. The money.

Shit. Twice as much now.

Caldwell continued. "But not today. Call me tomorrow morning, and we'll talk about a meeting then."

This time Steve heard the click of the receiver.

FIFTEEN

A lavender gray dusk veiled Manhattan Island as Steve walked toward Central Park West. Traffic had picked up.

It would be dark soon.

He couldn't walk forever. Eventually he'd have to go back to Sara's apartment, and try to explain. But what could he say to her that she'd believe?

Anyway, he just couldn't face the questions in her eyes, unless he knew the answers. Something he knew wouldn't happen.

A small crowd of tourists stood in a cluster near the corner of Central Park West and 72nd Street, staring up at the mysteriously exotic exterior of the Dakota building.

"That's where—" A small chorus of sighs and sibilent whispers swirled out

117

from the edge of the loose-knit circle of people.

Death, again. Death always command-ed a certain degree of morbid fascination, Steve thought angrily. A certain degree of relentless curiosity. Especially when it was the premature death of someone like John Lennon.

God, they make me sick.

He pushed past the small group, and crossed over to the park.

He wanted to be alone, away from peo-ple with their greedy staring eyes.

Voices bothered him, gratingly intrud-ing. Carefree voices that wondered out loud about the fatal shooting of their idol one minute, and talked of the cheapest place to eat sushi the next.

For some time now, ever since robbing Menket's tomb, in fact, he had stopped believing in the finality of death.

Death wasn't so bad anyway. The an-cient Egyptians had known that.

Life was the bitch. A confusing entity to be wrestled with. An endless battle to be won in a no-win situation.

His train of thought stopped abruptly, cut off in midstream.

Something seemed to be wrong with his vision. The trees blurred and shifted in front of him, until soon he could barely see their outline.

Jagged splinters of light flashed painful-ly bright, with an almost tactile sharpness.

Sounds of traffic faded gradually, like the tail-end of a symphony. Gradually he felt a sense of distance from everything around him.

A terrifying sense of being distanced . . .

Disembodied . . .

For a split second he understood everything.

Then . . .

Nothing.

Menket drew back under a tree, listening carefully to the rustling night sounds in the park. He had waited impatiently for the soft cloak of night.

Soon, now, he would usurp the useless spirit of the other man who shared this twilight existence with him.

For a time he had condescended to allow the one called Steve a facsimile of life. But only until he, Menket, could learn the ways of this new and inferior world. Then the other one would be done away with, cast off into the unsacramented void, to drift aimlessly in the dust of ages.

Above the Egyptian, the sky goddess Nut enshrouded the earth in darkness. Her children, the stars, pulsated faintly in the dark and exalted realm of the dead.

Was Nefrenofret amongst them?

An expression of pain crossed Menket's face as he looked up at the stars. Memories, aeons old but as fresh as if it were only yesterday, pierced his heart.

Do not weaken, he thought sternly. *Everything is in the hands of the powerful gods who rule over us. I, Menket, must command them to assist me. Only with their help can I protect the mysteries of Egypt.*

Throwing back his head, he flared his nostrils, breathing in the smog-tainted air around him. Over to the east he recognized the heavy musky odor of confined animals, carefully noting their direction by the familiar stars above him.

If he felt the raging need, he would be able to find their enclosure with ease.

Not yet, he thought. *Not yet.*

He had sated himself the night before, gorging on the human sacrifice that Osiris had chosen to send his way.

His head turned sharply, as though someone had called out to him.

Wait. Something just beyond a turn of the path.

He broke into a run, feeling an urgency that had to be satisfied.

Suddenly, he saw it . . .

His heart raced wildly, and an anguished cry tore at his throat.

Rage. Rage and hate that almost choked him with its intensity.

He threw himself down at the base of the obelisk, his eyes staring wildly at the ancient supplications etched in stone.

The final obscenity. What evil tribe had

dragged the holy Ben-ben so far from mighty Egypt?

He put out a hand to touch the dirt-encrusted monolith.

Where is thy temple, O Re?

What evil has befallen the holy temple of Heliopolis?

Menket sat back on his heels, arms outstretched, a timeless curse from the Book of the Dead on his twisted lips.

Re shall pierce thy head. He cuts through thy face, and it is crushed in his hand.

Thy bones are smashed, thou enemy of Re, and the black taste of death is on thy tongue.

He rose quickly to his feet as a low, barely audible mutter seemed to come menacingly from beyond the grassy hillocks and graveled paths to the south of the obelisk. Listening intently, he ignored the implicit threat.

He had no fear in the strange darkness.

What could a high priest of Hakau, the blackest of magic, possibly have to fear? Had he not traveled safely through the darkness of the grave?

He flexed his hands at his sides, feeling their power.

Somehow the skill of the old one had been cunning enough to find a human shell that boasted of great strength. That strength, together with the forceful influence of the art of Hakau, put him far above other men.

No matter that he had regained life in an unknown time. It was meant to be. Pre-ordained all those centuries ago, when the red earth and the black earth formed the center of the world in Egypt.

Isis, in her ineffable wisdom, had spread her wings, transporting him safely through the miasma of the netherworld to a time of great tribulation for the mystical dead of Egypt. He would bow to her superior knowledge.

He heard the sharp snap of a twig, announcing someone's furtive approach. Drawing back into the leafy shadows, Menket whispered the incantation for power.

He closed his eyes a moment, feeling the powerful strength gush through his body like a fierce tide, banding his muscles with sinews of steel.

Now, come.

As a threatening shadowy figure approached him down a small winding path, Menket laughed softly.

And waited . . .

Nothing had gone right for Larry Boudreaux all day.

Another bummer, in a month of bummers.

A month? Shit. A year. A goddamn *life.*

His pockets were empty again, and man

oh man, did he hate empty pockets.

His coarse, acne-pocked face screwed up into an expression of disgust. His old lady hadn't come up with any cash lately, and no amount of beatings could shake loose what ain't there. He'd told her—nice and slow, so she wouldn't say she didn't understand—no dough, no crack. And just so there'd be no mistake, he'd hit her one up side her head.

Shit. All she was good for was whining, and not much else.

If she didn't get off her ass and hustle pretty soon, he'd have to teach her a lesson she wouldn't forget.

Meantime, he was busted. Tapped out.

He walked furtively across a path, into a shadowy cluster of trees, hands shoved hard into the pockets of his leather jacket.

First son of a bitch that crosses my path, he promised himself, *is gonna wish he'd never been born.*

He felt a tinge of pleasure flush in his cheeks. His big hands clenched into fists. A switchblade knife lay cold and comforting inside his boot.

He'd had that knife a long time, had baptized it in blood way back when he was just a snot-nosed kid. He'd found out the thrill he could get with the first cut. Found out that just the sight of it gave him power over his victims, that he liked to hear them beg. Especially the women.

Bitches, all of them.

He saw something up ahead. Yeah, there he was. A fuckin' plum, just waiting to be picked.

"C'mon, asshole," he growled menacingly. "C'mon and show me what you got."

Lieutenant O'Reilly, of NYPD Homicide, cupped his hands around a match to light a cigarette, drawing the smoke deep into his lungs. He pinched the reddened tip of the match and slipped it into his pocket.

Poker Face. That's what they called him down at the station, and true to his name, his bland Irish countenance remained blank as he stared at the sickening mess on the ground.

In the early morning light, the body of a leather-jacketed man lay crumpled awkwardly in the wet grass, an expression of pained surprise frozen on his face.

As a macabre afterthought, the killer had gutted him like a sacrificial ram, dribbling the whitish-gray entrails across the victim's feet.

A trace of fecal matter tainted the air.

The surrounding area was still being combed for clues, and now O'Reilly waited to hear from the man who crouched by the corpse.

The gray-haired medical examiner straightened up stiffly.

"These early calls are murder on my back," he complained.

The lieutenant moved over to where the older man stood stretching gingerly.

"What have we got this time, Doc?" he asked.

"Something different, for a change. Never seen anything like it. Torso split down the middle like a piece of kindling. But no actual weapon used, that I can detect." The medical examiner paused, biting his lip, deep in thought. "Maybe a new form of martial art. I don't know. Have to see what forensics and an autopsy will reveal."

"Martial art? Looks like an axe job to me." The lieutenant took another drag on his cigarette, his green eyes narrowing imperceptibly against the smoke. "Hope to shit we don't have a vigilante running wild in Central Park."

SIXTEEN

Voices drifted down the air shaft to Sara Fenster's apartment. Happy voices, chattering in Spanish, coming from the Puerto Rican family on the floor above.

Sara lay in bed, half-listening, wondering about Steve. How could she have been so wrong about anyone?

Perhaps he had met someone else. It could happen. Someone mysteriously dark and exotic.

Someone Egyptian.

She bit her lip, trying to stop the tears. Damn it, it hurt. More than three months apart, and he preferred to go for a walk. He couldn't have made it any plainer if he'd told her flat out that he was through. That it was all a mistake.

It was a mistake, all right.

She hadn't even been able to tell him about the baby. Not an easy thing to

126

discuss when the father has other things on his mind.

She rolled over on her side, listening to the people upstairs, feeling lonely. Feeling so *alone*.

It couldn't be good for the baby, hurting like this, but she couldn't help it. If she didn't get to sleep pretty soon, she'd look like death warmed over in the morning.

Gradually, the sounds from upstairs died down, became muffled, softer. Somewhere a window closed quietly. A TV switched off.

She sighed, closing her eyes, but she couldn't go to sleep. Not until Steve came home.

If he *did* come home.

She dozed. Jerked awake. Dozed again.

Her head ached, but she didn't want to take anything for it. Not with the baby coming. She'd just put up with the pain. If only she could sleep . . .

A faint scratching sound came from the front door. Then a click, and the sound of it opening. So he still had the key.

She got up on her elbow to stare at the red digital numbers on her clock.

Where had he been until this early hour?

She might have understood it if he had been the type to frequent the clubs. But that kind of thing had never meant anything to him.

So where had he been since he left her at the door to go for a walk? Some walk. Over six hours.

She lay down again, trying to find a comfortable place for her aching head on the pillow, her eyes fixed on the bedroom door.

She heard him head for the bathroom, go in, and lock the door. That was the last straw. Since when did they need locks?

Since Egypt, that's when.

She swung her legs out of bed and ran to the bathroom, sudden anger lending speed to her feet.

Just to be sure, she tried the lock. Yes, she'd been right. The bathroom door became a massive wall of stone between them. She slapped her hand on it in frustration.

"Steve! Open up!"

Behind the door, silence.

She pressed her ear near the crack along the side. "Don't play games with me, Steve. We've got to talk."

Nothing. No faucet turned on. No flushing of the toilet.

She stood motionless, listening, struck by a mental picture of him on the other side of the door, listening to her.

"Oh, Steve." She turned her head slightly, resting her forehead against the cool white painted wood. "Okay. If that's the way you want it. Go ahead and stay in there all night. Or what's left of it."

She turned to go back into the bedroom, when she heard a slight noise. The straw laundry basket, rustling.

"Steve! Goddamn it! Open up!" How

much longer would he keep this up? Before she could stop herself, the sweet secret spewed out, transformed by anger into a weapon of assault.

"God damn you, Steve! I'm pregnant! D'you hear me? Don't you want to hear about it? Or don't you care?"

Silence.

The hurt felt like a lump of dry bread stuck in her throat.

"Screw you, you jerk," she muttered angrily, going back into the bedroom.

Tiredness and frustration made her weak. I can't fight anymore tonight, she thought wearily. She got into bed, turning on her side. She bent her knees up close to her stomach and closed her eyes.

After a long while, as if in a dream, she heard Steve come into the room. She felt him slip quietly into bed beside her, but by then, her fatigue had carried her halfway to sleep.

And well on the way to a nightmare of unspeakable dimensions.

Where did they come from, these voices?

Rising. Falling.

Surrounding her with a wall of unintelligible sound that assaulted her ears.

Where am I? she silently asked. No one answered.

She felt herself buffeted from side to side by sweating, surging bodies. Pulled along by clutching hands.

Her eyes felt weighted, as if sealed shut by metal discs. She tried to open them, feeling the muscles straining in her cheeks, on her brow.

No use. Her ears and nose tried to do the job that her eyes could not. Sensing the dust, the heat, the babbling voices, the hot breath on her face.

She cradled something in her arms. Something cold and hard, wrapped in fine cloth. Struggling not to fall, she felt herself pushed along roughly in the midst of the crowd.

The soles of her feet burned with the heat of what she deduced was sand. Hot, dry sand. Sifting in between her toes as she staggered along.

She wanted to speak, to cry out, but found that she could not open her lips.

There wasn't time for fear, only for a desperate need to survive the moment. Once she almost stumbled, and she clutched the bundle in her arms close to her breast, trying to keep her balance. The bundle chafed her skin, and she realized that her breasts were exposed.

The hot sand beneath her feet had given way to smooth sandstone. Square slabs of stone, almost slippery in their smoothness.

She smelled the cloyingly sweet perfume of flowers. Rough hands placed a garland around her neck. The soft petals fell gently onto her naked breasts making a whispering sound as they settled over the bundle she cradled in her arms.

Hands tugged at her hair, tweaked her breasts cruelly.

She tried to move her lips. *Leave me alone*, she silently cried.

As if on cue, the jostling crowd fell back, and she sensed that she stood alone in an immense silence.

Suddenly, a commanding voice somewhere in front of her came out of the stillness, the words harsh and guttural. She stood still, not understanding.

Someone touched her eyes and mouth with a feather, removing in a flash the suffocating weight that sealed them shut. The feather touched her ears, and she understood the words.

Her terrified eyes opened to a strange, exotic scene. Over her head, the burnished blue sky curved like a metalic lid to the horizon. The glare of sunlight struck her eyes like a blow, forcing her to close them again for an instant.

Opening them cautiously again, wincing as the harsh sun reflected off the pale yellow sand, Sara darted quick frightened glances around her. The crowd of half-naked people who had surged behind, pushing her forward, now held back.

They were packed tightly in a wide semicircle, and their voices rose and fell in a chant of excited murmuring.

An immense building, gleaming white in

the sunlight, rose before her. A man stood with his back to her in the wide entryway, arms outstretched to the heavens. His brown body, naked except for a thin pleated loincloth made of a fine white material, gleamed with a muscular beauty.

She tried to see who it was, but when he turned around, she saw that he wore a golden mask.

The crowd behind her roared, and with a gasp of surprise, Sara realized that the mask depicted Steve Harrison's features.

"Who are you?" she whispered.

Behind the mask, the glassy eyes burned with a reddish flame, through slits in the gold outlined with blue enamel.

It couldn't be Steve. His eyes were gray. His body didn't look like this stranger's body.

She felt an overwhelming sense of danger. "Who are you?" she asked again.

The glassy eyes seemed to bore into her innermost mind, until she thought her head would burst.

"What do you want?" she screamed.

"Follow me," the strange apparition said. The sternly uttered words resounded gonglike in her brain until she wanted to shriek with pain.

The crowds of onlookers began to chant again, the sound rising and falling in rhythmic cadence. Rising and falling to beat against her aching head like a harsh wind from the desert.

She tried to speak. To beg. To resist.

But the pain in her head became unbearable. A throbbing sledgehammer of agony against the inner casing of her skull.

"Follow," the apparition said again, turning away.

This time, almost fainting with the cruel pounding that had invaded her head, she followed, still clutching the mysterious bundle to her chest.

Through the massive portals, into the inner passageway lined with pillars. Ahead of her, the man walked on, never turning to see if she followed. Past chamber after chamber. Until, at last, the inner temple, open to the sky.

She looked up, feeling the hot sun on her face. The sky, a vivid blue heat, shimmered in undulant waves like a silken flag. The white hot glare cut like a knife across her aching eyes.

The apparition spoke again. "Come, bride of the Nile. The Time of Times is nigh."

He stood on a circular platform in the center of the temple, and as if mesmerized, she advanced and stood before him. His eyes captured hers, and to avoid his glassy stare, she looked down at the floor. Delicate mosaic tile had been arranged to form a map of the heavens. Stars fanned out away from the center, a red-gold disc that represented the sun.

Her head jerked up as the golden-masked stranger grasped her shoulders, his fingers digging cruelly into her bare flesh.

"Soon is the time," he intoned. The restless crowd beyond the portals, repeated the phrase over and over, their voices filling the air with a wail of sound.

An acolyte, dressed in a white transparent robe, advanced on Sara, sprinkling water on her head.

Sara raised her face to the cool water, and the water trailed down her cheeks like tears.

Suddenly the acolyte tried to tear the precious bundle from her arms, wrenching at the delicate cloth that bound it with grasping fingers.

"No!" she gasped pleadingly to the golden mask. "Help me, Steve!"

As if in answer to her plea, the man slowly removed the mask, revealing the horror behind it.

Dead. Decaying. The corpselike face moved with an imitation of life, to grin engagingly at her.

But it wasn't the necrotic flesh that moved.

Creamy maggots, avidly pursuing their busy trade, worked around the blackened flesh, stirring, moving, spreading the pus-filled lips in a facsimile of smiling goodwill.

He bent towards her like a bridegroom, as if to kiss her open mouth.

Shrieking in horror, Sara reached out to ward him off, punching out at the approaching death's-head with frantic hands. The bundle fell from her arms like a stone, to smash upon the colorful tiles at her feet.

In the instant before it shattered into dust, Sara saw what she had cradled so tenderly.

Too late, she tried to retrieve the precious load.

With a resounding crash, the alabaster baby shattered at her feet.

Lost. *Lost for all time.*

Sara jerked awake, her heart pounding, her body bathed in a cold sweat.

"Oh, God," she muttered, wiping at her mouth with a shaking hand.

Beside her, Steve still slept, his face strained and pale, as if his sleep were troubled by a nightmare of his own.

Couldn't be as bad as mine, she thought with a shudder. Nothing could be that bad.

Just a dream.

She got up carefully, trying not to disturb Steve. As she slipped on her robe, she glanced at the clock. Only 6:30 A.M. Still time for another hour's nap, if she wanted it. But then, the dream might come back.

She went into the kitchen and filled the

kettle with water. Why had she dreamed such a terrible thing?

She took a mug out of the cupboard and looked for the instant coffee. Measuring a spoonful of the coffee into the mug, she thought about breakfast, then decided against it. Her stomach felt upset enough. No use aggravating it further.

She shuddered suddenly, remembering the horror of the face behind the mask. Everything had been too upsetting the night before. No wonder she'd had a nightmare.

A sad feeling of disappointment filled her with depression. She had been so excited at the prospect of Steve coming home, had fantasized about the moment when they would be alone.

Nothing had turned out the way she hoped it would. Not even the moment she'd chosen to tell him about the baby.

She sat down at the kitchen table and took a careful sip of the steaming coffee.

Toughen up, girl, she thought to herself. *What did you expect? Happy ever after?*

A circle of bubbles floated delicately in the center of the mug. She watched it for a moment, trying to come up with a suitable answer to her question.

Yes, she thought finally. *That's exactly what I had been hoping for.*

Living with Steve, and the baby. Happily ever after.

SEVENTEEN

Morning sunshine didn't quite make it into Sara's bedroom. The large square window faced onto an airshaft between buildings, and the only view, day or night, was a dirty brick wall.

Steve opened his eyes slowly, glad of the dim light.

His mouth felt dry, coated and thick. He needed a drink of water badly.

What had happened last night?

He remembered crossing Central Park West and entering the park.

Then, nothing.

Not even a hazy memory, this time. Not until he came home. Then he'd slipped into the bathroom, avoiding Sara.

Something else. She'd pounded on the door, and he vaguely remembered her crying out, "I'm pregnant, Steve!"

Had she really said that? Oh, it was possible, of course. After all, he'd only left for Egypt three months ago. But, Christ. The timing couldn't be worse.

He remembered waiting for her to go back to bed. It must have been another half hour before he finally opened the bathroom door, and crept into bed beside her, careful not to wake her.

After that, he remembered nothing again, except a `dream, just before he awoke. A dream of water, cool and darkly shaded. Golden sunlight playing on the surface. Dark and mysterious in the depths. Cool green water.

Nile green.

He smiled wryly, savoring the last diminishing pleasure of it. He had dived in, opening his mouth wide to swallow the bittersweet waters of the eternal river.

Or had the river swallowed him without a trace, far below the golden flecks on the deep green surface?

Whatever the dream, he had escaped nightmarish reality for a few tranquil hours. He glanced at the digital clock on the bedside table. Ten A.M. Sara must have left for work at the New York Historical Society, and he felt a guilty sense of relief. Now he could forget about explaining until later on tonight. Thing was, he couldn't postpone it forever. He'd have to tell her soon. Better get it over with.

If she called the police and they locked

him up, so be it. He couldn't let the killing go on anymore.

A sudden thought struck him. Had anything happened the night before? He had to find out.

But how?

He swung his legs out of bed, and padded over to the bathroom. The clothes hamper was squeezed into the narrow space between the toilet and the sink.

Opening it up, he pulled out a wet towel, then a rumpled nightgown. Underneath, pushed down to the side, he saw the tightly rolled shirt.

His shirt. He'd worn it last night.

With a sick feeling of premonition, he pulled out the shirt and dropped it onto the floor.

It looked all right. Nothing wrong with it. Just a soiled shirt, with a trace of travel grime around the collar, crumpled up.

He almost laughed aloud in sweet relief.

Almost. But then he noticed something. It smelled . . . raw.

He touched it with his foot. The shirt unrolled slowly, and he saw the blood-soaked sleeve.

"Ah, shit, no," he muttered, despair overwhelming him. "Not again. Please, God."

He sat down on the toilet seat, half bent over, clutching his head in his hands. Slowly the dry, racking sobs grew louder, tearing at his insides.

Why? Why had it all happened? The questions had no answers.

No use trying to figure it out. It was a fact, that's all.

It couldn't be denied. There it lay, spread out on the floor. Like a scene in a horror movie.

Somebody's blood soaked his shirt in mute and terrible testimony to his insanity. His guilt.

Out of all the millions of suckers in the world. Out of all the centuries. *Why me? Steve Harrison?*

Who picked my name?

Why did I have to be the one to enter that tomb?

No good thinking about it. He took a deep shuddering breath. Breathing hurt. Thinking hurt.

Get rid of the bracelet. Get the money and give it to Sara. She'd need money now, for the baby.

Then turn yourself in. Get help. Soon.

Before some other poor bastard dies a horrible death at your hands.

He stood up stiffly, looking down in confusion at his bruise-blackened right hand. He shook his head, as if to clear his thoughts.

Better call Caldwell now. Don't waste anymore time in getting this whole thing wrapped up.

The phone rang sharply, jarring him out of his train of thought. He went back into the bedroom and picked up the receiver.

"Steve?" Sara's voice sounded hesitant, unusually so. "Steve, listen. I want to talk about last night. About the baby."

He felt a sudden despairing surge of love for her. She was going to be hurt, badly, and there was nothing he could do to shield her from the pain.

A foregone conclusion. Unless somehow he could kill Menket.

Send him back to that time and place that haunted him in his dreams. A time so far back that history itself seemed shrouded in the dust of centuries.

"Steve?" Sara again. "It's so nice out. How about meeting me for lunch? We could walk over to the Tavern on the Green for a quick omelet."

Food. He cleared his throat. "I don't think that I can face food yet, Sara."

She didn't say anything for a moment. "Okay, Steve. But come over to the Historical Society anyway. There's something I want to show you. Come at twelve."

She hung up the phone quickly, and he knew that it was so he wouldn't have time to make any excuses.

He wondered what she wanted to show him.

He thought about that a moment, then picked up the receiver again and slowly dialed Caldwell's number.

EIGHTEEN

Steve showered slowly, letting the warm water pour over him, sensually dribbling in and out of his open mouth.

I could stay in here forever, he thought regretfully. *Do they have an unlimited supply of water in jail cells?*

In psycho wards?

He closed his eyes, feeling erotically aroused. Time began to slip backwards. . . .

Nefrenofret holds the golden pitcher in her slender hands. Her naked thighs brush his lightly. O Menket, does this please thee? She laughs softly, showing her pink tongue between her even teeth. I am jealous of the water, Lord, for it goes where I would follow.

He turned off the water angrily, and got out of the shower. Glaring at his reflection in the mirror as he toweled off his body, he fought a sense of twofold loss.

I don't want your memories, God damn you! I want to make my own.

He shivered as cool air blew in the small window from the air shaft, and a sudden thought struck him.

What would happen if he got sick, caught pneumonia?

Would he survive because of Menket's power? Or would Menket suffer the illness too?

His mind took him one step further. If for whatever reason, the entity called Steve died, would Menket die with him? He couldn't risk Menket's survival. Couldn't leave that kind of a legacy to Sara and their unborn baby.

No, there had to be another way, another solution, even if it meant leaving Sara and never seeing her again. But not yet. First he had to get that payoff from Caldwell.

The New York Historical Society building faced the park at 170 Central Park West. Loud noises from a construction crew across the street filled the air with the clash of discordant sound, but inside the imposing building, an orderly hush reigned supreme.

Sara waited for him just inside the entrance, her eyes filled with a suffused anxiety. Her yellow linen dress looked wrinkled, as if she'd worn it one time too many.

"I wasn't sure you'd come." She made an awkward gesture, half reaching out to him, then changed her mind, dropping her hand back to her side.

"I'm here, aren't I?" He attempted to inject a teasing note into the question. But it was no good. It ended up sounding forced. "What is it you want me to see?"

"Upstairs. In one of the storerooms. Something we just got in." She led him down the hallway to an elevator. "I thought of you as soon as I saw the collection."

"Collection of what?"

She pressed the button to the third floor. "An old Armenian gentleman left the Society his collection of Egyptian papyri. Best I've ever seen, Steve. I'm no expert, but I know that this is important. I've been trying to get it into some kind of order, but it's not easy. I don't know where to begin. Someone from the Metropolitan Museum is coming over to look at it tomorrow."

"Brenholt," said Steve thoughtfully.

"Yes, that's right. Do you know him?"

"I'm going to see him sometime this week."

The elevator stopped at the third floor, and he followed her down the wide corridor into a storeroom. The collection lay stacked on a worktable lit by indirect lighting. Nothing protected the papyri from the air, and some edges looked frayed.

Colors jumped out at him. Colors and

words in the ancient hieroglyphic script.
He bent close to examine them, filled with
awe at their striking beauty.

In his mind he could picture the scene,
almost as if he'd been there, long ago. The
half-naked funerary scribe, brown shaven
scalp gleaming in the hot Egyptian sun,
had worked long hours to complete this,
he thought.

Tedious hours had extended into years,
until blindness took its toll. Until hands,
once supple and blessed with artistic skill,
had withered and curled with age.

But before that happened, the artisan
had created a timeless record to be used
in the netherworld by one deemed worthy.
The papyri had been intended for the
guidance of a High Priest, that much was
clear. A High Priest of Hakau magic.

"It shouldn't be left out like this. Why
isn't the collection protected in a sealed
container?" he asked.

"It will be, don't worry. But that's how
we got it, Steve. When the old Armenian
died, all this was found in a stone chest in
his home on Riverside Drive. None of his
family know where he got it from. Except
that he must have acquired the collection
in Cairo when he lived there some years
back."

Steve shook his head in wonder. "It's
thousands, thousands of years old. From
the Old Kingdom." His eyes drank in the
ancient words.

"I knew that you'd be interested." Sara

looked pleased. "What does it say?"

"It's from an ancient Book of the Dead. It's about resurrection. Secret rituals of resurrection and magic. And human sacrifice."

"Ghoulish." She shivered suddenly.

"God, what a discovery! I must call Dr. Peterson."

Sara touched his arm. "You look more like yourself again. Are you sure you won't go to lunch with me?"

He tore his eyes away from the ancient papyri. "No, you go, Sara. Let me stay here and examine this."

"I can't leave you here. I have to lock up when I go to lunch. Look, we've got to talk. Can't this wait? I've got to know what you think about the baby," she added shyly.

"Sara, I promise to talk about the baby all night, if you want. Only, right now, this is terribly important to me." He barely noticed the hurt expression on her face. She had to let him stay. Perhaps he could find an answer to everything among the spells and incantations spread out before him. It was worth a try. Anything was worth a try. "What do you think I'd do? Steal them? Come on, Sara. You know I'll be careful." He placed his hands on her shoulders, an expression close to desperation on his face.

She pulled away from his touch, disturbed by his intensity.

"Okay, Steve. But you know that I'm

taking a big chance. Just don't go crazy on me."

"What do you mean?"

"You've got a strange look about you. I don't know. You're just different, all of a sudden."

He forced a reassuring smile to his lips. "Go on, Sara. I'll lock up when I leave. You can trust me, can't you?"

"I guess." But she looked back at him as she left, doubt shadowing the worried expression in her eyes.

He listened to her receding footsteps a moment, before bending over the worktable again.

His eyes raced over the words. Dr. Peterson had been wrong about the younger man's knowledge of hieroglyphics. From the very first day in Peterson's Egyptology class, Steve had felt a certain affinity with the race of people who had developed their civilization along the Nile. Almost as if the good doctor had unlocked the knowledge that his student had been born with.

Now Steve shuffled through the papyri, until he came across the one dealing with spirit takeover. Without hesitation, he rolled up the papyrus and slipped it under his shirt. Then, filled with a sense of hope, a sense of purpose, he left the storeroom, locking the door behind him.

By the time Sara came home after work, he had figured out what had to be done.

The papyrus was his only hope for release. It shouldn't be too hard to follow the instructions. Only the time had to be just right. He quickly scanned the calendar tacked to the kitchen cabinet. The phases of the moon had been included, together with the days of the month.

Just one thing to wait for: the night of the full moon.

He heard the key in the lock, and went over to take the sack of groceries from Sara as she came in the door.

"Who did you buy all this for?" he asked. "I'm not hungry."

She began to put away the groceries, lining up the boxes and cartons carefully in the cabinet by the stove.

"You have to try, Steve. If you don't eat something, you'll only feel worse." She stopped suddenly, a look of almost comical dismay on her face. "Jesus Christ, just listen to me. I sound like your mother." He watched uncomfortably as tears filled her eyes. She sat down awkwardly at the kitchen table. "I don't understand what's happened. It's like there's a wall between us. Is it really because you're sick? Or is it something else?"

"Something else?"

"You know what I mean. When you went to Egypt, was it a case of out of sight, out of mind?" She stood up again, her face set in anger. "I just want to know, that's all. We haven't exactly been close since you got back."

"Why can't you understand? I'm not hungry." He spoke patiently, as if to an unhappy child. "I don't want to think about it. Why don't you leave it alone, Sara?"

She snatched a carton off the table and slammed it down in the sink, splattering the wall and cupboard with milk. "Goddamnit, I don't want to leave it alone! I want you to go to a doctor and find out what's wrong with you. Or don't you care?" He could see her mouth trembling. "Is it me? Is there someone else? Is that what it's all about?"

"Don't, Sara."

"Don't what? Don't talk about it? What do you want me to do, Steve?"

"I don't like to see you get upset." He went over to her and took her in his arms. "Especially now."

She resisted a moment, then relaxed against him. "This is the first time you've held me since you came back," she said softly. "I mean, really held me."

Suddenly she slipped her hand into his and began to pull him into the bedroom.

"Wait . . ." he said hurriedly. But it was too late. She had seen the papyrus on the bed.

"It's not what you think. I didn't steal it, Sara. Not for money. You've got to believe me."

Except for the angry flush of red on her cheeks, Sara's face seemed drained of color. Pushing him away, she walked over to the bed and touched the papyrus with a trembling finger. Then she turned and stared disbelievingly at him.

"You took it! Jesus, how could you? I can't even trust you anymore."

"I had to take it, Sara. I need it."

"Need it? For what? So you could be weirder than you are already?"

"You don't understand."

"You bet I don't. You risked me losing my job, Steve. And what about you? You risked going to jail. Or have you risen above the law now?"

"You just don't understand." He sat down wearily on the bed. "Even if I tried to explain, you wouldn't believe me."

"Try me."

"The one I stole, the papyrus—it has to do with Hakau, black magic."

She made an impatient gesture. "You told me that already."

"Yes. But this particular one deals with the termination of eternal life." He looked at her desperately. "I've got to learn how they did it!"

"You're really sick, Steve." She turned away from him, and began to walk out of the bedroom.

"Listen to me!" He got up from the bed and caught up with her at the door. He pulled her around to face him, his big hands holding her shoulders in a tight grip. "Oh, God, how I've wanted to tell you . . . Sara, for Christsake listen to what

I'm saying. I've killed people. Two, I think. But I'm not even sure of that. And animals." His face broke out in a sweat. "That's not all." He forced himself to go on, despite the horror in her eyes. "I've eaten . . ." He took a deep shuddering breath. "*Flesh.*"

Sara pushed him away violently. "My God, you don't know what you're saying!" She covered her ears with her fists, but he reached up gently, holding her hands down in front of her.

"Listen. You've got to listen. There's no one else that I can talk to." He drew her back to the bed, sitting down next to her, with her hands still captive in his. "Nothing that I've done is my fault." He saw the fear and distrust in her eyes as she tried to free her hands, and his voice became filled with despair. "Shit, I knew you wouldn't understand. Why should you? I can't understand any of it myself. But I'm going to try to explain anyway."

"I don't want to hear it!" she burst out.

"You've got to. You're the only one . . ." He took another deep breath. "Something, someone, is taking over my body. The spirit of Menket, a prince from the old kingdom, is controlling me. He makes me do things. Horrible things. Everything I do—bad—it's not me, Sara. It's Menket."

"Steve! What are you saying? What's happened to you? Oh, my God! Don't you see how crazy this is?"

"Listen. You've got to listen to all of it. Got to believe me. I even . . . I even remember parts of his life in ancient Egypt. There's a girl he loved." His eyes became distant, filled with pain. "I smell her skin, her perfume. Feel her touch. I don't want to, God help me, but none of this is my doing." His voice trembled with emotion. "It's not me, I swear. Please believe me. Not me. It's Menket. And I've got to find a way to kill him, or die myself."

"Oh, Steve. Oh, God." Her eyes searched his face for a long moment. Then at last she pulled her hands away from his grasp. "Don't worry anymore." Tenderly she put her arms around him, rocking him gently. "Don't worry, baby. Don't worry, Steve." She spoke softly, abject pity in her voice. "I don't know how this happened, but you're very, very sick. We're going to get you some help. Don't be afraid anymore. I'm going to help you get through this."

How could he make her understand? It wasn't his imagination. It was all real.

Somehow he had to kill Menket.

But could he do that—and still live?

Only the Hakau papyrus could show the way.

NINETEEN

Detective Inspector Ian Potter parked his car on a side street, and walked across Grosvenor Square to the American Embassy in London.

He needed a few minutes to go over in his mind the questions he had prepared, and anyway, it had rained earlier.

He never could resist a bit of a walk after it had rained. Supposed to be good for his heart too, just as long as he didn't overdo it.

Mustn't risk fainting again. Too embarrassing.

Officially, he wasn't on the Green Park case, but somehow he couldn't let go of the reins. It bothered him more than some of the other cases he'd worked on over the years.

Not that they had been less gruesome,

154   *Ehren M. Ehly*

except for the cannibalistic aspect. Still, this murder had an added touch of mystery.

How had the murderer crushed the victim's skull without any sign of a weapon? With his hands?

The forensic people hadn't finished their report, and they probably wouldn't send him a copy, now that he was off the case.

Stepping to one side of the sidewalk, he smiled briefly at a pair of secretaries hurrying by. A flash of pale sunlight glinted in their fair hair, and he wondered for the hundredth time if his and Molly's little girl would have been fair. Fair and blue-eyed like Molly? Or brown-eyed and square-jawed like himself? He hoped it would have been the former, though it didn't matter much, the way things had turned out.

He never blamed the doctor.

Molly had been just a slip of a girl anyway.

He plodded on, feeling bulky and awkward in his navy-blue serge. A fine film of perspiration dampened the pink expanse of his forehead, and his kind, intelligent eyes harbored a fleeting shadow of sadness.

But only for a moment.

Sick leave or not, there was a case to be solved, a particularly nasty crime. He felt the way he imagined a bloodhound must feel at the first scent of the quarry.

* * *

The tall, gray-haired man at the desk in the U.S. Embassy security office stood up and held out his hand, his eyes watchful behind the Navy-issue glasses.

"Have a seat, Inspector," said Captain Jamieson, Chief Security Officer. "I've got all the information you asked for. Do you really think that there may be some connection between the murder in Green Park and the mutilation of the dog at the U.S. Embassy in Cairo?

"There's a strong possibility of it."

The American shook his head slowly. "I don't know. I sure as hell hope that you're wrong. We've never actually tied Harrison in with the dog's death. There seems to be a difference of opinion about the hieroglyphic graffiti on the consulate wall."

"I understand that the young man's employer"—Inspector Potter checked his notes—"a Dr. Peterson, refuses to believe that Harrison might be knowledgeable enough for that."

"Well . . ." The Security Officer took a deep breath, then let it out slowly. "Once you accept that that's a possibility, the rest of the incident has to come under close scrutiny."

"So it should. It happened here too, didn't it? Only, no hieroglyphics, and it wasn't a dog, this time."

The American looked at the Inspector speculatively. "You're pretty sure Harrison did it, aren't you? But you're skating on thin ice. What real proof have you got?''

"He was here, in London, on the night of the murder in Green Park. Only a one day stopover, mind, but time enough for that. Then there's the raincoat.''

"But it isn't his. Your people didn't find anything on it except the victim's blood. I think that you're just playing a hunch, Inspector. Didn't someone else report the raincoat lost?''

"Or stolen. From a passenger on the same flight out of Cairo that Steve Harrison took. As for nothing on the raincoat except the victim's blood, you seem to have more information than I do. One thing troubles me. Why did your people over in Cairo let him leave so quickly?''

"Why shouldn't they? No reason to tie him into the dog's mutilation. The investigation revealed that it might have been one of the servants in the Marines' quarters. Moslems don't always like dogs. They consider them dirty.''

"Perhaps. But that would be a rather extreme way of showing dislike,'' said the Inspector dryly.

"Well, a couple of the kitchen workers had complained about the dog eating in the mess hall. Argued with the dog's owner, in fact. Then one of them left the embassy staff right after the incident. Our security people found out that he had a possible connection with a fundamentalist group. They weren't able to question him, unfortunately. We've just got word that he's dead. Cholera. So now we'll never know."

"How many kitchen workers do you know that have a fluent knowledge of the Book of the Dead?"

"I see your point, Inspector. Of course, it's conceivable that a cook might have known how to write hieroglyphic script, though I'll admit that part worries us. Something inflammatory in Arabic would have been more in character."

"Where was Harrison on that night?"

"At the embassy. You know that, Inspector. He attended the wake."

"But no one actually saw him at the wake."

"No one remembers seeing him that night except the Marine on duty when Harrison signed in at the gate."

"Isn't that a bit unusual?"

The American laughed good-humoredly. "No, Inspector. Everyone else at the wake was probably drunk. At a beer bust like that they're lucky if they remember anything at all in the morning. It's all in the file. By the way, how did you happen to find out about the dog?"

"I read about it in the paper. I like dogs, and this story caught my eye." The Inspector stood up and shook hands with the Security Officer. "Thank you for the copies of the report from Cairo. I'll return them when I'm done."

"You must forgive my asking," said Captain Jamieson hesitantly. "But you're not assigned to this case, are you?"

"No, you're right. I'm just following up on my own time. I'm semiretired. Heart problem. Police work is all I know, and I get in a lot of walking this way. It's good of you to have seen me." He sighed gustily. "They hardly let me into my old office these days. Oh well, mustn't complain. In a way, I'm almost like a free agent."

"Well, if there is anything else . . ."

"No, you've been very informative. Thank you again for your help." He paused reflectively at the door. "This isn't the end of it, you know."

"How's that?"

"If Harrison did commit these crimes, he's hopelessly insane, and he won't stop now. In which case, we'll be hearing from the U.S. one of these days."

"My God! I hope you're mistaken, Inspector."

"So do I," said the Inspector quietly. "But I'm afraid I'll be proved right on this one."

Captain Jamieson watched from his window as the Inspector crossed back over Grosvenor Square. He turned away from the window as his assistant came into the room.

"Anything to add to the Harrison file?" asked the young woman.

"No, nothing. But you'd better get Lieutenant O'Reilly, New York City Homicide, on the phone. We don't want this old guy to muddy the water. Ten to one he's booking a flight on the next plane to Kennedy. Scotland Yard asked me to put him off gently as he's on borrowed time." The American smiled wryly. "I hope to God he doesn't think we're as incompetent as I made out."

TWENTY

He couldn't remember how long he'd sat watching her. Sara slept quietly, breathing evenly through parted lips, one arm stretched out across her pillows.

Not dark yet. Better leave the light off.

Steve could hear the traffic outside in the city streets. The occasional jarring blare of a horn, the frequent screeching of hastily applied brakes somehow intermingled well with the normal hum from the living, pulsing machine called Manhattan Island. By the time the muted street sounds filtered down the airshaft to Sara's bedroom, they had become a soothing backdrop for what he hoped were pleasant dreams. Or better yet, no dreams at all.

He hadn't wanted to drug her coffee, but he had to be sure that she wouldn't try to follow him. Caldwell would never accept the extra company.

On the floor above Sara's apartment, a Puerto Rican family began to prepare their evening meal, sending the rich aroma of frying meat drifting into the airshaft.

Ah, Christ! he thought despairingly, as the familiar nausea rose in his throat. He hurried into the bathroom, wrenching at the cold-water faucet. Bending over the sink, he quickly doused his head in the stream of water, turning his head to catch some of the stream in his mouth.

Straightening up, he stared at the mirror.

The reflection in the mirror stared back coldly. Little rivulets of water ran down the cheeks, to hover in drops on the chin, before dripping into the sink.

That isn't my face! he thought suddenly.

I know you, you bastard! Leave me alone! For God's sake leave me alone, you murdering son of a bitch!

The eyes looked back, cold and disdainful.

Filled with a sense of dread, he leaned closer to the mirror.

Is that what I look like now? Can Sara see the other one? The other person straining to usurp the man I used to be, even to the point of stealing my face and turning it into his?

He raised a shaking hand to his face, cautiously touching the nose that to his eyes had become finer, more elongated, the nostrils curving with an almost aristocratic hauteur. Even the cheeks seemed thinner, drawn and taut.

He looked closer, his heart beating hard.

No way. No way. Pure fucking imagination.

The face staring back had his bone structure. His skin.

And yet . . . *It wasn't his face anymore.*

"I'm gonna kill you!" he screamed in anguish, bringing his clenched fist down like a hammer against the mirror. As the glass shattered, he saw his reflection in the jagged shards. In every section of broken mirror he saw the mouth that once looked like his stretch into a bitterly tormented smile.

"Oh, God," he groaned desperately. "Won't I ever escape you?"

The shards of broken glass seemed to glitter brilliantly, their points as sharp as daggers. Staring at them, he suddenly remembered the papyrus.

The ritual suicide at the full moon.

The only way out of this sickening mess. Do it. Get it over and done with.

What was it Shakespeare had said? Something about everyone owing God a death? Well, time to pay up.

He picked up a sliver of glass, testing the point against his thumb.

What will it feel like? Would he have the

strength to go through with it? Have to find the strength. No two ways about it.

No other way in hell to stop the killing.

He dropped the sliver of glass in the wastepaper basket under the sink. Better leave the rest of the clean-up until later. He had to see Caldwell first. And anyway, Sara wouldn't wake up for a while.

He went back into the bedroom. Sara hadn't moved. He hoped he hadn't put too much sedative in her coffee.

Kneeling down at the side of the bed, he touched her face lightly, brushing his fingertips across her forehead. She sighed softly, her lips parted in a smile.

God, how he loved her.

A fine beading of perspiration moistened the smooth skin above her lips, and he wiped it away gently with his thumb.

Suddenly he jerked his hand away from her face in horror.

Against her skin his thumb had looked black and rotted, putrid maggot-filled flesh falling away from the curved yellowed nail.

Stumbling from the room, he went into the kitchen and hurriedly switched on the light over the sink. Quickly rolling back his sleeves, he feverishly searched his arms and hands for a trace of the decay he'd seen in the bedroom.

Nothing. Sick imagination, nothing more.

But it had been there, he'd seen it.

Putrefication and decay.

He looked closer, fearful of what he might find.

His muscular arms gleamed in the light from the rose-toned bulb. The sandy hairs and smattering of freckles adding a touch of normality.

His jaw tightened in resolution as he fought a wave of dizziness.

Okay. So I'm hallucinating again. He glanced at the calender on the kitchen wall. The night of the full moon looked like an eye, staring back unblinkingly. It wavered as he stared at it, fading into the cloudy darkness that he seemed to be drowning in.

TWENTY ONE

Strange.

He almost seemed to be floating through space.

But where? When?

Something threw him off balance, and he felt his head strike the metal framework around the window.

"Sorry about that," said a voice, and within a flash everything became clear.

He must have caught the cab while in some kind of daze. Looking out of the window he saw that they were in Central Park, heading for the Upper East Side.

"Did I give you the address?"

"Sure, what d'you think?" The taxi driver looked back at him through the partition. "Forgetful, ain't you?"

Forgetful. If the guy up front only knew. The memories came frequently now, pushing aside the present as something unreal, unwanted. Sometimes the vivid images of that long-ago time held him in a powerful grip, luring him with their portrayal of sunlit pleasures, until he yearned to awaken from the nightmare of today.

Even if release meant dying, again and again.

Voices called to him, cajoling, threatening, reminding him of duties left undone. What did they want him to do?

Oh, God, who am I really? What have I become?

The driver jammed his foot on the brakes, leaning out to shout at someone blocking the way with a pushcart, and the familiar obscenity jerked Steve back into sudden awareness. He glanced at his watch. Better not be late. Caldwell was a real bastard when it came to punctuality.

Funny how worried he'd been about that loan.

Did it matter now? Maybe nothing mattered anymore.

Even if he didn't go through with the suicide, what kind of life could he look forward to? An existence full of fear and hate. And murder. Never knowing from one minute to the next whether the sickening urge to eat flesh would compel him to kill again.

He laughed bitterly. What was owing money to a loan shark, next to that?

* * *

The predictably vicious-looking hench-
man who opened the door to Caldwell's
apartment searched Steve quickly, then
motioned to a chair near the door.

"Wait here," he said.

Left alone, Steve looked around the foyer. The Egyptians claimed that Caldwell
bought or stole huge amounts of their
ancient treasures. Not a trace of art here,
though. Nothing but stark white walls and
a couple of solid-looking chairs.

The apartment itself probably extended
upward for two or three floors, but the
elevator from the street level didn't seem
to go beyond where Steve waited. Must be
a private elevator somewhere in back, he
speculated.

The hood returned, jerking his head at
Steve to indicate that he should follow
him. He led the way down a well-lit corridor, pausing in front of a bronze door at
the end.

"You can go in," he told Steve. "Just
remember that I'm outside the door, so
don't try anything. Anything! Hear me,
asshole?"

"Get off my back," muttered Steve irritably, pushing past him into the room.

Caldwell stood in front of a massive
fireplace, his cold hooded eyes staring
unblinkingly at Steve. His thin skeletal
frame seemed to be encased in layer after
layer of sweaters, culminating in a fine
Cashmere roll-collared cardigan. Sparse

gray hair had been carefully combed to hide the beginning of baldness, and his skull-like face had the unhealthy pallor of one near death.

A fire had been lit in the grate, and the room, furnished as a library, felt insufferably hot.

"I must apologize for any discomfort you may feel. But I suffer from the cold, and even though it is summer, I enjoy the warmth of a fire. There is another reason —you'll understand in a moment. First, however, we have business to discuss." His lips stretched in a grimace approximating a smile. "You have something for me, I believe."

"Yes." Steve found it hard to concentrate. The heat was making him thirsty again. He took a deep breath, and a faint trace of perfume in the room took him by surprise. Familiar and stirring, the scent pulled him back, back through time.

Oh, God, I'm drifting again. . . .

"Mr. Harrison, what is the matter?"

"Nothing. Must be the heat."

"Ah, well. I'll explain in a minute. But first, I believe this is what we agreed upon." Caldwell picked up a slim package of hundred-dollar bills off the desk, and handed it to Steve.

What was the old bastard trying to pull?

"What's this?"

"What does it look like, Mr. Harrison?"

"No way. This isn't enough. This doesn't even cover the bracelet."

"Ah yes. The bracelet. May I see it?"

Steve jerked it off his wrist and threw it on the desk. "What about the statue? The gold statue of Isis that Bill Evans sent you?"

"What about it?" Caldwell picked up the bracelet and turned it over to reveal the cartouche cut into the underside of the scarab. "This is a fine piece. It will look good on my princess." Caldwell replaced the bracelet on the desk, and took out another package of money. "All right, Mr. Harrison. There is another five thousand in that package. Seven thousand altogether. And, of course, we'll forget what you owe me."

"You're out of your mind! That statue of Isis is worth at least a hundred thousand."

"Then I suggest you try and sell it elsewhere." Caldwell smiled slyly. "What's the matter, Mr. Harrison? Cat got your tongue?" The smile faded abruptly as he continued. "You're lucky to get anything, considering the way you tried to avoid paying what you owed me. Still, the debt is satisfied now, and you may prove even more useful to me in the future."

Steve frowned in disgust. Seven thousand wouldn't be much help to Sara. Jesus, everything was turning out wrong. He made a quick decision.

"I've got something else. If you're interested I can bring it tomorrow."

The cold eyes sharpened greedily. "What is it?"

"A sheet of papyrus from the Book of the Dead."

"Whose tomb?"

"I don't know yet. I might even be able to get more."

"Mr. Harrison, you amuse me. Why should I be interested in one or two papyri of unknown source, when I have in my possession a complete Book of the Dead already? Not to mention the mummy that it was prepared for, and the tomb it all came in." He chuckled gently, a dry whispery sound like the crumbling of tissue paper. "I see that you are speechless. Good. Good. I have waited a long time to share a glimpse of the beauty that I possess."

"Where is it?"

"Patience, Mr. Harrison. If you only knew how tempted I've been to call Brenholt, or any of those other fools at the Metropolitan, to invite them to see what it must have been like, really like, in Egypt."

"What makes you think they don't know already? The Egyptian wing is one of the finest—"

"The Egyptian wing? Don't be a fool. What have they really got there?" A faint flush warmed Caldwell's face, and his eyes reflected the sparks from the fire. "A

few beads, a little jewelry, assorted statues, each with their neatly worded labels,
most under glass. And what about the
gaping hoi polloi who shuffle through.
What do they really learn? They can't
touch. Feel."

"If they did, none of it would last very
long," said Steve dryly.

Caldwell made an impatient gesture.
"They're missing all the beauty, the mystery."

"They all can't afford a private collection," replied Steve, a trace of bitterness in
his voice.

Caldwell turned to look at him. "Do I
detect a hint of envy? Well, no matter. All
the more reason to believe that you'll
appreciate what I have appropriated.
Come."

He walked over to a built-in bookcase,
touching a switch at the back of the third
shelf. "You must stand here beside me,
and don't move, until I tell you."

Steve walked over and stood beside
Caldwell. The lights in the library dimmed.
Moving soundlessly, the bookcase slid off
to the left, revealing a wide, pitch-black
opening.

"What—" began Steve.

"Say nothing, just watch," hissed Caldwell.

It's cold, thought Steve. Cold as the
grave. He shivered slightly, glad of the
warmth from the fireplace behind him.

"Now," whispered Caldwell. A faint glow, barely discernible at first, began to suffuse the room in front of them with light.

Pale, pale yellow light, that warmed to a soft rose, depicting a dawn. Gradually the light picked out the shape of stones that formed the inside walls. The ceiling had been painted a deep blue, and around it, near the edges, ancient spells pertaining to the goddess of the sky had been inscribed.

An army of gods, painted with gold, traversed the sky, creating a rich canopy for the age-old chamber. A riot of colorful hieroglyphics covered the stone walls, the paint as bright as if the scribe had just lay down his brush.

"Well?" Caldwell's voice gloated.

"It's a tomb!" muttered Steve angrily. "You son of a bitch, you've stolen a whole fucking tomb!"

"Mr. Harrison, your choice of language is not fitting in the presence of a lady." He gestured towards the sarcophagus in the center of the lighted room. "Whenever I open the door a new day starts for the princess, and I am able to see her again the way she slept in Egypt."

"How in God's name did you get all this out?" Steve stared around the room. Everything perfect. Not old and dust-ridden, but somehow fresh, as though she had just died, and a new tomb had just been readied for her long journey through the netherworld. "How did you get it?"

"Time and money, Mr. Harrison. Lots of money to grease the machinery. They shipped it across the desert in empty gasoline trucks to Suez, then on to a tanker waiting in the Canal."

"Who discovered the tomb?"

"You don't really expect me to tell you, do you? It isn't important, anyway. What *is* important, is that no one else in the community of Egyptologists knows about it. It is my secret." Caldwell smiled slightly, narrowing his eyes. "Like any secret, its value increases when it is shared. That's why I'm showing it to you now."

"How do you know that I won't expose you?"

"Not a very healthy suggestion, Mr. Harrison. And how on earth would you explain the two items stolen from the tomb about to be excavated in Saqqara? Not to mention using the U.S. diplomatic pouch as a means of shipping pilfered goods out of Egypt. No, no. I feel very secure in showing you this. One might almost say that exposing me would be the very last thing you'd contemplate." His laughter turned into a cough, and he pulled the shawl-like collar on his cardigan tightly around his neck. "If you take my meaning."

Steve clenched his fists angrily. The son of a bitch. He was right on the money, every time. No one, no one at all, could get the better of Caldwell. If they did, it was a temporary condition, culminating in a fast trip to the bottom of the East River.

"I keep it electronically monitored, of course," the older man went on. "The low temperature remains the same, even when I open the door. The slightest change, even our breathing or body warmth, is accounted for. Step forward, and you will walk through a current of air that resists the heat in the library."

Steve passed through the curtain of electronically controlled air. "It's freezing!" he exclaimed.

"Yes, but worth it, Mr. Harrison. Eminently worth it. Look around you. Every stone, every image, every tile is from the original tomb. Stone by stone. Piece by piece. Reconstructed for *me*. And, of course, the princess. Fascinating. I could tell that she had been beautiful before death worked its relentless destruction. Equal to Nefertiti, in my estimation.

"And she was mine! At first I felt satisfied. The image on the outer sarcophagus showed what she had looked like, but after awhile, that wasn't enough. Each time that I entered the tomb I became consumed with a burning curiosity. What did she really look like? Haven't you ever wondered? Don't you ever get tired of the desiccated skin, the worn linen wrappings? The putrid stink of death?''

Steve said nothing. What did the old bastard mean?

''Don't try to answer. You wouldn't be human if you didn't have at least a trace of morbid curiosity.''

''I'm as curious as the next man.''

''I'm sure you are. You probably have more than your share of weaknesses.''

''Leave me out of it.''

''Did I strike a nerve, Mr. Harrison? Well, as I was saying. Having the mummy wasn't enough. Oh, at first I was content to wonder about her. What shade of gold warmed the softness of her skin? How delicate were her curves? I wanted to see for myself, and as you know, money is no object.'' His mouth twisted with disdain. ''Plenty of fools in the world, ready to do anything for an easy dollar, no questions asked.''

''Forget that. Get on with the part about the mummy.''

''Caught your attention, haven't I? Well, I hired experts. Reconstruction experts, and more. The mummy has been sheathed in a silicon closely resembling skin. Her own cosmetics, antimony, scented oils, everything used as they used to be. A saline solution pulses through latex veins.'' The cold eyes shone with amusement. ''A Sleeping Beauty, made for me, Mr. Harrison.'' Caldwell walked over to the stone sarcophagus. "Look inside," he whispered. "Observe the miracle of science."

Steve couldn't move his leaden feet. His heart thudded in his chest, and a feeling of weakness washed over him, shrinking his genitalia.

I know what my saddened eyes shall see.

Even if I could not read your name and mine emblazoned on the walls around us.

Even if I could not smell the fragrance of myrrh, and cedar, and frankincense prepared for you alone.

Even if I hadn't read the story of your life set down in the ancient script wherever I look, I would know.

"As a thirsting antelope senses water . . ." Menket uttered the words aloud in the ancient tongue, and looked down at the recreated form of Nefrenofret.

TWENTY-TWO

A rushing sound. A wind.

Time unraveling through the centuries.

Back, back. Back to the days of blessed time, when unclouded light from the sun-god Re was like a falcon's shriek in the heavens. When the kite-hawk's wings swept the sky in ever-widening circles.

When the breath of the wind-god Shu emanating from the desert nights cooled the dampness of naked skin.

And love. Love that promised to survive the cold hand of death. Love that flowered like the fragrant primeval red lotus in eternity. Love that poured from one vessel into another, without repletion, without emptiness.

I am stone.

The disheveled hair and blue garments of mourning are not allowed me. In my mind is a secret place of sorrow, and there I sit in the dust, tearing at my face and rending my linen robes, O Nefreno-fret.

But to the world, my eyes are dry and distant, filled with hatred for the abomination of this time.

"Struck dumb, Mr. Harrison?" Caldwell beckoned him closer. "Touch the skin. It feels alive." He laughed softly. "Now try to tell me about the Egyptian wing at the Metropolitan. Nothing like this, eh?" Caldwell started to reach out and touch the lifelike skin on the naked breast, a fleck of whitened saliva moistening the corner of his open mouth. He half turned towards the other man, as though suddenly aware of a subtle difference, a sinister threat. "What—?"

The old man stumbled backward, a rasping cry for help strangling the breath in his throat.

But it was too late.

Muttering an imprecation, Menket grasped Caldwell's head in both hands. With a violent jerk, he snapped the scrawny neck like a chicken's wing, and the once-powerful loan shark fell at his feet like a heap of rags.

Slowly Menket raised his arms to the array of gods on the painted ceiling above him. Following the age-old rituals of a High Priest, he began to chant the words of power.

"Now, strength of the gods, come to my reddened heart. Let me destroy the head of my enemy, that he may lose his way to peaceful eternity."

He braced his foot on the dead man's chest, focusing his energy on the act to come.

Shouting the name of the sun-god Re, he bent over the body, and in a raging burst of power, ripped the head off its shoulders.

Holding up the dripping head, he stared into the half-opened eyes, muttering an ancient curse to seal the corpse's fate.

"I know your name, and I spit it from my mouth, that you may wander with the dust of jackals forever."

Looking around the tomb, he placed the severed head on a low stool at the foot of Nefrenofret's sarcophagus.

There is a thing to be done.

First, purification, as befits a princely High Priest. He stuck two fingers into an alabaster oil jar, and felt the silky liquid slide across his skin. Full. The evil one had spoken truth. Everything was as it had been, once.

In an ivory and ebony inlaid box, he found tweezers, a polished metal mirror, and a long, slender razor, still with the edge of sharpness.

Next, his garments. No wool or leather to shadow his skin. He stripped quickly, throwing his clothes and shoes back into the library.

Staring solemnly at his reflection in the mirror propped up against the ornate box, he picked up the razor and began to shave his head. As he shaved, he soundlessly repeated the incantation for the resurrection of the spirit.

Finally, he stood erect near the center of the tomb, his oiled skin gleaming in the soft indirect lighting. Flecks of blood beaded where he had nicked his skin, but no hair remained. Not on his head, his face, around his eyes, nor on his body. A thin trickle of blood from his pubic area eased its way into his groin, and down his thigh, leaving a trail of red against the hairless white flesh.

Moving quickly, he poured out all the oil in the deep alabaster jars around him.

"O Osiris, nourish the spark that I light for Nefrenofret. Let her become a shooting flame to the sky, and escape the lake of fire that must destroy my enemy."

He allowed himself a moment more, staring down at the still figure in the sarcophagus.

"Wait for me," he whispered. "And one day, time will stand still for us again in Egypt."

Now the ritual is done, yet all is not over.

Menket ran back through the current of frigid air into the library. He placed Caldwell's head on the desk, before seizing a burning log from the fireplace. Ignoring the searing pain, he lobbed it into the tomb, watching intently as the flames licked at the dead man's headless body.

He began to chant the song of purification for the dead, waiting as the conflagration grew to engulf the contents of the sarcophagus, then all the tomb, in a roaring fire.

As the blaze grew fiercer, a sudden bright flame shot upward through the ceiling, leaving a thick, shadowy pillar of smoke in its wake.

A series of electrical explosions from the tomb sent a billowing wave of fire curling through the wide opening left by the sliding bookcase. Like a horde of locusts, the hungry flames began to consume the edges of the carpet on the library floor.

The sound of fists pounding on the other side of the bronze door distracted Menket for an instant.

Fools. They would soon join their master in the fiery hell of Amduat. He ignored the threatening voices commanding him to open up the door. Soon the taste of death would be on their tongues.

He paused by the desk on his way to a small side door, glancing back toward the blazing fire. Then, grasping the blood-soaked head by its straggling tufts of hair, he moved swiftly to the side door. He wrenched it open, and found himself in another corridor.

A private elevator waited at the end.

Ignoring it, Menket raced to the narrow stairway at the side. Reaching the roof, he pushed open the door with his shoulder, clutching Caldwell's slippery head to his chest.

He paused a moment. Menket's face remained impassive when the cursing shouts turned into frantic screams below.

Then he ran to the edge of the roof, staring down at the sparkling city.

"Look on your domain, evil one," he raged, holding Caldwell's head up high over the parapet.

A thin stream of watery blood from his victim's mouth traced a pattern down Menket's arm.

The desperate screams mounted in anguish as the thundering rage of fire fanned out into the building like an uncorked scourge of the devil.

Pretty soon, the screams died away, leaving only the wail of sirens crying in the night.

TWENTY-THREE

In the building next to Caldwell's, four people sat at dinner in the penthouse apartment.

"Don't you think that we should leave?" The cooly elegant woman stared out of the wide French windows at the fire next door. "I don't like the look of it, John."

Her husband frowned slightly, white lines etched deep into his Caribbean tan. "I'm not sure. I think it's pretty much contained in that flat."

A second woman, petite, with auburn hair, laughed softly. "How clever of you to have arranged this, Leslie." She got up from the table quickly, and moved over to the French doors by the terrace. "When you said dinner at home, I never expected such a spectacular floor show. I think it's rather fun."

"You would," muttered the other man at the table wearily. "Let's leave now. It seems to be getting out of control."

"And that would never do, would it?" asked his wife, looking back at him from her vantage point by the terrace. "Whatever happens, don't let anything get out of control." She turned away again, staring out at the fire. "I want to stay and watch the whole marvelous show." She looked up suddenly as a white flash on the roof next door caught her eye. "There's someone up there. My God, darlings, he has nothing on!" She broke into a peal of laughter. "Let's invite him over."

"You're drunk," said her husband irritably. "I can't see anything."

"That's your trouble, darling, isn't it? You never see anything." She smiled at him spitefully as he glared at her.

"Perhaps we'd better leave," said their host uncertainly. "We could go to the Plaza, and wait it out. Looks as though it's spreading to the roof."

He stood up just as something landed with a crash on the terrace. "What the—!" Picking up a knife off the table, he began to move toward the French doors.

Like a ghastly video, Menket stepped into the open doorway, shocking the four people in the room with the horror of the apparition. For a long, sickening moment they stared at him, struggling to accept the reality of what it was that he held out toward them.

Wordlessly he stood there, naked, shorn of hair, holding up Caldwell's bloody head. For a heart-thundering instant, the only sound was the clatter of the knife as it fell to the floor.

Then the half-drunken man at the table threw up over the veal rosemary, and pandemonium broke out.

Terrified screams ricocheted around the room as the two couples forgot all decorum in the desperate scramble for the door.

Menket waited, listening intently. He could hear their panic-stricken footsteps skittering across the hardwood floor. Then the slam of a door.

He had no interest in them. Only in what the apartment could provide for his escape.

Glancing down dispassionately at his blood-flecked body, he knew that he had to have clothes.

He placed Caldwell's head on the dining-room table, then opened one of the doors to the side.

Soft lighting revealed a bedroom, and beyond that, a walk-in closet. He quickly pulled on a pair of jeans and a sweater. A pair of sneakers didn't fit, so he left his feet bare.

One other thing. Caldwell's blood would

soak through anything thin wrapped around it. He wrenched a short fur coat off its satin hanger, carrying it back into the dining-room.

It would serve the purpose well.

A quick search of the kitchen revealed a stash of brown paper sacks, folded neatly in a cupboard. He stuffed the fur-wrapped head into the largest one he could find, and made for the front door.

Smoke drifted in the terrace doors behind him, and as he left the apartment, a delicate tongue of flame licked at the draperies.

By the time Menket reached the street, the fire had spread down several floors. A roaring as thunderous as an oncoming train filled the stairwell, as air rushed up to join the flames.

Windows on the upper floors shattered explosively outward, loudly bursting with the eerily festive sound of smashed bottles of champagne.

Screams for help began to echo downward from people trapped in their apartments, and an old woman in a maribou-trimmed robe calmly jumped off her penthouse terrace. A fever of excitement gripped the crowds across the avenue, as the old woman seemed to float down towards them.

Suddenly, all the lights went out along most of Madison and Fifth Avenue, for a

ten-block area south of East 79th. As if a
giant hand had snapped a switch, Central
Park was doused in darkness.

One of the three buildings on fire
seemed to shudder as a portion of an
outside wall sheered off in an explosion of
smoke and dust and flames. The watching
crowds cheered, then pushed and surged
backward on the west side of Fifth Avenue
as a spray of red-hot sparks rained down
on them.

"Back off! Back off!" yelled a mounted
policeman, edging his section of the
crowd away with his horse's rump as another fire truck pulled up.

Menket stood in the shadowy darkness
of the park watching the fire. Light from
the flames danced on his face, highlight-
ing the hollow hate-filled eyes, the cheeks,
lean and tense. The bitter twisted smile.

Amduat, he thought exultantly, his dry
lips mouthing the word. *The accursed Lake
of Fire. May it swallow them all, O Re.*

He turned and ran swiftly across the
darkened park, toward the Upper West
Side, clutching the bag containing
Caldwell's head like a prize.

A huge cloud of smoke billowed out
over the park, drifting slowly in his wake.

Back in the apartment on West 80th,
Sara turned restlessly in her sleep. Her
hand reached out to the pillow beside her,
and she softly murmured Steve's name,
dreaming.

But it was too late.

Steve had entered a dream world of his own. Endlessly dark and terrifying. And one from which there could be no hope of awakening.

Pushing and shoving his way through to the front of the excited spectators on Fifth Avenue, an old man slipped on the curb, and fell into the gutter.

Someone in the crowd good-naturedly reached down and grabbed a handful of his ragged overcoat. "Up ya go, Gran'pa," he said.

"Lemme go, yer sum'uv a bitch!" the old man gummed indignantly.

"Just helping." The bystander grinned.

"Who ast yer?" The old man swung his arm in a wide arc, barely missing two or three in the crowd.

The mounted policeman danced his horse sideways over to the scene of the minor altercation.

"I should have known it was you," said the cop. "Can't you ever keep out of trouble?"

"Sum'uv a bitch," grumbled the old man, melting back into the mass of people.

See if he'd tell them anything now.

He could have helped the dumb bastards. Could have told them about the man running away across the park.

Hightailing it when everyone and his

fucking brother were shitting their pants to eyeball the fireworks on Fifth Avenue.

Well, they lost their chance now.

Screw 'em. He'd go to hell before he told them anything. See if he didn't.

A police car drove up and the officer driving leaned out. "Need any help, Tony?" he asked.

"Nah. Just Old Bleeder sounding off. One of these days, that old guy's gonna get himself into something he can't get out of. Then he'll be sorry."

A sound.

Not a big sound, nor even a frightening one. Just something that didn't seem right. Didn't belong.

A gnawing.

For a long moment, Sara wanted to forget she'd heard it. Pull the covers up over her head, and chance it. But she couldn't. She lay quietly, trying not to breath, straining to hear.

Then she saw the pencil-thin band of light at the bottom of the bathroom door, and knew that he'd returned.

Anger washed over her like a red-hot tide. She got out of bed and had her hand on the door before she realized it. She tried the knob, then thought better of it, and knocked.

Silence.

Then the gnawing sound again.

This time, she felt really frightened.

"Steve? Is that you?"

Silence.

"Steve! Open the door!" She heard a footstep, and the bathroom door swung open.

At first her mind couldn't grasp what she saw. Couldn't acknowledge it.

But it waited for her.

Waited while her mind put it all together.

Then she screamed.

Went on screaming. Until the screaming became part of the room, together with the blood, and the head, and the man whose face looked like Steve's, but wasn't, couldn't be.

Dear God in Heaven. He's shaved all his hair off, and there's blood on his hands, on his mouth.

And the thing in the sink is ripped and crushed, but I know what it is.

Oh, God, God.

I know what it is.

Suddenly she turned and tried to run.

Later, when she thought about it, everything seemed to have happened in slow motion. Painfully drawn out, like a nightmare that has no end.

The pounding chase with every step an age in time, stretched out from seconds to minutes to hours to aeons, until she almost reached the front door. Almost got away.

Her steps and his, slow, slow, like a macabre dance, somber in its majesty, terrifying in its resolute choreography.

No contest. He overtook her at the door.

His blood-slimed hand slid down her arm, pulling her toward the bedroom. At the bedroom door she gave it one last desperate try, swinging around and jerking her elbow back sharply into his gut. As he staggered back in surprise, she tried to slam the bedroom door against him.

No go. No way.

They both knew who would get the upper hand.

He threw her on the bed, knocking her breath out of her heaving chest. She felt her heart pumping wildly, charged up to the hilt with a desperate rush of adrenaline.

"Steve! No, don't!" she moaned, turning her head away from the cruel face so close to hers. His breath smelled fetid, stinking with the taint of the recent meal interrupted in the horror that used to be her bathroom.

Hands that had once stroked her to the exquisite point of no return now dug with venomous intent into the soft flesh of her thighs.

She fought back, straining to keep her trembling legs closed against him. He just laughed, his cold eyes filled with an unholy joy.

Why didn't he say something? Anything? Even words of anger that might help her to understand?

She felt her defense weaken as she struggled to breathe, the muscles of her legs faltered, and in that instant, he had her.

"Steve!" She screamed once as he plunged into her. A sharp pain cut high into her body.

Oh, God, how cold. As if love itself had turned to stone.

The room swung around like an unanchored vessel, tipping first one way, then the other, as he smothered her with his weight. How much longer?

Her eyes shifted, turning upward. A grey pall seeped into her consciousness.

Maybe I'm dying, she thought tiredly.

But you don't die from something like this. Do you?

An icy cold crept up from her feet, chilling her hands as she still tried to push against him. Still tried to fight. But weakly. Oh so weakly.

She felt an overwhelming sadness settle in her chest.

Maybe I am, she thought again.

Dying.

He stood and looked down at her. A faint emotion stirred within him.

Could it be pity? He rejected it harshly.

Pity was for fools. An unwanted residue of the man called Steve, still hovering like an eager shadow, ready to return and claim the unclaimable.

I am Menket, he thought arrogantly. *A prince of Egypt.*

A High Priest of the Almighty God Re.

Soon. Soon, shall I ride the crest of Time in the royal barque of ages.

Then glory shall be mine, and these poor fools no more than the dust beneath my feet.

So cold. So very, very cold.

Sara opened her eyes and saw sunlight reflected off the dirty brick wall. She ached . . .

I mustn't turn my head.

If I lie very still, he'll be gone.

Please, God, let him be gone.

It wasn't Steve . . .

Someone else. Someone insane.

She tried to moisten her cracked lips with a swollen tongue.

A murderer. A violent stranger.

She ran a shaking hand along the inside of her bruised thighs.

A rapist . . .

Please, God, let the baby be all right.

TWENTY-FOUR

"C'mon, Louie. I don't have no time to waste." The plump woman paused just inside the apartment building's glass security door, looking back impatiently at the boy on the stairs. "What's the matter with you anyway? We don't have all day."

The ten-year-old boy on the stairs tried to ignore her. He had just been watching a rerun of *Star Wars*, and hadn't come down to earth yet. Besides, he didn't want to go shopping. That was for girls.

Someone outside the main front door came in hurriedly and buzzed the buzzer. Louie's mother opened the glass door with a smile of welcome. The two women immediately became engrossed in animated conversation.

Left to his own devices, Louie practiced jumping off the last three steps of the stairway. He was tall for his age. His face showed the recent loss of baby fat brought on by a sudden spurt of growth. He'd combed his hair a new way, with the part real low. It drove his mother bananas. She really freaked out. Even though his red hair wouldn't lie down flat, he decided he'd keep on combing that way.

After a while, he began to explore the end of the corridor. A door stood ajar.

The voices of his mother and her friend purred on reassuringly behind him. They wouldn't miss him if he explored a little.

A frown of concentration creased his forehead. He touched the door with one finger. It opened slowly.

He looked back at his mother. Mouth parted in pleasure, she listened to the other woman's whispered words. Suddenly they both burst into laughter.

Everything was all right. She wouldn't be coming after him for a while.

He pushed the door a little harder this time, and went in.

The apartment seemed familiar, in a strange sort of way. The rooms looked the same as those in the one he lived in. But it didn't have the same furniture. It didn't look as bright as his mother's furniture.

His mother liked lots of red. His bedspread was red. The sofa that his father slept on sometimes was red. Sort of. And in the bathroom, the towels were as red as a fire truck. It looked good.

This place had soft colors. Okay for girls, but he preferred something brighter.

He wondered if the towels in this bathroom were sissy colors too. He screwed his face into an expression of disgust. Probably namby-pamby pink. Or (yuck!) purple.

He stood and looked in surprise. The towels weren't red. But the sink and the floor had streaks of red on them. Almost like the finger paint he used to use in kindergarten when he was a little kid.

A groan sounded behind him, coming from the other room. He turned around and went into the bedroom.

A lady lay on the bed, making the sound he'd heard. He tried to say something, but only a squeak came out.

She lay sprawled out like his cousin's rag doll, staring at the window.

Suddenly she turned her head and stared at him. Her eyes locked onto his. He found that he couldn't move. He didn't know how long he stood there, it seemed to go on and on.

Jeez. *He couldn't move.*

Maybe it would have gone on forever. But the almost magical silence was broken finally by the clickety-click sound of his mother's approaching footsteps.

"Hey, Fremont. Go get me a danish and coffee. Black, no sugar. I'll take it in my car."

``You sure, Lieutenant? You gonna be able to eat?''

``Just get it, okay?'' Lieutenant O'Reilly went back into Sara's bedroom and watched as the paramedics worked on the girl.

If the neighbor's kid hadn't been curious . . .

If the front door hadn't been left wide open . . .

But it was affirmative on both counts.

She'd be okay. Physically, anyway. At least the creep hadn't killed her. She wouldn't be able to sleep for awhile, he'd bet good money on that. Not if she'd seen what was blocking up the toilet, and he wouldn't ask her about that yet.

Later, he'd have to. But not yet.

He didn't show his anger, even though his throat felt tight with rage. That was part of him. Poker Face.

Still, none of this would have happened if they'd detained Harrison in Cairo, until they found out for sure about the dog.

TWENTY-FIVE

The doctor in the emergency room at Mount Sinai Hospital leaned over Sara encouragingly.

"You're doing fine, Sara. Just one or two more tests." He turned away and spoke quietly to the unseen nurses at the foot of the examining table.

If only she could hear what they said. But their voices were pitched just a fraction too low. Someone had thrown a heavy sheet over her raised knees, so she couldn't see beyond their double peak.

Had the baby been hurt? She closed her eyes wearily. Everything went on too long. If only they'd stop talking and get on with it.

"A little sting, Sara," murmured a technician soothingly, preparing her for the needle.

A little sting. Incongruously she felt her

198

mouth twitch, a crazy hysterical laugh try to burst out of her dry, compressed lips.

My God. A little sting.

A policeman came to the door of the emergency room, and she strained to hear, recognizing only the word "homicide."

Homicide. A breathy, sibilant word.

It wasn't strong enough for what she'd seen.

Homicide meant a stabbing, a gunshot wound. Even a strangling. Not what she'd seen last night. That was more. That needed jolting, ugly words.

Another thing. Was it last night? Or is right now still part of the same night? She began to drift.

What was in that little sting, doctor? Something nice for good little girls to dream on?

She shifted her right foot in the stirrup, and a calming hand patted her ankle.

"Feel cold," she murmured drowsily. Someone pulled the sheet up around her breasts.

"I don't have anything on," she explained carefully. "Nothing at all."

She tried to keep her eyes open, but someone must have weighted her eyelids with coins like the dead. Would Steve mourn for her?

"The baby?" she asked sleepily.

"Baby's fine," were the last words she heard before drifting off to blessed oblivion.

TWENTY-SIX

Lieutenant O'Reilly was feeling hungry again.

Funny how his mental processes seemed inextricably tied into his stomach. Maybe the act of chewing helped put his brain in gear. Or maybe the taste of sugar calmed his nerves, danish and sweet rolls being his favorite thinking foods.

His old Irish mother used to claim that sugar was good for what ailed you. Old-country recipes were brought out and dusted off at the first sign of a cold, all of them based on sugar.

Bad cough? Nothing, absolutely nothing, could beat the sweet brownish syrup obtained by boiling up a concoction of red onions and brown sugar. Even a regular prescription from the corner drugstore had to be doctored up with a teaspoon of finest white granulated. Only then could it do the trick.

No wonder he was hooked on the stuff.

He stood up restlessly, then reached for his jacket. If there was ever a time he needed a dose of the sweet stuff, this had to be it.

"I'm going out," he said to the sergeant at the desk outside his office.

The man looked up from his paperwork. "Want me to come with you, Lieutenant?" he asked hopefully.

"Just get that report finished, Robinow." The lieutenant went out into the street.

Everything should have fallen into place as easy as 1-2-3. But things had been messed up from the start, and getting messier by the minute.

Somehow the suspect had been permitted to leave Cairo without so much as a twenty-four-hour delay. Let alone a proper investigation.

Made you wonder what went on in the rarified atmosphere of embassy security.

If someone had been suspected of chewing up dogs in Manhattan, all hell would have broken loose. He could just see the headlines now. "Man Makes Meal out of Mutt." Dog-lovers from here to the Bronx would have tied up the lines to the Commissioner for days.

At the very least, the suspect wouldn't have been able to take a crap without one of New York's Finest looking over his shoulder.

Now it had become more than just the dog.

The lieutenant had read the report from London and wanted to puke. The dog was bad enough.

Then there was the girl, Sara Fenster. With her, the suspect had added rape to his rapidly lengthening list of criminal activities.

In view of Steve Harrison's proclivity for raw flesh and blood, perhaps she should count herself lucky that the son of a bitch had taken care of Caldwell first.

Forensics had already tied Harrison in with the job on the leather-jacketed guy in the park. Apart from having his guts strung out like a popcorn chain, the victim hadn't been interfered with in any way. No bones sucked clean, and his brains had been left where the Good Lord intended them to be. Perhaps Harrison had been interrupted before he could get down to business.

Or perhaps he hadn't been hungry.

The lieutenant's thoughts turned to food. A cinnamon roll, black coffee on the side, sounded pretty good at the moment. Thank God he didn't have a weak stomach. He might get a fleeting touch of the queasies now and again, when some psycho's imagination took flight. But nothing serious. Nothing permanent.

He went into a small coffeeshop around the corner from the station house. Entering the cramped interior, he immediately began to feel at ease.

The warm, familiar aroma of fresh bakery goods blended with stale cigaret smoke like a soothing elixir for his nerves.

A couple seated in a booth near the door interrupted their animated conversation as he came in. The woman's hair had been treated to an overdose of henna sometime back, and patches of gray roots gave her a piebald effect. She dabbed at her eyes a couple of times with a torn bit of Kleenex, before turning back to her companion. The man with her looked as though he'd been on a three-day binge and wasn't ready to face reality just yet. He stared at the lieutenant for a minute with sad unfocused eyes, before resuming the conversation in a quietly urgent voice.

The lieutenant slipped onto a stool at the counter, and the blonde middle-aged waitress poured him a cup of coffee.

"What'll it be today, Lieutenant?" she asked him, wiping the counter space around his cup with a damp cloth. "We got prune danish in fresh."

The lieutenant picked up the cup and stared morosely at the rich, dark brew. "How about cinnamon rolls?"

"Sure thing." The waitress looked as though she ate in on a regular basis. Her dainty white cotton apron, trimmed with red rickrack around the edge, was anchored around her ample waist by means of a large bow. On top of her stiff yellow curls, she had tucked another white bow, edged with a strip of the same red rickrack that adorned her apron. She opened the glass-fronted case behind her. "Raisin or plain?" she asked.

"Raisin." The coffee tasted hot and strong, and if the saucer had a chip in it, so what?

The lieutenant dug his teeth into the warm, doughy swirl. Nothing else like it. He jerked a white-paper square from the metal holder on the counter, and wiped a trace of glaze from his mouth.

"Been reading about that creepo in the papers," said the waitress, polishing a Coke glass with a muslin cloth. "When're you guys gonna get the bastard? A girl ain't safe anymore."

The couple by the door stopped talking and looked up, waiting for O'Reilly's answer.

He swallowed a mouthful of cinnamon roll before answering. His green eyes stared back at her blandly. No sign of anger. No flicker of frustration. Poker Face.

Only the green eyes looked hard, hard. Glacier hard.

"We're working on it," he said evenly.

"Sure," the big blonde waitress said, refilling his cup. "Meanwhile he's working on anyone he can get his hands on. You

and the boys'll have to put in some over-
time. Looks like this case is gonna be a
tough nut to crack.''

Lieutenant O'Reilly finished up the last
of the roll.

''Nothing I can't handle,'' he growled at
last.

TWENTY-SEVEN

Sara found the middle-aged heavy-set Englishman waiting on the doorstep when she got back from the hospital.

They hadn't wanted her to go home, but she'd insisted. They'd be watching from now on anyway. She could see the police car across the street. O'Reilly had told her that there would be a man watching her door all the time.

She hoped that they had managed to get someone to clean up the bathroom.

The solidly built Englishman looked nice, the way people used to look on family sit-coms. Friendly, and somehow trustworthy.

God, how she needed to trust someone.

"What do you want?" Something seemed to be wrong with her voice. She couldn't speak above a whisper.

"May I come in?" He was hatless, but

the polite way he spoke made her think of all the English movies where the men raised their hats to the ladies.

"I don't know you," she explained carefully, by way of refusal. Ever since the night before, she'd found herself speaking slower. Almost as if her brain had shifted into first.

The Englishman was trying to tell her something.

"Please forgive me for not making myself clear. I'm Detective Inspector Ian Potter, New Scotland Yard." He started to show her his identification, watching her calmly as she began to laugh. The hysterical giggles left her breathless and close to tears.

It must be a nightmare, she thought irrationally. A wild, crazy nightmare, all of it. Just like a third-rate movie with the monster from the Rue Morgue battling Sherlock Holmes.

"And I'm the star," she managed to say, gasping for breath. The wretched tears kept coming.

"Take it easy, Miss. Come on, let's go in." He took the keys from her hand, and opened the main security door. "Which is yours?" he asked, gesturing down the hallway with the key.

"The one at the end." She hiccuped gently.

"Something's happened, hasn't it?" he asked suddenly.

"You could say that." It struck her as

funny again, and she began to laugh and laugh until her chest hurt. "Oh, God."

"Now then, Sara. May I call you Sara?"

She nodded wordlessly, watching him as he opened her apartment door.

"Well now, that's better. Come on in, Sara, and sit down. I'll make you some tea." He paused, looking around. "Do you have any tea?"

She nodded again. "In the kitchen cupboard over the sink. Tea bags, though."

"That's all right." He went into the kitchen and busied himself filling the kettle, hunting for cups, opening the refrigerator, while she sat quietly at the kitchen table, watching him.

"Now. Drink this up," he admonished her kindly a few minutes later.

The tea was hot and sweet. He'd put milk and sugar in it, but it tasted good. Surprisingly good.

"What happened?" he asked at last. She found herself telling him everything, sparing herself no detail, staring at his kind tired face as the violently descriptive words poured from her lips like the bursting of an abscess.

Later, she cried. She went into her bedroom and lay down, and he sat on a chair by the bed.

"He's hopelessly insane," he said quietly.

"I know that. I guess I could tell that something was wrong as soon as he stepped off the plane."

"It's getting late. You'll need protection, not just a squad car outside. Let me stay here. I can sleep on the sofa."

"Do you think he'll come back?"

"I don't know, Sara. Do you?"

"No." She closed her eyes. "So tired."

"Go to sleep, then. I won't let anyone hurt you."

Just a little thing. A slip of a girl, like Molly, only dark.

Our little girl could have looked like that.

He got up quietly, and went back into the kitchen. He began to rinse out the cups, then something caught his eye on the wall by the sink.

The calendar looked askew.

He reached out to straighten it. Someone had circled something in thick, black pencil.

Who marked the calendar?

Wait a minute, he thought. That's more than just a mark.

He peered at the circle around the image of the full moon.

Not a circle. A rough-drawn eye, with the moon as the pupil . . .

The eye of Horus.

What's going to happen on that night? The night of the full moon?

He felt a twinge start up in his chest. Not now, he thought impatiently. I don't have time for that now. Later, after the blighter is caught, I can sit back and let the big one happen. But not now.

He shook two tablets out of the little bottle that he carried everywhere, swallowing them with a grimace. He filled one of the cups on the drainboard with water and drank it down slowly.

All right, that's better. Now then, what have we got? Deep in thought, he turned out the lights, and lay down on the sofa, staring into the dark, unable to sleep.

He wasn't much of a betting man, but he'd be willing to bet his first pension check that somewhere out in the night the murderer lay sleepless too.

Don't make any plans, he thought grimly. *Because sooner than you think, I'll be on to you, and that'll be the end of it.*

And the end of you, Steve Harrison.

On the other side of the bedroom door, Sara lay motionless on the bed. The Inspector had covered her with the light blanket that she kept neatly folded on the foot of the bed.

She couldn't seem to get warm. Her hands and feet still felt as though they'd been encased in ice. *Cold hands, warm heart*, she thought. *But that can't be right, because I know that my heart is frozen solid too.*

Better try and get some sleep. That's what everyone said. Only what are you going to do about the dreams?

She closed her eyes, willing sleep to come to her. To mend . . .

Face it, this is something that can never be fixed. She rolled over onto her back, staring up at the ceiling.

Every nerve seemed tensed, coiled and ready to spring. She'd always had trouble falling asleep, even when she was a little girl.

Her mother used to say good night, turn off the light, and before she got to the front room, Sara would be out of bed, playing with her toys. Rearranging the toy farmyard buildings, sorting out the animals.

Sometimes she'd wake up in the morning stretched out on the floor beside the straggling line of cows and pigs, the carpet pattern creased into her flushed face.

High-strung. That's what her mother had called her. She guessed that she'd always be that way. Especially now. Oh, God, yes, especially now.

She turned her head restlessly on her pillow, biting her lips.

Get over it, she thought fiercely. *At least it wasn't a stranger.* But that's what he'd seemed like. A cruel, heartless stranger. Even his face, so close to hers, had looked different.

Something about the eyes.

What could have sent him over the edge like that?

What had happened in Egypt?

She remembered the first time she met him. He'd seemed so wholesome. So different from the guys she'd gone out with in

New York. So different—and yet so ordinary.

Well, he wasn't ordinary any more.

It hurt to think of him somewhere out there, sick, confused. Needing shelter. Needing treatment.

She guessed that pretty soon she'd have to face up to the fact that nothing could ever be the way it was before.

But not yet. For a little while longer, she needed to hope. To remember the way it used to be, before he got so terribly sick. Before the horror in the bathroom.

Before Egypt.

She could hear the Englishman in the other room. His steady breathing reassured her. Funny how well they got on. Something about him had clicked with her right from the start.

If someone had told her a couple of days ago that she'd be entertaining a Scotland Yard detective on her living-room couch, she wouldn't have believed it in a million years.

That's how crazy things have become, she thought sadly.

And no amount of wishing would change the fact that she had lost Steve forever.

TWENTY-EIGHT

"None of the girls want to go out. Not with that goddamn freak on the loose." Polly Winslow frowned delicately, then hurriedly pressed the frown line away with a firm finger. The wretched lines were always waiting for a chance to deepen, and the Park Avenue madame had had enough surgery lately, thank you. The plastic surgeon's wife had a new full-length sable coat from Bergdorf's to prove it.

"You can hardly blame them," said the other person in Polly's bedroom, a rather precious black man under 30, with a light complexion. He was Polly Winslow's righthand man, but had cleverly managed to become even more than that.

It beat being a street whore's pimp. Besides, he had developed a taste for caviar.

He sat back in a peach damask easy chair beside Polly's bed and watched her drink her early morning coffee. No doubt there were worse things than dancing attendance on a rich old madame, but he had no intention of finding out what they were.

She wasn't too demanding, not that he cared one way or the other. He did as much as he could to please her, and all in all he felt he earned an *E* for effort.

Now, he reached forward and solicitously filled her cup from the silver coffeepot on the tray. "Sugar?" he asked, a slightly flashy smile on his handsome face.

"I really shouldn't. I don't want to get hippy." She stared morosely at the full cup, the lines tight around her petulant mouth.

"You'll never be hippy." *Ain't that the truth. Old bitch look like a fuckin' skeleton.*

She drank the coffee slowly, the frown sneaking back quietly between her penciled eyebrows. Her heavily made-up face, with its low-slung jaw and cap of red-gold curls, gave her the appearance of an aging clown.

"Be a dear, Raul, and find out who's available," she said finally.

"Tamara is free," said her fancy man, checking the register. "You did promise her the weekend off, but I suppose, in a pinch—"

"You can forget Tamara," said Polly

coldly. "She's finished, as far as I'm concerned. And don't think that I haven't noticed the way she looks at you." She replaced her cup in its saucer with a little click.

"Polly, darling, I swear—" he began.

"I said, forget her. Anyway, her aunt called and told her to stay out of Manhattan for a couple of weeks." She laughed slightly. "Told her there would be a killing in Central Park. Said she read it in the tea leaves. Said she saw the body of a woman in the goddamn orange pekoe." Polly laughed out loud, the sinews in her scrawny neck standing out like telephone cables.

Raul joined in the merriment, the streetwise guttural snicker belying his carefully cultivated upscale demeanor.

"Besides, Tamara wouldn't do. She's too dark," Polly added spitefully. "This is a specialty deal. The customer in question is flying in from Washington for a couple of days. He wants someone very fair. An ice-princess type. He was very specific about the requirements, and believe me, he always gets what he wants. I'm not going to put my head on the block by spoiling his record."

"Loren is a blonde."

"She's been booked by that Arab sheik. We won't see her for a month." Polly gestured irritably at the silver tray on her lap, and Raul jumped up to remove it.

"Sometimes I wonder what they expect of me." She got out of bed unsteadily, and went over to an antique liquor cabinet. She opened the cabinet and took out a large bottle of Bombay Gin. "I'm not a goddamn miracle-worker."

Raul composed his not-unattractive features into an expression of exaggerated commiseration.

"How about Dulcie Bennett?" he asked, consulting the register again.

"Dulcie!" Polly paused in the act of pouring out a shot of gin. "She won't do at all."

"She's got that fantastic white skin," he countered. "And she could always lighten her hair. She'd be fierce as a real light blonde."

Polly took a sip of gin, neat. "There's something about that girl I don't like. A lack of class. Not only that, she's hardly trustworthy."

"C'mon, Polly. You can trust her for one night!"

"Maybe. Maybe not. Everything has to be exactly perfect for this particular gentleman."

"Hey, it's just a one-night stand. So she isn't a debutante." Raul grinned, showing off his perfect teeth. "After the first few seconds, he'll never know the difference."

Polly swallowed the rest of the gin in her glass. Her face took on a calculating look.

"Oh, Raul. Have you got a lot to learn."

He smiled sweetly. *Old bitch. Acts like*

*she knows everything. She don't know
nothing.* "Well, we don't have any other
blondes. And if that's what the client
wants . . ."

Polly didn't answer. She let her cream-
silk kimono slip to the floor, and walked
naked into the bathroom.

He heard her gargling and spitting into
the sink. *One day the old bitch gonna
choke.*

The sound of the shower came next.
Maybe she drown. Then you be out, man.
He giggled slightly.

"Raul!" Her raspy voice broke into his
thoughts.

He sauntered into the shell-pink bathroom. "Did you want anything, darling?"

"Call Dulcie. Tell her what the deal is.
And while you're at it, call that friend of
yours at La Coupe and set up an appointment for her this morning. Did you get
that?"

"Sure, Polly." The bathroom filled with
steam. He could just barely see the outline
of her scrawny shanks.

"Tell him I don't want her to look cheap.
I want him to use a little Ash Blonde with
the lightener. Platinum, but toned down.
Can you remember all that?"

"I believe so, my love." His smile
stretched into a secret snarl of rage. "Anything else?"

"Yes. While you're in here, you can
scrub my back."

TWENTY-NINE

Money used to just flat out slip through
Dulcie Bennett's greedy fingers.

Didn't matter how many tricks she
turned, she had always felt a trace of
disappointment when she'd added up the
actual figures. Lately, though, things were
looking up.

Men liked Dulcie. They liked her rather
cool Nordic features, her white skin, her
delicate mouth that had an almost cruel
twist to it sometimes. In fact, there were
quite a few men who were turned on by the
trace of spiteful cruelty that she sometimes revealed.

Sometimes there were regrets. But not
on her part. Never ever on her part. Some
men had accused her of having no heart,
but that didn't bother her either. It wasn't
her heart that they were interested in.

From her very first day on the streets, she'd realized how much men liked her. They showed it in several ways. The main way was money, but even when she wasn't working, they couldn't seem to keep their hands off her slender body. Not that she was really thin. Just that the soft white flesh was attractively spread over a tall frame. Attractively enough, in fact, that she couldn't ride in a crowded elevator without some handy guy showing his appreciation of her.

At first, she'd practiced flirting, but it didn't take her long to realize what a waste of time that was. Men didn't need any come-on. Not with her. She just had to be who she was. Dulcie Bennett. A cheap whore who'd made the transition to big time.

She never missed the streets. Never looked back. Except for the occasional john who wanted something a little out of the ordinary. Then she'd dig back into her bag of memories and show him a time he'd never forget.

Most times, she didn't bother, though. Didn't have to. She got a bang out of the other girls who worked for Polly Winslow. "Work" seemed to be the key word. A word Dulcie didn't bother with.

She knew when she had a good thing going. Yes indeed.

Now that she had come under Polly's wing, things were looking better all the time. For one thing, she didn't turn "tricks" any more. My goodness gracious, that was a four-letter word in Polly's book.

Dates. That's what Polly called them. And sometimes, when the john was a really big fish, Polly's young ladies were given *appointments.*

Just like going to the dentist, only better. You got the same feeling of numbness, *and* you got paid too.

Money was the only thing that counted anyway. The only thing you could really depend on. Dulcie didn't believe in love. No way. That was for suckers. She had seen what it did to her mother all those years ago.

After Dulcie's father died, her mother had gone bananas at first. Dulcie remembered how the house had been shut up in the daytime. Curtains drawn against a hint of sunlight. No movies. No radio. No TV. A child's idea of hell. But that had been before Dewayn came on the scene.

Overnight, her mother had bloomed. Nothing was too good for Dewayn, and wasn't it nice to have a man about the house?

Well, it had been nice, at first.

But then Dewayn started to walk in his sleep. At least, that was what he called it.

Down the hall and up the stairs to Dulcie's room. Night after night after night after night. Four years of it. Until at last she upped and ran away for good.

She'd been only ten when it began. Dewayn's sleepwalking. When she cried and tried to push him away, he had slapped her and told her she'd better be quiet or he'd tell her mother.

I'll tell, I'll tell, he said over and over. Funny how *he* did it to her and *she* felt guilty.

As she grew older, she just lay there and thought about killing him. Sometimes she thought about killing them both. Her mother and Dewayn. She thought about the different ways she could do it.

But in the end, she tried to kill herself. Scared Dewayn shitless.

That was when she found out about the power she had over him.

No more trips up the hallway without a payoff. Not just nickles and dimes either. First it had been a new watch. A bracelet. Then the real stuff. Money, honey.

But never enough. She always wanted more. As though a purse full of dollars made her worth something.

Even though Dewayn kept telling her that she was no good, wasn't worth a damn; the money proved him wrong. She could go into a store, any store, open up her purse, and all the dumb salesgirls would sit up and take notice.

A shrink that she'd screwed once tried to tell her that she substituted her purse for the other thing, but she'd just smiled and held out her hand.

She had been on her own for six years now, and her appetite for cash just got bigger and bigger, her bank account fatter and fatter.

She felt almost grateful to Dewayn. The son of a bitch had opened up new vistas for her. At least she wouldn't end up a loser, like her mother. She'd never have to be a doormat for the rest of her life, which is all the old lady ended up being.

Dulcie began to rub some Revlon Moondrops into her white skin. Got to take care of the merchandise. Tonight would be a very important night for Dulcie, according to Polly. An appointment had been set up for eight P.M. sharp at the Essex House on Central Park South.

A certain Someone, in New York for a much-needed twenty-four hour R & R from Capitol Hill, needed the gentle ministrations of a very special girl to take his mind off things.

Dulcie had smiled sweetly at that. Seemed to her that he wanted his mind *on* things. Not off them.

Polly had said that she thought Dulcie would be just his type, *if* she played her cards right and didn't forget to show some class.

Dulcie had snickered quietly. In her quite extensive experience, she had discovered that, as far as her customers were concerned, the higher they reached on the ladder of success, the lower they wanted to wallow on their days off.

Everything was set, anyway. She'd had her hair done that morning at La Coupe, lightening it from its usual honey gold to a silvery blonde.

That particular shade of platinum would be a bitch to keep up. But if the guy became a regular, Dulcie guessed it might be worth it.

Polly had given her a list of other requirements, up to and including the silvery frosted polish on her nails. All ten of them.

She held out her hands and stared at them musingly. She was used to fire-engine-red nail polish. Men liked it too. Liked to feel the delicate scratches she drew on their backs.

Now her fingernails looked pale and colorless. *Drained* of color. Almost . . . *ghostly*.

For some reason, the goose bumps crept along her waxed arms, an army of tiny dots on the hairless white skin.

She shuddered suddenly, feeling chilled. Then shrugged carelessly.

No need to get spooked, she thought with a thin smile. *It's only someone dancing on my grave.*

A fair distance away from Dulcie Bennett's Hudson Street apartment, Old

Bleeder had shuffled into the southern end of Central Park. Bottle in hand, he found a secluded area suitable for his particular needs. Bleary eyes vague, he paused to pick his nose speculatively. If he went out on Fifth Avenue, he might be able to panhandle off the still-curious onlookers. On the other hand, he had his bottle, so what the hell.

Drifts of old leaves lay scattered across a small clearing. The old derelict kicked at them haphazardly, staggering about in a kind of tipsy choreography.

He raised the bottle in a good-natured salute to his surroundings, before downing a swig of the cheap, sour wine.

A police car raced along Central Park South, sirens blaring, reminding Old Bleeder of the recent excitement on Fifth Avenue.

"Sum'uv a bitch," he muttered, remembering the wild-looking man running across the park. "Goddamn shit-bird went and outsmarted 'em." He felt a slight discomfort somewhere in the vicinity of his stomach. Opening his mouth, he emitted a rolling, gullet-rattling belch, and an almost misty miasma of alcohol fumes hovered around his face.

He frowned, trying to think. Trying to remember what the mutha-fucker had looked like. The bottle almost slipped from his hand as he had a sudden jolting recollection of cruel maddened eyes glaring back at him.

Clutching his bottle like a fractious child, Old Bleeder crouched back under a convenient bush, trying to hide from a danger he couldn't define.

"Goddamn boogeyman," he muttered. He took another drink of the wine, letting it dribble slowly down his throat. The cheap wine warmed him inside, fortifying him with a reckless courage. "Ain't no boogeyman gonna git me nohow."

Shadows shifted among the leaves on the ground. The sun's rays slanted across the low green hills and sheltered hollows in the park. Night came softly, hard on the heels of a beautiful evening.

"Ain't no skinheaded mutha gonna mess with me," said Old Bleeder, taking another drink.

THIRTY

Menket lay rigidly still in a ditch in Central Park. Hidden from sight by a blanket of leaves, he breathed shallowly, slipping into an almost trancelike state.

He must not move. Not yet.

If he felt the raging need, he would take whatever he could find around him. Until then, he would not drink, nor urinate, nor defecate.

He smiled to himself, remembering his childhood training.

Even then, a priest.

And a hunter . . .

How many times had he gone hunting in the mysterious red desert. How many hours had he waited eagerly for his prey, ignoring the ache in his bladder, the urgent gripe in his bowels.

Now the waiting became ever sweeter.

Soon his Ka-spirit must journey onward. In three more days the moon would wax full, signifying the victory of life over death.

I know what my shell had planned for me that night. The fool, he had only hastened his own destruction.

Now the spirit and shell are one, and soon there will be nothing more of this life for the man called Steve, except the child.

Except the child . . .

He drifted deep into the trance, his heartbeat slow and steady. Gradually the rigidity left his limbs, as with infinitesimal shifting movements, his supine body sank further into the ditch. His flesh, beginning to show the relentless signs of decay, settled with an awful yearning to be one with the earth, and the jutting ridges of his vertebrae took on the contours of the rough, uneven ground beneath him.

Soon his breathing was all but suspended. The clenched mouth slackened, and under his slitted lids his eyeballs rolled back into his skull.

Memories, sharp and poignant, enveloped his somnambulant mind with their seductive balm, and once more he walked the sands of Egypt.

As if awakening from a hated nightmare, he recalled the hot Egyptian sun on his face, smelled the desert's harsh perfume, and an inward shout of triumph filled him with its warmth.

A tremor passed across the half-closed lids as Menket strained to see beyond the gulf of years. The sea of centuries.

Come, now it is clearer.

The slackened mouth curved in a fraction of a smile as the beloved images sharpened.

The burnished gold disc is held up high to reflect his visage. His shaven skull has already been anointed with the fragrant oil, his loins encircled by the cool, pleated linen. The bronze face retains its haughty demeanor, and his eyes, outlined with the blessed wand of antimony, gaze sternly at his reflection.

The highborn and the humble alike await his coming. For he is a prince of Egypt and a priest of the sun god Re. The art of Hakau keeps no secret from him, and the gods of Egypt reach out to touch him with their beneficence.

O thrice blessed city of On, where the red desert sand stretches to the edge of the earth, prepare for the flight of the sacred beetle as the sun blesses you with its glory.

It is morning, the time of the sacred Phoenix, the bennu bird that dwells on the holy ben-ben stone in the temple of Re.

Menket trembled, and his inert limbs began a palsied twitching as the vision faded. His lips moved rapidly, mouthing a prayer to Osiris, the god of resurrection.

Why couldn't he see the acolytes? Where

were the slaves? His eyelids flickered again, and a vein pulsated in his temple.

No matter. A white antelope had been brought forth for the slaughter, and now waited, tethered to a willow, proud head bowed for the sacrifice.

He approached it on feet that seemed to float across the fine desert sand.

Why is everything fading? His heart began to pound. Do not go, beloved Egypt.

He stretched out a cruel hand, grasping the wild beast by its delicately curved horns. With a sudden downward stroke, he plunged the sacrificial knife into the quivering throat, uttering an ancient paean that echoed the white antelope's scream.

A shuddering thrill racked his body. With a wrenching groan, his eyes jerked open again, staring, fiercely alert, and ready for the hunt.

Ready for the sacrifice.

Again.

THIRTY-ONE

Dulcie Bennett smoothed her long ash-blond hair back into its loose knot, anchoring it with a silver clasp. Everything had to be perfect.

She turned sideways, carefully examining her slender reflection in the bedroom mirror with coldly speculative eyes. Her hands fluttered restlessly over the white strapless evening gown, tugging at the heavy satin until she felt satisfied with its appearance.

Don't mess up, kid, Polly had told her. This client is very important. Could mean mucho repeats. But it has to be kid gloves all the way. No flash, no dash. And for God's sake, don't recognize him. Even if you do.

Well, she had.

The luxury suite at the Essex House on Central Park South had probably seen

more than its share of well-heeled men.
More than its share of discreetly high-class
call girls.

But not all of the clients were as famous
as the man who waited impatiently in the
living room of the $600-a-night suite.

Dulcie traced her lips with gloss, her
rather thin mouth curving into a smile.
Polly hadn't mentioned the kinks that the
client had requested, but then maybe she
hadn't known about that.

All in a day's work, thought Dulcie carelessly. She sat down near the head of the
king-sized bed and emptied a small plastic
packet of white powder onto the top of the
bedside table. Using the long, frosted
pearl-laquered nail on her little finger, she
separated the powder into four thin lines.
Then she delicately licked the tip of her
finger.

A respectably thick pile of 100-dollar
bills sat next to the cocaine lines, and with
an expertise born of long habit, Dulcie
rolled one into a tube.

A hesitant knock at the door interrupted
her mid snort.

"Just a *minute*," she said sharply. There
was silence from the other room, and she
chuckled spitefully.

Polly would just *shit* if she heard her
now. But Polly only heard as much as she
wanted to. She didn't want to know the
details. Especially when they involved
someone as powerful and wealthy as the
man in the other room.

My stars, that would *never* do.

Polly dealt in a classy service for gentlemen. Nothing *common* under any circumstances. Just give them what they want and always remember to be top-drawer. It pays well.

Sure, Polly, thought Dulcie. *But sometimes they want something a little different, a little lower on the scale. A little less Upper East Side. And guess what, Polly? That pays even better.*

She snorted the rest of the coke quickly, rubbing her nose with the back of her hand afterwards, and breathing deeply. Then she stood up and glanced at herself in the mirror once more.

Okay. Here we go, boys and girls. Lights, camera. Action.

She walked imperiously to the door and opened it wide. Moving with a graceful hauteur, she went into the other room and sat down in the chair that had been readied for her.

The man groveled on the floor in front of her. He was naked except for an adult version of a baby diaper.

"I really appreciate this, Dulcie," he said humbly.

"Don't mention it," she said regally. "It takes all kinds. Let's just get on with it."

Long after midnight, in the early hours of the morning, she went back into the bedroom to get her white Chinese lambskin wrap. She picked up the pile of bills and put them in her purse. She dabbed at the trace of white powder on the bedside table, sucking her finger reflectively.

In the other room the man sobbed uncontrollably. "Do you forgive me? I must know that you forgive me. Oh, God!"

What a drag, she thought irritably.

"Say that you forgive me, Dulcie," he begged.

She walked to the door and looked at him. "Of course I do," she said, smiling sweetly, her thin lips curling upward.

Outside on the sidewalk some of the streetlights weren't working, and the air was still heavy with smoke. The street looked deserted.

"This town is going to the dogs," grinned the old doorman cheerfully. "Need a cab, miss?"

"What I need is some fresh air," said Dulcie.

"Doubt if you'll find any tonight." He touched his forefinger to his braided cap and turned back to the hotel.

Dulcie crossed over to the north side of Central Park South, and began to walk toward the West Side.

The almost full moon shone fitfully through the clouds that drifted across the sky, turning her fair hair to a silvery white.

Suddenly she felt afraid.

She turned quickly to look behind her.

Why hadn't the goddamn lights been

fixed? She began to run awkwardly, hampered by the long white-satin skirt and thin spike heels.

What was that?

Was that just the sound of her own footsteps echoing behind her?

A cab drove by, speeding toward Central Park West. She ran out to the curb, trying to flag it down, but it didn't stop.

A shred of conversation came from a couple hurrying along on the other side of the street, and for a crazy moment she wanted to run back and join them.

Don't leave me alone, she mouthed silently.

Damn. Her heel felt loose. Must have happened when she was trying to stop that cab. Polly will have to reimburse me for these shoes, she thought with a nervous giggle. They don't exactly give them away at Bergdorf's.

The giggle turned into a sob. What a bummer. Only the fat roll of bills in her satin purse stopped the night from being a complete washout. Goddamn wimp, she thought, remembering the man asleep at the Essex House. Just like all the others. Well, she was going to get fat off their quirky jollies, any way she could.

She limped over to the stone wall that hemmed in Central Park, wondering if the shoe could be saved. Leaning against the cold stones of the wall, she wondered why she felt so breathless.

Never realizing for a moment that soon she wouldn't be breathing at all.

As she bent over again to look at her shoe, she caught sight of something out of the corner of her eye. A flash of pure blind terror gripped her in its icy talons as she saw the hand on the wall.

Adrenaline rushed to fuel the machinery of flight as she tried to run, but not soon enough. Not nearly soon enough.

Wall-eyed and panting like a hunted doe, she felt herself dragged into the park by her unraveled hair.

She tried to fight. When she saw the shaven head with its scabbed-over nicks and cuts, she felt a fleeting burst of hysterical anger.

Another goddamn kink, Dulcie thought furiously.

She dug her long nails into his arm, and his flesh seemed to break away under the shirt sleeve like well-ripened Brie. And what was that awful smell?

She was still wondering about that as the final swift blow fell, settling her confusion once and for all.

Now come, Osiris. Come, Herakhty-Re. Partake of this sacrifice that you may fulfill my command when the time for rebirth draws nigh.

Menket stood motionless, arms outstretched to the moonlit sky above.

O Victory, how sweet thy taste.

Joy filled his heart. Once more, even in this accursed place, he had performed the sacred ritual. Lacking the ceremonial flint knife, he had struck a lightning blow to the jugular, and now the red blood pulsed darkly across the pure white skin, the heavy white satin.

Shuddering as the waves of hunger engulfed him, Menket fell to his knees and tore at the still-warm flesh. A bone cracked sharply, filling the night with its brittle sound.

No one came to disturb him. Strong now, he mouthed a bitter curse to confuse and waylay the paths of his enemies. Then he turned back to the work at hand.

Slowly the pale moon faded, readying for the approach of the sun god Re, as Menket raced back to his leafy ditch.

Across from the park, the man lying awake and distraught in his $600-suite at the Essex House would not have recognized Dulcie Bennett now. Not in a million years.

Flanks stripped to the bone, what was left lay in her shallow grave, wrapped in the blood-drenched satin, a shattered remnant of an ancient ritual.

A carefully placed layer of leaves hid the site. As if to add to the camouflage, a light scattering of rain began to fall, pattering on the thirsty trees and bushes in the park.

*   *   *

A large drop fell on Old Bleeder's red-veined nose as he slept curled up beneath a bush. Muttering obscenely, the old derelict sat up slowly, bleary eyes staring vapidly at nothing. Another patter of rain lightly bathed his deeply crevassed face.

"Shit," he said amiably. Rain didn't bother him. Not unless it was a thunderstorm. Encased in his thick layers of ragged clothing, Old Bleeder was impervious to the vagaries of weather.

Clinging to the overhanging limbs of the bush that had sheltered him throughout the night, he stood up unsteadily, still clutching yesterday's bottle. He held the bottle up high in front of his unfocused eyes. He shook it a couple of times, then drained the last few drops before discarding it, smacking his lips.

Breakfast over, he fumbled in the musty layers of tattered clothes, searching for the source of urgency that demanded his immediate attention.

He urinated lengthily, the yellow stream, pungent and steaming, creating its own puddle in competition with the rain. Rearranging his clothing with care, more out of concern for warmth than modesty, he paused to turn aside and blow his nose through his fingers. As he wiped his hand down the front of his overcoat, he recollected that once, way back in the dusty reaches of his past, he used to use a handkerchief for that purpose.

"Shit," he said again, amused.

Having attended to the necessities of the morning, he set out with his peculiar shuffling gait to look for new supplies.

The rain stopped, and the sun came out strong over Manhattan.

Bleeder didn't care. The dirty layers of clothing were insulation against heat as well as cold.

And anyway, he had something to figure out.

Something that clung like sticky cobwebs to the part of his brain that attempted memory.

All in white, like a fucking bride. Or one of them ghosts. Maybe that's what she was. And what about the other one? What was he?

What was it that had happened in the night? Must have been a goddamn dream.

His laughter bubbled thickly in his rheumy lungs. Goddamn spook.

Only . . . if it was a dream, why did he dream about *that?* He shuddered, hurrying towards Columbus Avenue as though the devil were hot on his heels.

People were going to work, faces already set with an almost predatory focus. Muttering barely audible insults, Old Bleeder pushed past them roughly, shuffling up Columbus as he headed for the Hayden Planetarium. An old bench on the sidewalk outside the planetarium drew him to its bosom like a mother's arms.

But first, fresh supplies. He stopped at a familiar liquor store, entering his holy of holies with the slightly proprietary air of a regular customer.

Behind the counter, the real proprietor sat reading a day-old paper. He looked up as Old Bleeder shuffled in, then returned to his perusal of the pictures of the fire on Fifth Avenue. An artistically touched-up photo of Caldwell stared up at him with cold eyes.

On the counter near the register, a tray of stale-looking sandwiches offered a semblance of nourishment to the unwary. Old Bleeder looked them over critically, unwrapping the Saran Wrap to smell them before making his selection. The choice was simple. Tuna salad or processed cheese. Old Bleeder chose the tuna.

"I seen something in the park last night." Old Bleeder's hoarse whisper carried with it the decayed fumes of the earlier bottle. The man behind the counter turned his head away slightly. His thin face wore the cynical look of a man who had to deal with drunks and losers every day of his life.

"Shouldn't wonder," he said absently, still looking at the newspaper with interest.

"It wasn't no dream. I seen the blood." Old Bleeder hawked a clot of phlegm into his toothless mouth, working it around

thickly with his tongue. "I seen him do it,"
he added importantly.

"Sure, pal. What d'you need now?" The
owner stared hard at Old Bleeder. "You
gonna buy that sandwich?"

"Gimme a bottle o' Ripple."

The owner reached over to the shelf
behind him without getting up and took
down a bottle of wine. He put it down on
the counter by the register. "Four bucks,"
he said.

"For what?"

"For the booze and the sandwich."

"My ass," said Old Bleeder indignantly.
"Them tuna sam'itches look like puke."

"Out," said the owner, reaching for the
sandwich.

Old Bleeder dug in his pocket, bringing
up a handful of change mixed with bits of
fluff and loose tobacco. Grumbling to himself, he slowly counted out some coins
and slammed them down next to the register.

"You're short a dime," said the owner.

Old Bleeder counted out another nickle
and five pennies, then headed for the
door, clutching his bottle and the sandwich. "Sum'uv a bitch," he muttered as he
left.

"Up yours, pal," said the man behind
the counter, picking up the newspaper
again.

THIRTY-TWO

Sara awoke to the pleasant aroma of eggs frying. Coffee too. The warm, familiar smell of toast came next, making her hungry, and she sat up, yawning, stretching, still half asleep.

Then she remembered.

It had been bad from the very moment he got off the plane at Kennedy Airport. He had looked shockingly different, thinner or something. Anyway, different.

If only she could go back and change everything. Make it run right this time. Smooth out the kinks. Erase the tape and start over from scratch.

But she couldn't do that. Somehow she had to find a way to live with the memory of what had happened between her and Steve. A way to go on, to put it all behind her.

Fine words, she thought helplessly. *One way or another, I have to go into that bathroom.*

"Sara, are you awake?"

She smiled in relief at the sound of the Englishman's voice. "Yes. I won't be a minute," she said.

"There's someone here to see you. Come on out, I've made breakfast."

She pulled on her bathrobe, hesitating at the bathroom door.

I can't put it off, she thought unhappily. *I have to go in there. I have to. But I can't.*

"Oh, there you are." Inspector Potter came up, and casually reaching past her, opened the bathroom door. "I hope you don't mind. I took a nice, cold bath this morning, *and* had a shave. Set me up marvelously."

A faint whiff of toilet soap and aftershave freshened the room. A brightly striped towel hung neatly folded on the towel bar. "Is it all right to leave my towel there, Sara?"

She nodded wordlessly, smiling her thanks, grateful for what he'd managed to achieve. The bathroom looked normal again. A little bit untidy, a little bit damp, but just a bathroom, after all.

"Don't let the eggs get cold," he admonished, as he closed the door.

The medicine cabinet's mirror had not been replaced, and the Inspector's round shaving mirror lay face down on the back of the toilet tank.

Just as well. She didn't want to see her reflection yet. Didn't want to see the fear that she tried so hard to suppress.

She quickly washed her face and hands, pushing back her short hair with damp fingers. *I'm hungry,* she thought with surprise. *Really hungry.*

"Ah, there you are." The Inspector greeted her with a smile as she joined him in the kitchen. "You know Lieutenant O'Reilly, I believe."

"Yes." She stared at O'Reilly unhappily. "Do we have to talk about it now? I don't think . . ."

The lieutenant shifted uncomfortably in his chair.

"I know that it's hard for you, Miss Fenster, but I can't wait around anymore to find out what you know about Harrison. The clothes he took with him, for one thing."

"I told you people everything yesterday. What more can I say? I didn't notice what clothes he took with him. Didn't want to look at him, don't you understand? I just wanted him to leave." She picked up her fork and began to eat the scrambled eggs on the plate in front of her. "Is there any coffee?"

"Made it fresh this morning." The Inspector beamed, pouring her out a cup.

"I don't get it," said O'Reilly, a trace of irritability in his voice. He glanced at the Englishman. "Shouldn't you be out chasing down clues?"

"All in good time," said the Inspector placidly. "First things first."

"There's an original thought." The lieutenant pushed his cup forward for a refill, and the Englishman filled it with coffee. "I don't suppose you have any danish?"

"Sorry. Haven't had time to do any shopping yet."

"Tell me, Inspector." O'Reilly took a careful sip of the hot coffee. "Does Miss Fenster know that, strictly speaking, you have no authority in this case?"

"No." The Englishman looked steadily at Sara. "But since you've brought it up, I'll tell her now. He's right, you know. I'm actually on sick leave, and it won't be long before they pension me off."

"Then why—?" Sara began.

"I read about the dog. The one in Cairo. I like dogs. Stands to reason. I'm English, aren't I?"

"I don't understand," said Sara faintly. "What dog? What are you talking about? What's that got to do with—"

"Let him finish," O'Reilly interrupted. "Go on, Inspector."

"Well." The Inspector sighed deeply. "Then there was that boy in the park in London. Poor little bugger never hurt a soul. I couldn't let that happen. I put two and two together. There were certain similarities. I made up my mind to stop Harrison before he did any more damage.''

''You didn't make it,'' said O'Reilly quietly.

''No. But neither did you. He's still out there, isn't he? And you've got a whole police force behind you.''

''We'll get him,'' muttered O'Reilly.

''Yes. But tell me this, Lieutenant. How many will he get first?''

The early shower of rain had not managed to clear away the smoke that hung low over the Upper East Side.

In her luxurious apartment on Park Avenue, Polly Winslow clutched the phone in her glittering clawlike hand. She knew that diamonds weren't suitable at breakfast, but they made her feel so *secure*.

''It's not like her,'' she said petulantly into the mouthpiece. ''There just isn't anyone you can trust nowadays. No ethics at all.'' She removed a cigarette from the pack on the table, then crushed it in the ashtray without lighting it up. ''Dulcie Bennett is one of my most reliable girls. Or, at least, she has been up till now. She's supposed to check in as *soon* as she leaves the client. I mean, what do I have the answering service for?''

She sighed impatiently, listening to the voice at the other end. Her free hand crept up to pat her red curls.

"I *know* that she's probably got a good excuse," she interrupted. "Put another way, she'd *better* have a good one. The client called an hour ago. Not once, but twice. He wants to see her again. Says he owes her an explanation." She rolled her eyes upward, sighing again. "God only *knows* what that means. I really thought that she was reliable. Now I'm not so sure. For some uncanny reason, I can't help thinking that we've seen the last of Dulcie Bennett. So inconsiderate, when all is said and done."

Polly replaced the receiver firmly and stood up, smoothing the seat of her well-tailored skirt. She walked over to the window and looked out at the spectacular display of flowers along the avenue below.

Her skin-tight, unlined face, a survivor of untold lifts and tucks, took on a spiteful cast.

"Well, Dulcie my girl, wherever you are, you can be absolutely sure of one thing." Her rather childish mouth drew back in a delicate moue of displeasure. "If you don't check in soon, I give you my word, you'll never, never work in *this* town again."

THIRTY-THREE

Detective Inspector Ian Potter rolled up his sleeves and began to wash the breakfast dishes. He added a squirt of detergent to the sinkful of hot water, and reached for the dishrag.

"You don't have to do that," said Sara gently. "You've done so much for me already."

"It depends on how you look at it." He began to scrub a plate. "After all, you're helping me by letting me stay here. Maybe Harrison will try to contact you."

"I don't think he will. I don't want him to."

"But if he does, I want to talk to him before O'Reilly gets to him."

"Why? What difference does it make?"

"Maybe more than you realize." He

rinsed the plates and put them on the rack. "I think that I can handle him better if I get to him first."

She stood up, frowning, remembering something she had to do. "I've got to go into work today." She paused at the kitchen door, looking back at the Englishman. "I'll see if I can find another key to the front door. I don't want you to be locked out." She smiled crookedly.

He turned away from the sink, drying his hands on a dishcloth. He looked worried, his kind, brown eyes full of concern.

Concern for me, she thought, surprised. He doesn't even know me.

"Look, Sara. You don't really have to go into work today, do you? I mean, isn't it a bit . . . Isn't it too soon?"

"I've got to. If I don't return the papyrus . . . If they find out, I could lose my job." She shook her head despondently. "I should never have left Steve alone with the collection. Something about the way he acted should have tipped me off."

"Don't take it back today, Sara."

"Oh, I won't stay there long, believe me. I don't feel up to facing all those sympathetic friends just *dying* to know the gory details."

He folded the dishcloth neatly, putting it back on the counter near the sink. "That's not what I mean. I want you to let me keep the papyrus for a while."

"I can't do that. I can't let you have it."

She felt tired again. Tired and afraid. Unconsciously she placed her hand on her stomach and leaned against the kitchen wall. "I wish that I'd never called Steve that day. If anyone finds out about it, I just know they'd fire me." She sighed softly. Don't you understand? I don't have anyone now. I've got the baby to think of."

"I must have it, Sara. Just for a day or two. Only until I find someone to decipher it."

She looked at him incredulously. "Don't tell me that you believe all that crazy supernatural stuff?"

He shook his head. "Of course not. But Steve does, doesn't he? He must have thought it was very important. If I'm to stop him, I've got to find out what it says."

She said nothing, closing eyes that stung with sudden unshed tears. Then, "It's so unfair."

The Englishman came up to her quickly, and took one of her hands in his two. "That's what I want to change, Sara. I want to make everything right for you and the baby."

She looked at him then, scanning his face for a trace of duplicity. But there wasn't any.

He really gives a damn, she thought, surprised by the intensity she saw in his eyes. It's not just another case for him. An awkward shyness overcame her, and she tugged her hand gently out of his.

"Let me think about it," she said weari-ly. "Funny, I feel so tired. I think I'll go lie down for a while."

"Best thing for you," he said quickly. Almost too quickly.

He listened for the sound of the bed-room door closing behind her, then slowly let out the breath he'd been holding in.

What's got into you now? he wondered, confused by a fleeting emotion he couldn't quite focus on. *Getting balmy in your old age, are you? There's serious work to be done, my lad. Never knew you to be the one to play up to a pretty face. Better get a move on, because it's odds on that Harri-son isn't going to let the ground cool under his feet.*

His eyes lost their confusion and be-came clear and determined once more. First thing to do is call some of the local museums. Find out which one might have an Egyptologist on the staff. Make an ap-pointment. Then insist on Sara letting him have the papyrus.

Insist? *Yes*, he answered himself firmly. *Bloody well insist.*

That's better, he thought with deep re-lief. *Now you've got the right attitude. Wasn't like you to mince matters just be-cause the witness—the only living wit-ness, mind you—rolled her pretty eyes.*

He smiled to himself, suddenly warm with an unfamiliar feeling of happiness.

* * *

Old Bleeder watched the heavy-set man walk to the corner of West 80th and look uncertainly at the traffic speeding down Columbus Avenue.

Safe on his favorite bench, the old drunk loved to watch people go by. Especially those who seemed to have a purpose, a destination that creased their foreheads and tensed their jaws. Time-card punchers. Or to give them the descriptive label Old Bleeder preferred, fucking idiots.

He'd decided at an early age that he wasn't going to be one of them. Not if he could help it. Drifting from menial job to menial job had suited him just fine, providing him with a kind of arrogant independence that those who drew a regular income couldn't afford.

And there was more. Life became sweeter, freer, as old age decended upon him. In exchange for a tiny stipend, an old retired whore in the village lent her address as a receptacle for a Social Security check. A check that arrived with more punctuality than anything he'd ever earned before.

Sometimes the booze and the cold brought on a fit of depression. Then he'd wildly brandish an old rusty potato-peeler and threaten to kill himself. It usually brought him a warm bunk in the station house, plus medical treatment, if he needed it.

But most days he drifted, choosing a

favorite bench or bush to call his own.

One of these was the bench near the Planetarium now being approached by Detective Inspector Ian Potter.

Sum'uv a bitch better keep away, thought Old Bleeder sullenly. *Don't want no mutha in a shit-brown suit sitting next to me.* He shuffled his feet in his old black oxfords and edged toward the middle of the bench.

"Excuse me. Mind if I share your seat?" The Inspector took the old man's acquiescence for granted. He sat down heavily, calmly gazing out at the passing parade with more than a little interest, one hand inside his jacket gently massaging his chest.

Old Bleeder's deeply crevassed face took on a look of outraged incredulity. The red veins cobwebbing his bulbous nose and sunken cheeks seemed to pulsate with an angry warning.

A fucking Limey, for Christsake.

He searched his feeble mind for something scathing to say to the foreign interloper. Something to show the bastard who he was dealing with.

Before he could come up with anything, the Englishman stood up and left, moving on down Columbus.

One after the other the sidewalk restaurants lined the avenue, offering a selection of food that impressed the Inspector. But

Potter wasn't hungry. Not yet, anyway.

Something else demanded all his attention. All his concentration. O'Reilly wouldn't tell him much. Well, that didn't matter. Before leaving Sara's apartment, he'd made an appointment to see someone at the Metropolitan Museum the next day. Someone called Brenholt.

The Egyptologist hadn't heard a word about any papyrus. Which could mean that O'Reilly didn't know about it. Or, didn't think it important enough to be deciphered.

Whichever it was, O'Reilly was missing a good bet.

As the Englishman walked down toward Lincoln Center, his sharp eyes took in the details of every face that passed him by. Habit, pure and simple.

If a crime were to be committed right then, he'd be able to give the police a pretty good description of the perpetrator. Or at least of those in the vicinity at the time of the crime.

And it wasn't because he had a photographic memory. No, nothing like that.

Observation, that's all it took.

He felt a twinge of regret that he wouldn't be able to use his powers of observation much longer.

How would he be able to stand retirement? *Suppose I'll be reduced to reading murder mysteries*, he thought gloomily. Trouble was, he always solved the case long before the fictional sleuth.

He sighed, plodding along the sidewalk.

Still, he should look on the bright side. If he had to choose a final case, he couldn't have done better if he'd dreamed it up himself.

Back at the Yard they wouldn't be pleased. Not the ones in charge, anyway. And they were right, as always. Only, being right wasn't always enough.

They hadn't seen what lay in the grass one early morning in Green Park. And they hadn't heard the dead boy's mother screaming, screaming, until someone came and took her away.

The Inspector crossed over the street and began to walk back the way he came. No point in overdoing it. He wanted to take it easy, but somehow he felt that he couldn't waste any time. This case would haunt him till the day he died, if he didn't get to the bottom of it. He knew full well that this would be the last bit of action for him. That was okay, as long as he got what he wanted.

And all he wanted in this life was to make sure it was the last bit of action for Steve Harrison. Ever.

THIRTY-FOUR

By noon the last traces of the early rainfall had evaporated under the hot sun. The temperature hovered somewhere in the 80's, and despite the layer of smoke that hid the blue sky, people lay about on the grass, hoping for a tan.

Away from the crowded pathways and grassy knolls, Menket lay silently in the ditch.

Something was happening to the body that sheltered his spirit. Something immutable and relentless, that pursued its own timetable of rot and decay. The sickly sweet stench grew thicker as he lay in the hidden ditch, only half-aware of the slow, tedious hours to nightfall.

Menket moved his lips feverishly in constant exhortation, lips that now swelled with a festering suppuration of pus.

Glide across the sky in your barque of gold, O Re. Bring me closer to the sheltering arms of night.

Twice more must the sun god traverse the sky, before the eye of Horus moon lights the night in spherical perfection.

And then . . .

Then shall this accursed shell be cast off like the dried-out skin of a serpent.

The festered lips creased in a bitter smile. *The hand of Osiris is on me, and I shall arise again, and leave my enemies to wallow for eternity in the cursed Lake of Fire.*

But first, the knife . . .

The knife of flint, and the ritual. Both must be used that I may regain life.

He tensed as shuffling footsteps came close to his hiding place. His hands clenched, ready to kill if need be. But after a pause the footsteps passed on, and his cunning mind turned back to plot what he must do to get the knife.

THIRTY FIVE

Diane Mason pushed her way into the grocery store on the corner of West 80th and Columbus and began to hunt for the orange juice in the big freezer. Looked like everyone in New York had the same idea, she thought irritably. The place was packed, with a line forming up at the register by the door.

Her fine silky hair, nudged to a golden sheen with a little help from Clairol, hung straight to just below the tip of her ears. She looked younger than her 30 years. But the youthfulness of her soft features had been tempered lately by lines of stress.

Why does it always have to be this way? she wondered. *If I'd only thought about it sooner, I could have asked Maria to pick some up at the supermarket.*

Guess Jerry's right. I should be more organized. Maybe then he'd quit complain-

ing, which is all he seems to do lately.

It wasn't all Jerry's fault. And lots of women had husbands who dumped on them occasionally. Only why did it have to be now, this week? With the meetings at work leaving her drained each night.

If Jerry would only try to understand her position. Just once, try to see it from her side.

She didn't want to give up her job. Not now. Not when she was finally getting somewhere.

It wasn't as if he ever had to do anything around the apartment. He didn't really have to help out with Todd. That's what they'd hired Maria for.

Someone jogged her elbow as she reached into the freezer for the low-acid orange juice. She broke a nail, muttering under her breath. Funny how Jerry had the ulcer that had to be coddled, while she struggled along trying to be Super-Mom. Maybe she should let him pick up a few things after work. See how he liked it.

She found the green can. Okay, now what? She opened her purse to take out the scrap of paper she'd made a list on, then realized she'd left it at the office.

"Oh, *shit!*" she said out loud, to the amusement of a couple of kids buying candy.

Finally she made it up to the head of the line, and grabbed up a newspaper from the rack.

"What d'you think about that guy who

set the fire on Fifth Avenue?" asked the man behind the register.

"I haven't had much time to read about it," said Diane, opening her purse. "Seems almost unreal. I mean, *Fifth Avenue.*"

"You never know what some people will do." He made change for her five, putting the can of frozen juice in a brown paper sack. "You take care, now."

"Thanks." She hurried out onto Columbus Avenue, anxious to get home, the paper folded under her arm. Thank God she had the next day off. Perhaps she should take Todd to the park.

That was another problem. She loved Todd, but . . . Always that one word. But.

Three little letters that added up to another word. *Guilt.*

Because she really hadn't wanted children just yet. Children, nothing. Let's be honest, she hadn't wanted a single child. Hadn't wanted Todd. When you came right down to it, that was the whole problem in a nutshell.

She hadn't wanted Todd, and Jerry had.

Why not, after all? He didn't have to take maternity leave. He just went on climbing up that goddamn ladder of success. Hand over hand, up we go. While she had a burden to drag up with her, and its name was Todd.

A sudden rush of guilt washed over her. *Oh, God. Why do you even think things like that? You love Todd. You'd die if any-*

thing happened to him. You know that you would.

She crossed Columbus against the light, ignoring the shouted comments of an irate cabdriver.

Eff you too, she thought, without looking back. Somedays she'd give her right arm to get out of the city. Get away from the pressures at work, the crazies on the street, and—*yes, while you're at it, why not go ahead and admit it.* Get away from Jerry and his constant bitching. Jerry and his receding hairline, his relentless workouts, and his nightly dose of Zantac. That last was almost a status symbol. You'd really reached the pinnacle when you had to take Zantac for your ulcer. She could just picture all the young execs in Manhattan popping their little pink pills every night before servicing their wives.

Never mind, she reassured herself. Tomorrow is another day. She'd make every minute count. Isn't that what the child experts always stressed? Quality over quantity?

Well, okay then. Tomorrow would be a quality day in the park for just the two of them. Sunshine, fresh air. She felt better already. Nothing would spoil their day together.

Nothing.

The two guards stood talking just inside the entrance to the Metropolitan Museum of Art. Tuesdays the museum closed at 8:45 P.M., and the older of the two looked bored and tired, just putting in his time until he could go home. He had a long rubbery-looking face that managed to maintain a constant expression of pained boredom, and arms that almost reached to his knees, giving him a faintly simian appearance.

The younger guard had a round, pimply face, distinguished by slightly protruding teeth. His tall gangling frame still crackled with nervous energy after eight hours on the job. He looked with a kind of innocent interest at the crowd of people still in the museum.

"It's an art form in itself, people-watching," he asserted enthusiastically.

"Yeah, sure." The older guard took out a large, slightly soiled handkerchief and blew his nose loudly, examining the results with cynicism. "I knew I was coming down with something. What time is it?"

"Almost eight-thirty. Not much longer to go."

"You'd think people would have sense enough to know we're closing in a few minutes. Why don't they go home? Are they deaf?"

"Trouble with you is, you've lost your enthusiasm," said the younger man. "Now as I see it, once you lose that, you're dead."

"Yeah? Well, I'm dead, all right. Dead

tired of listening to all your bullshit. What time is it now?''

Silently the younger man held out his left arm with the Timex strapped to his wrist, so that the other guard could see the dial.

''Okay, okay,'' said the other man irritably. ''I just asked.'' He jerked his head at the entrance. ''Go see what that joker wants.''

Menket stared with a cold unswerving gaze as the young guard approached him.

''What d'you want, pal. We're getting ready to close up,'' said the guard.

Menket came close to him and muttered a few words, just as a large group of tourists pushed out of the open doors.

''What did that guy want?'' asked the older guard.

''Said he was looking for his wife.'' The pimply youth grinned widely, showing his large uneven teeth. ''Must be some kind of foreigner. Did you see his haircut? I thought he said `knife' at first.''

The older man sneezed mightily. ''Jeez. I knew I was coming down with something. You should'na let him in. Place is closing, for Christsake.''

''He'll only be a minute. Funny thing about foreigners. They smell different. I mean, this one really stank, you know?''

''They should try taking a shower once in a while.''

''So should you, pal.'' The young guard

grinned and ducked as the older man faked a body punch.

Menket walked quickly into the Egyptian wing. No need to ask for directions. The ancient display drew him like a homing pigeon.

As he entered he saw on his right the elaborate chronology of the history of Egypt. It contained nothing that he wanted. He went in further, rage building in his gut as he saw the desecration spread around him in case after case of artifacts.

What accursed people were these who usurped the sanctity of sacred tombs? Where wandered the souls of those whose holy relics had been plundered by the barbarians?

Sorrow mixed with rage as he thought of the scattered dead carelessly separated from their necropolis on the west bank of the Nile.

Who would feed their Ka-spirits now? Without the sustenance prepared for its long and arduous journey, the spirit would falter and lose eternity.

He ground his teeth with fury, his fever-ish eyes searching for the sacrificial knife.

A few desultory stragglers remained in the Egyptian wing, drifting aimlessly to-wards the exit. They looked at the strange, evil-looking man with vapid curiosity, then looked away rapidly as they caught the gleam of murderous wrath in his eyes.

Suddenly, he saw the knife. Surrounded

by stolen treasures from another age, it lay resplendent on a soft black cloth. He approached the heavy transparent case carefully. It was as it should be, the carved handle a creamy ivory, the blade a magical flint.

How he ached to hold it. To wield it in an exorcism of death eternal.

His tongue felt thick and swollen in his mouth as he muttered the sacred words of supplication to the mighty god Osiris. As if in answer to his prayer, a group of high school students converged on the Egyptian wing. The slightly harried-looking man in charge of them began to argue with a guard.

With a blood-curdling roar, Menket smashed the case with a powerful blow from his fist, and after a heartbeat of stunned silence, all hell broke loose among the students.

As he fled the Egyptian wing, he could hear the hysterical screams and yells, the violent sounds of destruction erupting behind him.

He had the knife.

A feeling of elation carried him out swiftly ahead of the panicking crowd, past the two guards standing frozen at the entrance with shell-shocked expressions on their faces.

Out. Out into the safety of the night.

I am a prince of Egypt, Mother of the World, and her enemies are mine. He felt the words rise jubilantly to his lips as he raced down the steps in front of the museum.

O gods of Egypt! Her enemies are mine.

Slipping the ritual knife into his shirt, he ran deep into the park, only resting when he reached a place north of the lake that few ventured into.

He leaned against a tree trunk, panting breathlessly, the harsh gasps forced in and out of lungs already beginning to blacken with decay. He must get back to the ditch and wait.

Isis, Isis, protect me, he whispered fiercely. *Spread your wings and waft the breath of life into my nostrils that I may survive.*

He raised his face to the sky above as a breeze blew softly over him, cooling his tortured throat, filling his lungs with the soothing balm of life.

Above him, the moon looked down with its tranquil eye.

Its beauty pierced his aching heart once more, as he remembered the moon's silver reflection on the waters of the Nile.

How cool the water. An elixir for all time.

And the moon.

Yes. Yes. Now the blessed moon traverses the sky in Egypt.

The pain in his tormented body faded away, as if it were all a dream. As if dream became reality.

From a long way off, lost in the rushes by the river, he hears the voice of Nefrenofret. She calls to her lord. Singing his name as the songbird in the acacia bush calls to its mate.

His tortured face became intent, straining to hear the words.

An agonized cry burst from his swollen lips.

Come closer, O distant one. Beloved, do not leave me in this accursed land of darkness.

O Nefrenofret. You are the red lotus that shelters my heart.

Without you, must I endlessly travel the years?

O Nefrenofret, show me the journey's end.

Or has my time come to journey to the land of silence?

He lifted his head to gaze at the moon again, and this time, he smelled the perfume.

It must have been the wine. A slight indisposition.

The women have gone down to the banks of the Nile. And now his friends and servants await his pleasure.

Gesturing regally, as befits one so highborn, Menket indicates that he too will bathe.

Startled by the women's laughter, a bird flies low across the river, its wings skimming the dark waters.

As his servitors remove his robe, Menket's eyes search for the girl. His heart beats rapidly as he looks for the one they call Nefrenofret, but his stern face does not reveal the inner turmoil.

"Yonder, Lord," whispers Amnet, his personal servant, hovering close by. For he has seen the desire in the fierce eyes.

Nefrenofret rises from the shallow tide, droplets of water cling to her dark hair. She laughs with the other women, shaking her head, and the drops of water shine like amethysts in the moonlight. Her breasts are bare and gleaming with the anointing of perfumed oils.

She glances at him artlessly, then stoops to splash the blessed water on her arms.

How young. How pure. His breath comes fast, and he frowns to hide his consternation. But Amnet knows.

"She is very beautiful, Lord. A princess amongst other women. Surely her eyes are as the eyes of a doe." Amnet murmurs the words for Menket's ears alone. "See how she smiles for you, Lord. Her heart is in her mouth."

"Enough." His voice is harsh, but his soul is like a quivering bird.

A breeze fans the rushes that grow by the river. They whisper a song of yearning for my love.

Somewhere downstream a lone fisherman casts his net, calling on the river god to guide his hand. So I call on Isis to guide my love.

Menket steps into the water, his naked

body hot and restless. How cool the water as it swirls around his loins.

O Nefrenofret, your eyes are filled with shyness.

How soft the glances from your dark-rimmed eyes.

Softer than the wings of the gray-feathered dove.

Sweeter than the purple fig that opens its blushing heart to be devoured.

O Nefrenofret, let me press the fullest honey cakes to your lips. Let me gather the white grapes for your wine.

Nefrenofret approaches through the silver tipped water.

Her voice is as the playing of a harp.

"Come, Lord, join with me in the blessed river, that I might bathe you with its cooling mud."

Surely all the waters of the Nile cannot quench his singing blood.

Her breath is hot upon his cheek as she spreads the silky mud across his shoulders, and her hand is like the zephyr that caresses the dawn.

"Lord, let my life run with yours forever, until . . ."

Until . . .

Where have you gone, O Love?

Groaning with a desperate grief, he swayed his head from side to side like a wounded beast.

Don't look back, he thought with bitter

desperation. The Time of Times is past, but will come again.

Onward, ever onward. Think only of the journey soon to come, under the cover of night.

Pain crawled its way through his anguished body.

He crouched down, resting his head against the thick base of the tree. Beyond the environs of the park, the big city pulsed, alive and awake. But the lamps in the park were out. And some of the streets on the Upper East Side were still without normal lighting.

Menket looked down at his hands. They gleamed a wormy gray in the pale moonlight, and his fingers had started to swell. Under the torn sleeve of his shirt, the wound inflicted by Dulcie Bennett had begun to shed strips of sticky black flesh in an advanced stage of necrosis.

Soon, very soon, the rotting body that housed him would need fresh nourishment to sustain it.

He closed his eyes a moment, summoning strength.

Then he stood up stealthily, and crept back towards the southeastern end of the park.

The cage cleaner at the Central Park Zoo filled his bucket with water, and picked up a mop, grumbling quietly to himself.

"That's all you bastards can do, is shit. Night and day, that's all you think about. Eat and shit." He walked along the pathway, taking his own sweet time. "Ain't gonna hurry for no one. Least of all youse bastards." The water sloshed over the rim of the bucket and into his rubber boots.

There's gotta be a million jobs a man could do. A million ways of making a buck. So what did I do? Become a nursemaid to a bunch of fucking animals.

He looked up as he came to the orangutan enclosure.

"Jesus H. Christ!" He dropped the slopping bucket with a clatter, eyes bugging out of his head.

Something had smashed the plexiglass that sealed off the cage and bent back the bars. Blood had splashed over the shards of plexiglass like sauce on spaghetti. Nothing remained that looked remotely like the man-like apes.

Only the skins, ripped and torn, strewn among the shattered bones.

And the skulls, empty and staring.

Staring and empty.

THIRTY-SIX

Mayor Theodore Tanner smiled grimly at his young assistant, Tommy Jefferson, and tried not to look too annoyed. His thick iron-gray hair grew back in a wave of almost theatrical exuberance from his high forehead, and his pugnacious jaw jutted with something close to belligerence.

Everything about him said, "Take charge."

Well known for his aggressive temper and biting wit, he nevertheless earned respect as a man who got things done.

And, by God, there were a few things he wanted done *now*.

The Police Commissioner had already received his call, and there were quite a few names and phone numbers left on the list that would be receiving His Honor's attention before the day was out.

This was his town, and everyone had better get the message. He wasn't about to sit back and let some degenerate asshole with a penchant for arson and unholy appetites give it bad press.

A hefty chunk of one of the most famous avenues in the world had suffered a serious blow. God only knew how long repairs would take. In the meantime, a brownout of some of the most exclusive streets on the Upper East Side had turned the area into something of a no-man's-land.

And now, the Egyptian wing of the Metropolitan Museum of Art, beneficiary of his wife's particularly well-publicized activities, had been vandalized.

The Mayor loved his wife. Not a very fashionable stance, he knew, but one that kept his very busy life on an even keel.

Anything else could turn out to be very messy, if not downright dangerous to a man in his position. He certainly didn't want to be like that idiot from Washington who, it was rumored, spent an inordinate amount of time at the Essex House engrossed in questionable activities.

So now he smiled grimly at his young assistant and tried hard to keep his voice within an acceptable range of decibels.

"Run that by me again, Tom. Who did you say I'm having dinner with?"

"The Chief of the Egyptian Mission to the United Nations, Ramsy Serafin, and his wife, Madame Serafin."

"That's what I thought you said. See if

you can get my wife on the phone. And while you're at it, get me a drink."

"It's only ten o'clock."

"I believe I asked for a drink, Tom, not the time." The Mayor's gray eyes glinted dangerously. He liked to think of himself as the captain of a very tight ship. Under no circumstances would he allow anyone to forget it. All it took was a little muscle-flexing. Up till now, anyway, that's all that had been needed. At the moment, things in the city had gotten a little out of hand. But nothing that he couldn't handle, given the right cooperation from all quarters.

He drank down the glass of Teacher's with a grimace, then took the receiver from his assistant for the call to his wife. He didn't want to start an argument with her. But it did strike him that with all due respect, and considering the destruction of irreplaceable Pharaonic treasures at the museum, this was hardly a felicitous time to break bread with an Egyptian.

The child threw the green tennis ball up high into the air. He stretched out his fat little arms, and his hands made clutching motions over his head. But the ball slipped through his fingers, and fell to the ground.

Red-faced and puffing with ecstatic exertion, the excited toddler scrambled on all fours.

"Mama, look!" he crowed joyfully. "Ball."

His mother, Diane, lay back on the grass, eyes closed against the hot sun. "I see you, Todd baby," she said languidly.

The grass had the sweet smell of new-mown hay. The green perfume of clover.

Nearby, a bee droned lazily, drowsy with the heady scent of summer. It felt so good.

Perhaps I need more time off, thought the mother absently. *More time to unwind, spend with Todd. Play Mom.* She yawned luxuriously, and the yawn turned into a laugh as she pictured herself coming to Central Park every day, watching soaps, gaining a little weight. Being a housewife.

No way. Even if her husband did like his women a little on the plump side. She'd go nutty. Right out of her mind. And she had a good mind. Too good to waste on a continuous diet of Pablum and Pampers.

"Don't go off too far, Babe," she said dutifully.

"Ball," said Todd, without looking back.

Diane Mason plucked a blade of grass and chewed on it reflectively, wondering if she would be offered the promotion tomorrow. If it came through, she'd take her husband to lunch at Woods. First class all the way. Jerry would go for that.

If she didn't get the position she'd been angling for over the past six months, then forget it.

Forget it, nothing. They had to give it to her. She'd earned it. Paid her dues.

She could hear Todd crashing about in

the undergrowth. The natives are restless, she thought with a smile.

"Todd," she called. Why do they always wander off?

The little boy was getting tired. He threw the bright green tennis ball into the air, and it bounced off a tree. Gathering speed, the ball rolled down an incline, coming to a stop by a mound of leaves.

"Ball," said Todd. His chubby face took on a seriously intent look as he half slid the foot or two down to the ball.

The ground here was uneven, and he squatted down awkwardly to pick up the ball. His fingers touched the ball and it rolled a little further, disturbing the leafy pile with a dry breathy rustling sound.

A fetid stench arose around him, and Todd wrinkled his nose in disgust.

"Poo-poo," he said sternly, just as the rotting hand came out of the leaves and grabbed his bare leg. The cruel bonelike fingers dug into his soft child's flesh, until losing his balance, he sat down heavily on the twisted wrist, and managed to squirm free.

His scream cut sharply across the balmy languor of the afternoon. For a sickening moment Diane could not see her son, and her throat constricted so tightly that she couldn't swallow.

Then he came pounding towards her, his sturdy little legs working like pistons.

"Man!" he shrieked. "Man!"

She held out her arms to him, her eyes searching behind the child for his attacker. Damn it, she couldn't see the bastard. A sick feeling in the pit of her stomach made her want to vomit. Fear changed to anger, then mixed with relief as Todd flung himself into her arms, bellowing the same word over and over.

"Man!"

"Did he hurt you, Todd? What did the man do? Tell Mother what happened. Don't cry, don't cry." She held him tightly to her breast, her mouth close to his ear, his legs wrapped around her as he tried to escape the horror.

After a while, his screams subsided into a snuffling hiccuping croon. He held on tightly to his mother, refusing to be put down.

"Come on. Let's go home, Todd." There wasn't anyone suspicious-looking nearby. But what did that mean? The bastard probably took off like a shot when the boy screamed. That type were all cowards anyway. Else why would they go for children?

Propelled by anger, she managed to carry him all the way to the front door of the apartment building on West 81st. The doorman hurried forward to help, but at his touch, the child screamed and screamed until people across the street turned to stare.

"Don't worry, John. Just get the elevator for me, will you?" Her arms felt numb, and she couldn't tell if it was from the child's weight, or her feeling of shock.

The elevator seemed to crawl up to the fourth floor, creaking and groaning slowly all the way. The child clung to her desperately, his head turned sideways as he leaned against her.

"Look at your face," she murmured softly, soothingly. "All covered in dirty tear streaks." She wrinkled her nose suddenly. What was that smell? "Did you step in something, Todd?"

He brought a thumb up to his mouth and began to suck.

The elevator stopped with a lurch at the fourth floor, and the doors glided open silently.

Now that she had reached the familiar safety of home, Diane felt weak with exhaustion.

"Maria!" she called, kicking at the door. Her purse was slung over her shoulder, and the child wouldn't let her put him down.

"Maria! Open the door! Quickly!"

The young maid had thick wavy hair worn in a braid around her head. Her dark eyes looked anxiously at her mistress. "*Señora* Mason! What happened? What happened to the baby?"

"A man. In the park." Diane felt breathless, the words came out in gasps.

"My God! What did he do?" The maid followed Diane and the little boy down to the kitchen. "Let me take him from you."

"No, it's all right. I just want to wash his

face and give him a drink of water." She set the child on the kitchen counter and turned on the faucet. "Get him some cold water from the refrigerator, would you?"

She splashed a little water from the faucet onto his face, then turned her attention to the little boy's leg.

"What's this all over your leg?" She pulled a sheet off the roll of paper towels and wet it under the stream of water. She wiped the boy's leg, then stared closely at the shreds of something sticking to the towel. "Oh, my God!"

"What is it?" The maid came up to the child and looked at his leg. "Ugh! It smells bad. Rotten. Like pork gone bad, or something."

"It's flesh. Rotted flesh. And pus." She felt faint. Where had it come from?

Was that why Todd had screamed?

Had he somehow come across a body? A decomposing corpse left in the park for an innocent child to fall on? To be terrified by?

"I'll call the police," said the maid quickly.

"No!" She saw the shock in Maria's eyes, and spoke quietly, urgently. "What can the police do for him now? Anyway, we don't know anything."

"But, _Señora_—"

"No! I don't want you to call them. Whoever it is, they can't help him now. And I don't want Todd mixed up in it." She caught at Maria's arm, a desperate look in her eyes. A rising sense of panic made her feel faint. She didn't even understand it herself. She just knew that nothing was to be said. Nothing at all. Not even to Jerry.

"I'm afraid, Maria," she said shakily. "We mustn't say anything to the police, or something will happen to Todd. I know it will." She stared out of the window toward the park. "I know it will," she whispered.

Who had screamed?

He had reached out to grab at something. He couldn't remember.

Steve Harrison stared up at the sky through a delicate mosaic of leaves, and wondered if he were dreaming. Something had happened to his memory, but he felt too ill to care. Too weary to do anything but drift on a sea of feverish pain that threatened to drown him in its glassy depths.

His mouth felt thick and swollen, his tongue coated with a putrid layer of coppery scum that seemed frighteningly familiar to his taste.

A moan escaped his lips, shaping a half-forgotten name.

The blue sky above blended easily with the greenish-brown of the leaves, fading into a cloud of black that he struggled to resist.

A quivering spark of life persisted in his mind, and in the darkness he strove to remember something. Someone . . .

His tongue moved behind his teeth, trying to say the name, the urgency of it making him tremble.

The darkness enshrouded his consciousness, and the name spun off into space at last, leaving its shadow to hover in his tortured mind.

Sara.

Oh, Sara.

Too late. He could barely remember her face. Barely remember the warmth of her eager flesh. The soft curve of her breasts, her thighs.

Or had it been the other one? So long ago.

Had it all been a dream, turning to dust like a moldering corpse?

Somehow he must have died, long, long ago, in another place (yes, yes, remember?), and this reality was just a vapor, clinging tenaciously to his decaying body like a ghost.

Gritting his teeth, he conjured up Sara's face for a fragile instant, clinging with the desperation of a drowning man to the translucence of her smile.

The fading images passed in disarray against the backdrop of his quivering eyelids, and again, he tried to speak.

No use. He felt it all slipping away, quickly now, like the dry desert sand, through his trembling fingers, and his rotting hands clenched and unclenched uselessly at his side. He'd lost, and the horror that was Menket had won at last.

THIRTY-SEVEN

"Good of you to come in," said O'Reilly, green eyes masking his thoughts.

"Well, I had to, didn't I?" Detective Inspector Ian Potter settled his bulky body carefully in the chair near O'Reilly's desk, staring back blandly at the American. "That's only common courtesy, isn't it? I mean, since I am a policeman also."

"Yeah. You could say that. But the little matter of you not being over here officially does bother me."

"Oh, that." The Englishman smiled good-naturedly. "Well, you know how it is. It's hard for me to throw off the habits of a lifetime. I'm just not ready to retire yet."

"You won't be able to keep this up much longer. I mean, once you *are* retired. I don't have to tell you that the average police department doesn't share much information with outsiders.''

Potter shifted in his seat uncomfortably. "Hardly an outsider, Lieutenant. I should think that my record speaks for itself.''

"No offense meant," O'Reilly said quickly. "But let's be realistic. If you were assigned officially by Scotland Yard, we'd be able to tap into any information you manage to gather. And vice versa, of course. But at the moment, you're a free agent, more or less. We can't really force you to divulge what you've found out. Not that we'd want to use force," he added hastily. "But you could be charged with withholding information."

"I intend to file a complete report, once this case is solved."

"Sure. But the key words are 'once it's solved.' What happens before that? What if you find out something that could help us? Would you come to us voluntarily with any pertinent information?"

Detective Inspector Potter hesitated slightly. "I might," he said.

"Not good enough," growled O'Reilly.

"Best I can do, I'm afraid. I've got to follow my leads. You wouldn't begrudge me that. That's only fair."

O'Reilly stared at him in amazement. "Fair? What the fuck has fairness got to do with it?"

"No need to get nasty," said the Inspector mildly. "I've never felt the need for language like that myself."

"Bully for you!"

The Inspector stared at the backs of his hands. Hands that he had placed squarely down on his knees, not hiding anything.

An honest man's stance, thought the American. Cards on the table. No sign of artifice whatsoever. Almost *too* innocent. Which was why the lieutenant suspected that the old bastard had an ace or two up his sleeve. Ten to one he wouldn't play them until the very last minute. The very last instant.

But who could be sure what might happen before that? Murder isn't a game.

O'Reilly had quite a few years as a policeman under his belt himself, and a reputation as a tough cop. He knew what his men thought about him. Goddamnit, they trusted him to bail out the whole department in this mess.

And he would. He felt it in his bones. Just as long as the old limey didn't shift the target before he had a chance to line it up in his sights.

Moving in with Sara Fenster had been a stroke of genius on Potter's part. But then, the old guy didn't have to play by all the rules anymore, did he? Or was that the current Scotland Yard procedure with regard to victims and witnesses? Sure beat putting a tail on them, or calling them in for questioning.

"I want to know, right up front, if you intend to withhold any information from this department," said O'Reilly grimly.

"Up front? You haven't been completely honest with me, have you, Lieutenant?" countered the Englishman.

"In what way?"

"You've had me watched from the moment I arrived in this country. Spotted your man at Kennedy Airport. You probably were tipped off by the gentleman in the U.S. Embassy in London. It would have been nice if you'd contacted me right away, so that we could pool our information. But you didn't, did you? What did you think I'd do? Spoil your act?"

"How did you know that the embassy in London contacted me?" asked O'Reilly lamely.

"I've been a policeman a long time. I knew that the gentleman at the embassy had more information than he was willing to divulge. I could tell from his behavior. He probably knew that Harrison was a prime suspect, and was on his way to New York. I'd lay odds that he called you before I stepped out on the street." He grimaced slightly, his calm brown eyes shadowed by hurt. "It's amusing in a way. I spent all those years as a copper, and now that my heart's gone bad, I'm supposed to forget everything I do best. Well, it doesn't matter really what you or Scotland Yard or that johnny at the embassy thinks. I've made up my mind. I'm going after the bastard and I'm going to bloody well catch him."

"Thought you didn't use nasty language like that," said O'Reilly, half-smiling.

"I make an exception, now and then," said the Englishman. "And this is an exception, if I ever saw one."

Inspector Potter stood on the sidewalk in front of the Metropolitan Museum and looked around. Not bad, he thought. Not quite up to the British Museum. But not bad.

He liked the benches lined up under the trees, just off to the side. He liked to see the children, banded together in colorful groups, being escorted into the museum by good-humored young teachers. He'd always had a soft spot for children. Molly used to tease him about it, but he'd known from the very first that she felt the same.

Maybe Sara would bring her little one to the museum, one day. He tried to picture it, smiling gently to himself. *Oh, Lord, there you go again, becoming sentimental, when you should be concentrating on the immediate problem.*

There would be no safety, no peace, for Sara, until Harrison was put away where he could do no more harm. The suspect was still in the park. The Inspector felt sure of that, even though O'Reilly doubted it.

Still, the Inspector had years of experience under his belt. Years of plodding legwork, painstakingly following every clue, every hunch until the case had been solved. Sometimes you couldn't tell where logic left off, and pure gut instinct took over.

Right now he could swear to being on the right track. Knew it. Felt it. Like an old bulldog with a one-track mind, he'd follow the scent to the end.

Not very scientific perhaps. But you can't teach an old bull dog new tricks.

He'd better get a move on. Brenholt had said twelve o'clock, and it was already five to.

He went on up the wide stairs, looking with interest around him. As he walked back toward the administration offices, he noticed several policemen in the area. Could Harrison have slipped in?

If Harrison thought that he had become an Egyptian priest, would he frequent the display from the one place he revered? Or would he detest the sterile assemblage found in the museum?

Maybe Brenholt could help.

Maybe the papyrus stolen by Harrison would be the key. The Inspector hoped so.

His heart beat rapidly, and he tried to calm its agitation by breathing slowly, carefully, willing the pain away.

Not yet, damn it. Got a job to do. Can't waste any time coddling the old ticker.

He saw a bench against the wall of a

corridor, and sat down with a sigh of relief.

There seemed to be a lot of coming and going, with workmen carrying in broken parts of statues and artifacts, all of them looking Egyptian, ancient Egyptian.

Hello, hello, thought the Inspector. *Had a spot of trouble, have we? Who could have caused all this, I wonder?*

He got up, pain temporarily forgotten, and followed a workman to a door at the end of the corridor.

"Just a minute, if you don't mind," said a young woman. She was young and earnest, and was barring the Inspector's progress with an outstretched arm. "No visitors allowed in this section. You'll have to go back down the corridor to the main area."

"I'm here by special invitation." The Inspector showed her his Scotland Yard identification. "Mr. Brenholt. That's the name of the gentleman I've come to see." He pushed past her into the stockroom. Someone had done a hell of a lot of damage.

"Mr. Brenholt is in his office. He's not expected in here till later. If you like, I'll show you where his office is, Mr . . ."

"Detective Inspector Ian Potter."

"Yes." The young woman frowned perplexedly. "Are you investigating the vandalism? I mean, why Scotland Yard?"

The Inspector turned and smiled at her.

"Oh, no. I don't know anything about this. I've come to see Mr. Brenholt about another matter."

"Well, if you'll just follow me, I'll take you to his office."

The pain in his chest started up again. "Just a minute, miss." He quickly swallowed two of his pills, downing them with a gulp of water from a water fountain while the young woman waited impatiently. "All right, lead on."

She smiled at him fleetingly, as if humoring a child. "I really am very busy, Inspector. We all are, including Mr. Brenholt. We don't have much time to spare. So if you'll just come this way . . ."

Not much time to spare.

Apt phrase, under the circumstances. He sighed.

The ancient Egyptians thought of time as endless, but for the Englishman, time was running out.

THIRTY-EIGHT

John G. Brenholt looked up sharply at the bulky man standing in the doorway.

"Well, come in, come in. And shut the damn door, will you?" The man's wispy gray hair and vivid blue eyes were in striking contrast to his lined, brown face, weatherbeaten by years under the desert sun. He punctuated his abrupt, staccato way of speaking with jerky motions of his brown hands, giving him an air of almost electric vitality.

"Terrible thing to have happened," he went on. "Everything smashed. Years of work down the drain. Who are you?" He uttered the last question with no change in inflection.

"Detective Inspector Potter, Scotland Yard. I called you earlier. About the papyrus."

"I can only give you half an hour at most. We're in the middle of a crisis. Someone vandalized the Egyptian section."

"It's very important," the Englishman said quietly. "Urgent, in fact."

"Yes, yes. But aren't the police here handling that case? I should have thought that New York was out of your jurisdiction."

"I'm carrying out my own investigation. A crime was committed in London too."

"I see. You want me to decipher something, is that it?"

"That's right." The Inspector removed the rolled up papyrus from his inside pocket, and spread it open carefully on the desk. "This was left by the suspect at the last place he was seen. I believe that it has some significance, and I must know what it says."

Brenholt moved around the desk and stared at the colorful hieroglyphics on the papyrus. "Yes. Yes. Mm. Hmm." He pursed his lips, whistling soundlessly. "Where did he get this?"

"I'm not at liberty to say."

"Really? Why not?" Brenholt looked up sharply at the Englishman. "Well, don't tell me. I'll tell *you.* At least, I'll tell you where it came from originally." He touched the ancient document with a finger. "See here? This indicates a Pharaoh."

He pointed to a small rectangular mark enclosing five hieroglyphic symbols. "That's his name. Not a familiar one. This papyrus was probably stolen years ago from a tomb at Saqqara. Happened all the time." He smiled cynically. "What would the English have done if people came over and started carting off bits of Stonehenge? Well, I suppose we're all guilty one way or another."

"What else does it say?"

"Details of incantations. Spells. Black magic spells to do with spiritual transference. Very interesting papyrus. Part of a Book of the Dead prepared for a Pharaoh called Ankhset-Re. Short reign, according to this."

"Why black magic?"

"That is part of the ancient religion. Don't laugh. Much of our culture has come to us from ancient Egypt. Religion, medicine, architecture. The list is endless."

The Inspector hid his impatience. "But what does this one say? Specifically."

"Specifically? Well, in the proverbial nutshell, it says that a ritual suicide committed during a certain phase of the moon will rid a reluctant host body of its unwanted guest spirit. Without killing the host, I might add."

"What phase? A full moon?"

"Well, yes. It mentions a grave danger,

though, besides the obvious one that accompanies a suicide."

"What would that be?"

"If the unwanted spirit is powerful—a high priest of the inner temple, say, or someone well-versed in Hakau magic—it could transfer to another body."

"And the host body?"

"The most it could count on then would be a quick trip to eternity."

"He'd die, in other words?"

"Yes."

"One more thing. Who vandalized the Egyptian wing?"

"I wish that I knew!" Brenholt glared angrily. "There are a lot of crazy people out there, but for the life of me, I can't think why anyone would do that!"

Perhaps not, thought the Inspector shrewdly. *On the other hand, I can.*

The sun felt pleasantly warm as the Inspector left the museum. He smiled to himself as he turned into the park. A bit of a walk would help him think, and he had a lot to think about.

Everything seemed to be falling into place. Just like a jigsaw puzzle.

It had happened that way in his other cases over the years. Ideas came to him out of thin air, aided by good, solid legwork, and before you could say Bob's-your-uncle, the most tangled web unraveled, and the case would be solved.

This particular case had seemed more difficult than the usual, with its strangely mysterious undertones. But just now he'd had a beaut of an idea, and the mystery had begun to evaporate like fine rain on a summer's day.

The papyrus *was* the key. Harrison, in his poor deluded condition, thought that he had been possessed by an ancient spirit. The next step, then, would be to get rid of the evil interloper.

Harrison had already decided when. The eye of Horus inked in on the calendar in Sara's kitchen showed that.

Next question: Where?

The Inspector plodded on resolutely, his jaw jutting out at a determined angle.

All right, now. Let's look at things through Harrison's insane eyes. Where in all of Manhattan would an ancient Egyptian priest perform an act of holy magic?

Not in the museum. The Inspector didn't doubt for a moment that Harrison had smashed the Egyptian wing up in a raging fit of hate.

No. He'd want somewhere quiet. Somewhere secluded, where he could spout his incantations freely without attracting attention.

Somewhere out in the open, under the magical moonlight.

But where? Where?

The Inspector looked up to cross the road in his path, and suddenly the answer loomed up before him, rising like a massive stone sword from a knoll just ahead.

Lieutenant O'Reilly sat behind his desk and waited while the last man squeezed into his overcrowded office. Then he began to speak quietly. He was always quiet, but he didn't fool the men around him. They knew full well that the shit was about to hit the fan.

"The Chief called me in today. I'm not going to bore you with the details, but it wasn't a cozy chat, if you get my meaning." O'Reilly took out a pack of cigarettes, carefully lighting one and inhaling a couple of times before continuing. "I can't blame the Mayor for being irritated either." He blew out a stream of smoke, staring around the room at the silent men. "Someone goes and murders a couple of guys, and we have a solid lead but the suspect gets away. Doesn't look good. Not for us, and not for the Chief. Especially when the suspect indulges in a little arson and vandalism, not to mention a few other nasty tricks on the side. And when I say arson, I'm not talking about some warehouse out by the docks. Oh, no. The Mayor turns on the eleven o'clock news, and the first thing he sees is Fifth Avenue going up in smoke." O'Reilly's voice took on a deceptively calm tone. "Fifth Avenue." He looked around his office slowly, staring at each of the men in turn. "The Mayor's a patient man. He's willing to wait until

tonight's eleven o'clock newscast to see
the suspect apprehended." He raised his
voice a fraction. "Personally, I'm a little
more demanding. I want you to get your
asses in gear and go out and get the son of
a bitch. I don't want any more trouble at
the Metropolitan Museum. No more trouble on Fifth Avenue." He ground out his
cigarette in the ashtray on his desk. "And
no more sicko homicides. Now go out and
do your job. Not you, Johnson. You wait."

"Something special you want me to
do?" asked Johnson as the other men
filed out.

O'Reilly stared at his subordinate. "Better call your wife. No time off from now on.
You're going to shadow Harrison's girlfriend. I want to know everything. Where
she goes, what she does, and who she
does it with."

"What about the guy who's tailing her
now?"

"Never mind him. I'll put him on to
something else. I want *you* on this. The
two men in the squad car can continue to
watch her apartment."

"Is that all, Lieutenant?"

"If you do the job right, that'll be
enough. Whatever happens, don't lose
her."

"You think Harrison'll try to get to her
again?"

"Maybe. Or she'll try to get to him.
Women are funny that way. And she's still
in love with the creep. Either way, I want to

know as soon as something breaks."

Johnson got up quickly and left the room, and O'Reilly looked up expectantly as another man came in, shutting the door behind him. Tall and blond, with short hair, the newcomer moved with the ease of a natural athlete.

"It's about time, Schwartz. What have you got on Harrison?" asked the lieutenant.

"Nothing. The guy's clean. Not even an outstanding parking ticket." Schwartz sat down on a straight wooden chair in front of the desk, and began to loosen his tie.

"What else did you find out?"

"Average student. Well-liked by his peers at school and college. Professors liked him."

"Women? Drugs?"

"I'm telling you, Lieutenant. Harrison's the original All-American Kid."

"Next you'll be telling me his mother baked apple pie." O'Reilly shook his head impatiently. "No. There's got to be something on him." He paused, deep in thought. "How about psychological problems? Breakdowns, outbursts? Anything of that nature?"

"Nah, nothing like that. He played football, went to the beach. Liked everyone. Had a special girlfriend in high school. Betty Something-or-Other."

"And then he came to New York and met Sara Fenster."

"Yeah." Schwartz frowned slightly, gnawing at his lower lip. "Here's the crazy thing about it, Lieutenant. They lived together. She loved him. Gonna have his baby, for Christsake. He didn't have to rape her."

"Perhaps he forgot where he was," said O'Reilly dryly. "What about his job? How long had he been working for that guy in Egypt, what's-his-name?"

"Peterson."

"Yeah. What about that?"

"Like everyone else. Peterson didn't have anything bad to say about him. The old guy still can't believe about the dog. Thinks it must have been a terrorist or something."

"Sure," said O'Reilly sarcastically. "They always go around knocking off dogs."

"The professor did mention something, though. He didn't want to at first. I had to dig it outta him. And the phone connection was bad."

"Get to the point, for Christsake. Do I have to dig it out of you?"

"Well, he said something about a bracelet."

"A bracelet? What the hell does that have to do with anything?" O'Reilly's upper lip twitched in disgust.

"Maybe a lot, Lieutenant. He explained it to me."

"Do I get the explanation now, or must I

wait for tomorrow's episode?'' asked O'Reilly. His green eyes stared hard at the other man. ''What about the bracelet, Schwartz?''

''Peterson thinks he stole it. Harrison, I mean. Not Professor Peterson.''

''I figured that much out for myself. Go on.''

''Well, he only saw the bracelet once, on Harrison's wrist.''

''Harrison wears bracelets?''

''An ancient Egyptian bracelet. Very special. Worth a lot of bucks to a collector. Or someone that sells it to a collector. Peterson thinks that it may have come from a tomb they were working on.''

O'Reilly got up from his desk and walked over to the water cooler by the door. He filled up the paper cup and drank it down slowly, thinking. ''So Harrison could be a smuggler, as well as a murderer. He didn't only go to see Caldwell about a loan. Your All-American Boy has been very busy lately.''

''And don't forget about the arson, Lieutenant.''

''O'Reilly smiled humorlessly. ''I'll try not to. Okay. So here we have a lily-white kid, a regular Boy Scout according to you, who suddenly taps into an inexhaustible source of big bucks. He has a hungry buyer, but something goes sour. Perhaps he wants more cash, or the buyer backs out of the deal. So he kills Caldwell and sets the fire to cover up the crime."

"It all fits, Lieutenant," said the other man.

"Not quite. How do you explain his little trick with Caldwell's head? Sudden attack of the munchies?"

Schwartz looked sick.

"And," O'Reilly went on thoughtfully, "what would you call his mutilation of the dog in Cairo, not to mention the kid in London? Practice? No. No. There's more to this than just a bracelet."

"Maybe the limey knows."

"Yeah," agreed O'Reilly. "Maybe he does."

The child sat bolt upright in his bed and screamed. A high-pitched feral shriek that seemed like an alien sound in the bright colors of the cleverly decorated room.

"What the—?" exclaimed Jerry, spilling his drink over the kitchen counter. "Damn, look at that."

"Don't worry, I'll see to him," said Diane Mason hastily. She hurried down the hallway and opened the bedroom door just in time to see her son getting ready to emit another scream. His sweaty hair stuck up in spikes, giving him the almost comical look of a miniature punk-rocker. But his face was a mask of terror, dominated by unseeing eyes that glittered with fear.

"Todd! Baby, what's wrong?" His mother tried to pick him up, and he jerked his body back stiffly, striking his head on the cartoon-decaled headboard. He lay there staring up at her blindly, his head pressed up awkwardly against the wood, his body rigid with fear.

"Jerry!" yelled Diane. "Come help me!"

"What now?" her husband muttered to himself in the kitchen. "I'm fixing my drink," he called out to her. "Can't you handle it?"

"Jerry!" Her voice held more than a trace of panic, and her husband sighed with exasperation.

"I'm coming," he said. "Hold your horses." He took a long drink from his glass before putting it down on the counter again. Then with the air of one used to dealing with unruly subordinates, he went down the hallway and into Todd's room.

"Come on, fella," he said firmly, his square-jawed face set uncompromisingly. "Time for bed. No more playing around now."

Diane Mason turned and looked at her husband with something close to hatred in her eyes. "Just once I wish you'd try to understand that he's just a baby. Look at him. Something's very wrong." She turned back to the child and tried to pick him up again.

"*No!*" shrieked the child, his pudgy hands trying to push her away. "No! No! Man! Boo-boo!"

"Wait a minute here," said Jerry, suddenly alert. "What does he mean? What man?"

"There wasn't anyone." Diane bit her lip nervously. "No man at all. Todd just stepped in . . . something at the park. There was *no* one around. I checked, believe me."

"So what's he doing? Making this up?" He bent over his son. "Show me where he hurt you, Todd."

The little boy moaned softly, not answering, and his father pulled back the rumpled covers to look at him.

"Oh my God," breathed Diane faintly.

The child's right ankle had swollen into a grotesque lump of yellowish purple flesh. Five black indented bruises clustered together, showing the cruel pressure from Menket's hand. A thin crust of dirty-white matter rimmed the bruises.

"How did this happen, Diane? Who did it?" Jerry Mason glared at his wife furiously.

"Honest to God, I don't know, Jerry." She heard the hysteria in her words, and tried to think what to say. She wasn't going to tell him about her unreasoning fear of whatever it was that Todd had seen in the park. He'd think that she was crazy. "I'll put some ice on it," she said hurriedly. "It's just a bad sprain."

"Did you call the police?" Her husband followed her into the kitchen, staring at her angrily. "Did you at least think about doing that?"

"No. There wasn't anyone there. Todd must have imagined the man." She opened a cupboard quickly and took out a plastic bowl. "Honestly, he just made it up." She opened the refrigerator freezer and grabbed a handful of ice cubes from the ice-maker. Some of the cubes slipped out of her hand and scattered across the floor. She put the bowl on the counter, and got down on her knees to pick them up. Her hands were shaking, and the wet ice slipped out of her grasp.

"Oh, for Christ's sake," said her husband impatiently. He took the bowl of ice off the counter, and went back to Todd's room.

Diane opened her hands slowly, and let the rest of the melting cubes slide out onto the floor. She sat back on her heels, fear making her short of breath.

She couldn't tell Jerry about the nightmare.

About the swollen, decaying face that glared at her from the darkest reaches of her dreams the night before.

Only a crazy dream, he'd say in his superior way. You're a little too old for that, aren't you?

But she had felt the danger from the first. Knew it, without even understanding it. Night had come again. And she wasn't going to let her husband or her maid or anyone else in the whole fucking world stop her from protecting Todd.

She could hear her husband now, loudly

questioning Todd. There wasn't any time
to waste.

She stood up awkwardly, holding on to
the counter, forgetting everything except
the nameless horror in the park.

Moving about the apartment with an
almost hypnotic deliberation, she carefully drew the curtains on all the windows.
Then, with a strength that came from
something wild and primitive deep within
her, she began to push the furniture
against the front door.

The little boy lay quietly in the dark, and
listened to them fighting.

His father had refused to leave the light
on, calling him a baby. But that didn't
matter now, because Mommy was taking
him away.

She hadn't said so yet, but he knew she
would. She felt frightened too.

Maybe she could hear the voice.

The one that kept calling, calling. Wanting him to go back to the park. Wanting
him.

He scrunched down under the covers,
and squeezed his eyes shut.

After a while they stopped fighting, but
that only made the voice seem louder,
until its sound seemed to fill the room.

Todd's father stood outside Lieutenant
O'Reilly's office and pointedly looked at
his watch.

"You can go in now," said the sergeant,

opening the door and ushering him in.

"Sit down, Mr. Mason," murmured O'Reilly. "I'll be through with this in a minute." He indicated the report on his desk. "You caught me at a bad time."

"Look, I don't know why they sent me to you anyway," grumbled Jerry Mason. "This has got nothing to do with homicide."

"Ah, but you're wrong." The lieutenant closed the report with a snap. "I suspect that your son . . ."

"Todd."

"Todd . . . had a very narrow escape."

"Some escape. His ankle swelled up to twice its size."

"But he'll get over that," said O'Reilly quietly. "It could have been much worse."

"How worse?" Todd's father had a sudden vivid picture of his wife's terrified face, his son's catatonic blank stare. "It was daylight, for Christsake."

"I don't think that would have mattered to the man we're after."

"A murderer?" Jerry Mason nervously wiped at his mouth with the back of his hand. "Are you telling me that Todd could have been killed?"

"Among other things," said O'Reilly dryly. "Where is the boy now?"

"His mother's taken him to California. She has family there." Mason ran a hand through his hair. "Jesus. How could she have known?"

O'Reilly shrugged. "Mothers have a way of knowing sometimes. Just be glad, and tell her to keep him in California out of harm's way until this is over."

"How long will that be?"

"Wish to Christ I knew," said O'Reilly. "We'll let you know." He nodded at the boy's father, who left the room in a daze.

"Well?" asked the sergeant, coming back into the office. "What d'you think, Lieutenant?"

"I think that guy doesn't know how lucky he is."

"Kid could have been murdered, huh?"

"Murdered?" The lieutenant stared at him with his hard green eyes. "Remember Caldwell's head? Remember the report from London? Not to mention the dog in Cairo. What do you think his son would look like after something like that?"

"You don't mean—"

"Sure, I mean. We're dealing with a psycho. According to this report, Mason thought it was just some pervert playing grab-ass in the park. He owes a lot to his wife. God knows how she guessed what might happen." O'Reilly stood up and began to put on his jacket. "Maybe she didn't guess. Maybe she just sensed it. Whichever it is, that guy better never forget birthdays or anniversaries. He owes her." He picked up the report and made for the door. "That woman saved her son's life."

THIRTY-NINE

The long gray limousine entered the park at East 79th Street, driving a short way before coming to a stop not too far from Graywacke Knoll.

"Should I wait for you, sir?" asked the driver, opening the door for Ramsy Serafin.

"No. I'm going to walk home. A beautiful day, isn't it, Bender?" The slender, middle-aged man alighted carefully, carrying a honey-colored Pekingese dog in his arms. His dark, evenly featured face relaxed in a smile. "Besides, Ptolemy needs the exercise." He put the dog down, snapping a chain leash onto the green leather harness. "Please tell Mrs. Serafin that I shall be back in plenty of time for dinner."

"Very good, sir." The chauffeur, resplendent in a pale gray uniform, touched the bill of his cap, and got back behind the wheel, leaving his employer, the Chief of the Egyptian Mission to the UN, standing in the roadway.

"Well, Ptolemy," murmured the Egyptian, "which way shall we go today?"

The little dog, red tongue hanging out as it panted eagerly, began to pull the man toward the Knoll.

"Ah. So it's to be the obelisk today, is it? Well, let's go. But remember, no bad manners. An obelisk is not a tree."

Smiling to himself, Ramsy Serafin allowed the dog to pull him toward the ancient monument. No doubt the smorgasbord of canine smells around the base acted as a powerful magnet for the little fellow, he thought indulgently.

Ptolemy would probably have preferred to be off the leash, but laws must be obeyed. And anyway, Mr. Serafin would have to answer to his wife if the dog got away.

Soon his beautiful young wife's maternal instincts would be focused on the child that she carried. For the moment, however, the dog's needs held sway.

Slightly bulging eyes glistening with anticipation, the Pekingese snuffled its way around the bushes, tugging gently on the leash.

The Egyptian diplomat sat down on a bench and allowed his thoughts to wander. Funny to see an obelisk here, of all places. How sad it looked, a gray somber stone, planted incongruously amongst the bushes in Central Park.

It belonged in Egypt. Side by side with its sister monument, in stately majesty, pointing upward to the hot blue sky of Heliopolis, the sacred City of the Sun. Ah well. *Sic transit gloria mundi.*

Come to think of it, he missed Egypt too. His wife, on the other hand, had embraced Manhattan with open arms. The shops. The new friends. Even the cold winters.

You and I, he thought, mentally addressing the obelisk. *Strangers in a strange land indeed.*

He looked around as a yelp disturbed his thoughts.

Something was wrong with Ptolemy.

The dog suddenly uttered a series of shrill cries, and tried to hide behind its owner's legs.

"What's the matter, Ptolemy?" the diplomat asked anxiously. He picked it up. There was no other dog in sight. Just as well. He'd hate to be confronted by a hostile animal with this jerking, struggling little creature in his arms.

But something had frightened the little dog. A smell perhaps? What could have caused this sudden fright? This violent trembling?

What had passed this way, leaving a trace so menacing that the Pekingese

seemed stricken with an uncontrollable
bout of terror?

Hurrying away from Greywacke Knoll,
Mr. Serafin wished that he'd instructed
Bender to wait. As it was, he'd have to walk
home to his apartment on Park Avenue
with the shuddering ball of fur in his arms.
The dog literally shrieked when he tried to
put it down, its hysterical yelping echoing
through the trees.

"It's all right, little fellow," muttered Mr.
Serafin, trying not to trip over the dangling
leash. "Soon be home."

The dog whimpered, burying its head
under the man's arm.

What *had* passed that way?

Mr. Serafin glanced back uneasily at the
obelisk.

Gray and somber, the ancient monument seemed to point upward accusingly,
keeping its own silent counsel.

As silent as the grave.

FORTY

"Hello, Sara." Inspector Potter smiled cheerfully and fell into step with Sara as she walked down West 79th toward Columbus Avenue. "How are you feeling this evening?"

"Where did you come from?" Her face seemed pale to him, tired and drawn, with delicate purple smudges under her eyes.

"I've been waiting for you to get off work. I want to talk to you. Maybe we could get something to eat."

"I've been thinking about Steve all day," she said, "I can't concentrate on anything else." She glanced sideways at him, a worried look in her eyes. "Tell me honestly, what's going to happen to him?"

"Sara, you don't want to think about that," he said firmly.

"But I *do* think about it. I don't want to,

but I can't help it." She began to cry effortlessly, tears streaking down her face. "He was so special. I don't understand why it happened. It's all so crazy."

"Nobody understands." He took a large white handkerchief out of his pocket and handed it to her. "But I do know that anyone can get sick. And that's what he is. Very, very sick."

She stopped suddenly, turning towards him, and clutching his arm. "What will they do to him?"

"Put him away where he can get treatment. Where he can't hurt himself, nor anyone else."

"I don't believe that I can stand it anymore," she said softly. "God knows I'm trying to handle it. Trying to rationalize. But I keep imagining him out on the streets somewhere, confused and afraid. Hunted. Even you're hunting him down," she added accusingly. "Like an animal."

"He's dangerous, Sara. He's killed people. He almost killed you."

"No, he didn't. He hurt me, sure. But he didn't kill me. He still loves me."

"Sara."

"It's true." She shook her head stubbornly. "I can't expect you to understand. How could you? You don't know him the way I do."

They reached the intersection of West 79th and Columbus, and she stopped uncertainly on the corner.

"I don't know what to do. I don't even know who to trust anymore," she murmured softly.

"You've had a big shock, Sara. And I think that it's only just beginning to hit you." He took her arm, gently maneuvering her down the crowded sidewalk towards Ruelle's. "Come on, a nice steak dinner is what you need. Nothing like good food to scare away the cobwebs. My treat."

"How did you ever decide on this place?" She half smiled sadly as they were seated in the sidewalk section of the restaurant. "Somehow I never expected you to be so trendy. This is where all the singles come."

His square-jawed face broke into a pleased grin. "Well, to tell the truth I just followed my nose. Everything smells so good." He looked around the restaurant with interest. "Looks nice in here too. Flowers on the table. Sort of place my Molly would have liked."

"Funny. You know so much about me, but I don't know anything about you. You haven't talked about yourself at all. Who's Molly?"

"Was," he said gruffly. "She was my wife. She . . . died."

"I'm sorry." Sara reached across the table and touched his hand lightly. "I'm so wrapped up in my own problems that I haven't really thought about anything else. It's pretty obvious that you haven't gotten over her.''

''Well, you've guessed right there. Don't want to get over her either.'' He sighed. ''She was the only girl that I ever felt serious about.'' He laughed softly, remembering. ''Funny, really. I'm so large, and she was so small. Dainty. Like you, in a way,'' he added shyly.

''I'm flattered. She must have been special,'' she said gently.

''Yes.'' A faraway look came into his brown eyes. ''I met her at a dance. All of us young policemen used to go to dances at Trenchard House hoping to meet girls. And vice versa, I suppose. I enjoyed those dances.'' He laughed again as memory became stronger. ''You'd never guess to look at me how light I am on my feet. Or was, anyway.''

''I can imagine you being a good dancer. You're a sensitive person in many ways.''

''Well.'' He flushed slightly, toying with his fork to hide his confusion. ''Anyway, Molly came with a friend. She hadn't planned on going out that night, but the friend persuaded her. I saw her standing talking to a couple of other chaps, and that was that. Luckiest night of my life.'' A sad look came into his eyes. ''Sometimes I wonder about her, though.''

''In what way?''

''Well, if she hadn't met me, things might

have been different. She died so young."

"You mustn't think that way. It's too morbid. It could have happened no matter who she married. And she could have married a real bastard." Sara squeezed a wedge of lemon into her glass of water. "Or someone sick. Like Steve."

"Let's not talk about that now." He picked up the menu, scanning it hurriedly. "Come on, Sara. I'm going to order you a big dinner. It's amazing what a meal can do for your spirits."

"And guess what?" she interjected. "I *am* hungry after all."

"Of course you are. Stands to reason, doesn't it? You being in the family way."

"You know, Inspector . . ."

"Call me Ian."

"You know, Ian. You're really an old dear."

He blushed again, clearing his throat. "Well. I hope that you don't mind sitting out here, by the way. Makes it easier for the poor blighter across the street who's been told to follow us."

"Where?" She scanned the opposite sidewalk. A drifting crowd of pedestrians merged and parted in a steady stream. "How can you tell?"

"Oh, I can tell another copper a mile away. I'll have to commend O'Reilly for the competence of his man."

"He won't like that."

"I think that you're wrong there. I'm

sure that he expects me to spot his man."

Her expression became sad again. "I'm so afraid that they'll shoot Steve."

"Sara, he must be stopped. They'll try to apprehend him without any trouble if possible. But I won't lie about it. They may shoot if he attacks first."

Tears appeared in her eyes. "Isn't there something you can do to help? Anything at all?" She wiped her face with effort. "Jesus, I wish I wouldn't keep crying this way. I feel so damn weak. I'm not the crying type, usually."

He looked at her steadily. "I'll do what I can. I promise you that much."

"Oh, God, it's all so horrible. Sometimes I wish I'd never met him. But then I remember how it was before all this mess started. And not knowing whether he'll ever be cured . . . whether he'll ever be my Steve again . . ." Her shadowed eyes took on a haunted look. "How can I go on, day after day, not knowing what tomorrow will bring?"

"You've got the baby to think about, Sara. That's your future. Your hope."

And the immediate future, the Inspector added to himself grimly, will bring the night of the full moon.

FORTY-ONE

Patrolman Anthony Tirelli sat in the kitchen of the small apartment he shared with his wife, chewing on a meat-loaf sandwich. He swallowed a large mouthful reluctantly.

First thing his old lady had done wrong, he thought, was make the sandwich with white bread. If she didn't know by now that white bread was so much crap, it wouldn't do any good to tell her. Crap—unless you toasted it first. Even then.

Thirty years they'd been married, and her meat loaf still tasted like something you'd strap on a horse's back.

"What did you put in this meat loaf?" he asked sarcastically. "Besides sawdust."

"Same as always," his wife answered absently. She had a copy of *People* maga-

316

zine open on the last page. An item about
Bruce Willis caught her eye. She liked
Bruce Willis. He had a nice smile—sweet,
kind of. He reminded her of Mickey
Rourke. He had the same smile, even
when he played that drunk with Faye
Dunaway. She'd walk a mile to see Mickey Rourke. Funny her liking a Mick, and
married to an Italian.

She wondered if Bruce Willis was Irish.
He sure wasn't Italian.

"You put ketchup in it?"

"Ketchup, meat, onions. I don't know.
How come it's so important all of a sud-
den?" She took a long drink from a can of
Pepsi.

"You shoulda tasted my mother's meat
loaf." Tirelli stuffed the rest of the sandwich into his mouth. "Two kinds of sau-
sage meat. Green peppers. Tomato sauce.
You could live off the smell alone."

"Ah, yes. Your mother's meat loaf."

"What does that mean?"

"Nothing. Only your poor father, God
rest his soul, never went to bed without a
dose of baking soda from the first day he
met her."

"That's a terrible thing to say!"

"Oh, sure. How come you can say stuff
about my meat loaf, and I can't say nothin'
in return?"

"My mother was a saint." Tirelli stood
up angrily and put on his uniform cap. "If I

was you, I'd throw that meat loaf out. Just don't let the neighbor's cat get it. I wouldn't want you to be accused of murder."

His wife made a rude gesture as he left. Sometimes she wondered how she'd ever put up with him all those years. Now that the children were grown, she could easily leave and start a new life.

So could he, if it came to that, she thought. But he still kept coming home. Still handed over his paycheck, only asking for coffee money and a handful of small change to buy treats for his horse, Ebony.

She began to clean up the kitchen, hesitating a moment with the plate of meat loaf in her hand. On a sudden impulse, she dumped it into the garbage pail.

No use in forcing it on him. It wasn't that great anyway.

She finished wiping up the kitchen counter, then dried and put away the dishes.

Two plates. Two sets of knives and forks. Two cups. Regular Darby and Joan, she thought, smiling for the first time that evening.

She went into the tiny room they called the den and switched on the TV set. Turning the channel dial, she wondered if they could get another set soon.

A console. She'd seen one at Sears &

Roebuck. All rich-looking walnut wood. Simulated, but what the hell. In addition, it had a remote control. Tony would go for that.

Maybe they could get it before he retired. Wouldn't be long, now, thank God, and then he could come home smelling of something other than goddamn manure.

She turned up the sound. Dan Rather was reading the news, his square, pleasant face serious as he reported the latest information about the fire on Fifth Avenue. Lights still out in the park. For some reason, they couldn't be fixed yet.

She sat back in the recliner, worried lines etched deep in her forehead.

Tony would be patrolling in Central Park tonight. Her heart pattered lightly in her chest.

Of course, except for an occasional dust-up with that drunk they all called Old Bleeder, he never had any trouble. Not often, anyway.

Her hands clenched in her lap.

Nothing would happen to Tony, would it? *Would it?*

Suddenly she felt sorry about the meat loaf. She should have put some more stuff in besides ketchup. Sweet Italian peppers, or something. He liked peppers.

The tears came to her eyes, spilling onto her cheeks, blurring Dan Rather's image on the screen. She felt the first sharp pinch of fear in the pit of her stomach. Why couldn't they catch the madman who set the fire?

A policeman's wife never sleeps easy.

She remembered some smart-alecky neighbor telling her that when she was just a bride.

But everything would be all right, once he'd retired. That's what he'd been working for, all these years. A nice pension. Evenings together, at last.

It would all be worth it, once he retired. Only a few more months, now.

Nothing to worry about, was there?

Was there?

FORTY-TWO

And how do you find our city?" asked
the Mayor's wife, ignoring her husband's
meaningful glare. "I mean, I know that it's
hardly showing its best side at the moment—"

"Not at all," interjected Madame Serafin
tactfully. "I find it totally fascinating." Her
large brown eyes, accented by a blue-
black eyeliner, were filled with a moist
compassion. A simple blunt-cut hairstyle
softly framed the high cheekbones and
slightly elongated nose of a face that
could have been the model for paintings
on a temple wall in Egypt.

"My wife has a sympathetic nature,"
said the Egyptian woman's husband with
a smile. Ramsy Serafin, the Chief of the
Egyptian Mission to the United Nations,
paused as the gold-rimmed dinner plates

were removed from the table. He glanced shrewdly at Theodore Tanner, his small, rather neat features arranging themselves in an expression of concern. "It must be extremely difficult for you at the moment, Your Honor. Such a cataclysmic disruption."

"Only temporarily," said the Mayor icily, trying out a smile. "Nothing permanent, I assure you."

"Of course not," the Egyptian hastily agreed politely. His nearsighted eyes narrowed slightly as he contemplated his guest's dilemma. "Still. One can't help but wonder. Especially in view of the unusual aspects of the situation." He picked up the white linen napkin and dabbed delicately at his mouth.

"Unusual?" Mayor Tanner began to eat the pale lime-green dessert that had been placed in front of him. "Are vandalism and arson so unusual in your country, Mr. Serafin?"

The Egyptian smiled gently. "Well, one hopes not in such a spectacular fashion. Forgive me. I do not wish to pursue so painful a subject out of idle curiosity."

"My husband is something of an amateur Egyptologist," explained Madame Serafin.

"There," said the Mayor's wife eagerly. "Perhaps Mr. Serafin can give you some advice, Ted."

"I don't see how. The suspect is an American, Susan." He softened somewhat. "It's kind of you to be so concerned with our problems, Mr. Serafin. But, as I said, I really don't see . . ."

"I have to tell you that I have some knowledge of this case," the Egyptian said. "Not much, but enough perhaps to help you trap this man before it is too late." His breath came a little fast, and Tanner looked at him sharply, wondering why Serafin seemed so agitated.

Madame Serafin threw down her napkin and stood up gracefully. "Shall we have coffee in the drawing room? We can continue our conversation there." She took the middle-aged American woman's arm, smiling in a friendly fashion. "At home in Egypt we often read our fortunes in the coffee cups. But not, I'm afraid, when our husbands are present." She laughed softly. "They might learn too much about us."

Susan Tanner glanced back at her husband fondly, her fresh, unlined face pink with a shy emotion. "Ted knows all there is to know about me anyway."

Mr. Serafin went over to a small Turkish table by the window, and brought an ornate ivory box over to the Mayor. "Would you care for a cigar, Mr. Mayor? I can assure you that these are some of the finest made in a country that I wouldn't dream of mentioning."

Mayor Tanner smiled politely, holding up his hand. "No, thanks. I'm cutting down. I shouldn't even have indulged in that excellent chardonnay served with dinner."

"Why not? Wasn't it St. Paul who said, 'Take a little wine for your stomach's sake'?"

"Very apt. Perhaps I'm mistaken, but shouldn't I feel surprised at the quotation, and the wine?"

"Ah," said Mr. Serafin, "but I am not Moslem. I am a Copt."

"A Copt?" asked the Mayor's wife. "I'm not sure that I—"

"We are Christian," Madame Serafin said, interrupting. "Copts were among the earliest Christians. And before that—"

"Before that," said Mr. Serafin quietly, "Copts lived and ruled along the Nile in the ancient land of the Pharaohs. We are the descendants of the builders of the Pyramids. Even our Arabic name is borrowed from a Greek word meaning Egyptian. Which is why I may be able to help."

Tanner shook his head impatiently. "All very interesting, but, as I said before, the young man in question is an American. Our Police Commissioner thinks that he is just your average psychotic, if that isn't a contradiction in terms. Anyway, we have an excellent man on the job. Lieutenant O'Reilly. The suspect should be apprehended any day now."

"You seem very sure," said the Egyptian.

"O'Reilly has been in contact with our embassy in Cairo. Of course, it's no secret that the case has some connection with Egyptology. But only in a peripheral way."

Ramsy Serafin's eyes became sharply intense. "The young man was involved in the excavation of tombs?"

"Yes. He is . . . was Professor Peterson's assistant. Perhaps you've heard of this Peterson?"

"I've met him, yes. A very capable man."

"Well," said the Mayor, "apparently the young man was more impressed with ancient Egypt than might be considered normal."

The Egyptian raised his eyebrows slightly, saying nothing.

"The stories in the newspapers talk about a rather nasty murder," said Madame Serafin eagerly.

"Meena," murmured her husband reprovingly.

"No, it's all right," said the Mayor. "There *was* an unusually violent murder, but I won't go into details. I'm sure the press has covered them adequately."

"In spades," Mrs. Tanner interjected with a laugh.

"I thought they'd make more copy out of his shaven head, though," said the Mayor cynically.

Mr. Serafin became alert. "He shaved his head?" he asked quietly. "I had not heard about that."

"But that is nothing out of the ordinary here," said the Mayor's wife. "You should see what goes for fashion in the Village."

"No need to put down the diversity of our city, my dear." Tanner smiled tightly, and his wife shrugged.

"Did you hear what Tanner said?" Ramsy Serafin stood in the middle of the room and watched his wife get ready for bed. "A shaven head. And the newspapers mentioned cannibalism."

His wife sighed with fatigue. "I don't want to talk about that now. It's getting late. Let's go to bed, Ramsy."

"It can't be," he muttered to himself, wringing his hands nervously. "And yet, he is wreaking havoc upon one of the greatest cities in the world." He felt faint. It wasn't possible.

"Who is?" asked his wife, alarmed at her husband's appearance.

"Someone. God alone knows who. Perhaps only a madman. Or perhaps . . . someone who has succeeded at last in using the ancient spell." Serafin's normally healthy tan face took on a yellowish cast. How could it have happened?

As a young man in Egypt, he had dabbled in Egyptology. Filled with an intense desire to know, to understand, his forebears, he had learned to read the ancient hieroglyphics.

At first, he had read only entreaties to the gods for a safe resurrection on the walls of the tombs.

Once, only once, he had seen a Hakau spell that had shocked him with its potential for evil. The tomb had been little more than rubble, the artifacts stolen by grave-robbers centuries before. And the mummy, desecrated and exposed, had long since turned to dust.

But what if one of the ancient priests had succeeded . . . ?

No. His logical mind rejected the possibility. No. Pure evil fancy. It just couldn't be.

But, what if . . . ?

"How could it have happened?" he groaned. Sweat ran down his face in little rivulets.

"Darling, you're ill. Delirious," said his wife anxiously. "You must be running a fever." She tried to place a cooling hand on his forehead, but he pushed her arm away, dark eyes showing the white of terror.

"No. No. My God, can't you just listen to me? There is evil out there. In fact, it would be safer not to go out. You mustn't go out anywhere."

"But darling, I can't stay in all the time. Be sensible. Besides I want to go to that gourmet food place tomorrow. You know, the one Mrs. Tanner told me about. Park 75. Now that I'm pregnant, I seem to have the most exotic fancies." She smiled, trying to cajole him out of his strange humor. But it didn't work, and now she became really frightened. "What is it, Ramsy? Why are you acting so strangely?" She stood up quickly, her face set with unaccustomed determination.

"I'm going to call the doctor," she said firmly.

"No." He reached out and grasped her arm. "No doctor."

She winced in pain. "You're hurting me, Ramsy. I don't understand what is happening."

He let go of her arm and walked over to the window like a man in a dream. The street outside was dark. Dark . . . and threatening.

He felt a fearful helplessness in the face of what he suspected lurked outside. Was it all part of what had frightened Ptolemy in the park? Dogs knew. They could sense things that humans had no idea of.

He remembered the terror in the little dog's eyes. The rush to escape from something unseen but sensed. Or smelled.

Everything that had happened would be within the power of a priest of Hakau. If you believed in that possibility, you would believe in anything.

Well, *he* believed. What had happened at

the obelisk that very morning had been
the deciding factor.

Where else in the whole of Manhattan
would an ancient Egyptian priest go? And
Ptolemy had known.

"There is something immensely evil at
large, Meena. Something evil and uncon-
querable." He shook his head in despair.
"And I don't believe that anyone here has
any idea what they are dealing with." He
turned away from the window and faced
his wife. "I have to make some calls. You
go to bed now. I'll be in later."

"Where are you going?" Her dark eyes
widened in alarm. "Surely you're not going out at this hour?"

"No. I'm just going to telephone someone. I'll be in my study." He paused, his
hand trembling on the doorknob. "I don't
want to be disturbed, Meena."

He hurried along to his study and went
in quickly, closing the door behind him.

Someone had to be told. But who? The
police?

No. They would just laugh at him. Not in
front of him, of course. But certainly behind his back. *Another crazy foreigner.*

No. No. It had to be someone who would
understand. Who would have some knowledge of the ancient ways. Someone who
could help.

He sat down at his cherrywood desk and
snapped on the green-shaded lamp.

What was the name of that man in

charge of the Egyptian wing at the museum? The man who had been so kind as to give him a personal tour, culminating in the spectacular remains of the Dandur temple? He had seen the man's eyes lit with fervor.

Yes. That man would understand. Would *believe*. Would warn.

But what was his name?

He dug into a side drawer, looking for his extensively cross-referenced address book.

Quickly, quickly. Look under *M*.

His small hands fluttered over the turning pages and at last found what he was looking for.

Metropolitan Museum of Art. John G. Brenholt.

Ah, yes. *Brenholt.*

The authorities would believe *him*. The Egyptian flipped back to *B*.

Could Brenholt be persuaded of the nature of the danger at large? He must be made to understand.

Drawing in a deep, shuddering sigh, Ramsy Serafin reached across his desk and picked up the phone.

No answer, of course. The museum had closed up long ago. He left a message on Brenholt's machine, trying to keep his voice as calm and reasonable as possible. Better to explain face to face. He suggested an appointment for the following day, hoping against hope that Brenholt would be free.

Having left the message, he returned to the bedroom. Closing the door quietly behind him, he glanced at his wife. She lay on her side, with her back to him, a silken mound beneath the covers.

"Meena," he said softly.

He stared at her unresponsive back, a sad look in his eyes.

"Meena, I know you're awake." He went around the bed and touched her cheek. "Don't be angry with me."

She rolled onto her back and stared up at him, eyes wet with tears. "I don't know what's wrong with you. Frightening me like that. Weren't you pleased with the dinner?"

"The dinner has nothing to do with it. Everything was perfect. It always is." He stood looking down at her, a worried frown creasing his forehead.

"Well, then I don't understand . . ." she began, somewhat mollified.

"Of course not." He sat down on the bed, next to her, gnawing at his lower lips. "Of course not," he repeated, speaking more to himself.

How could she be anything but confused? He loved his wife passionately. He was proud of her beauty, her gentle nature. She would make a wonderful mother.

Although their marriage had been arranged, he had never been anything but thankful that she had been the one. It had seemed like a miracle that she had shown a reciprocal depth of feeling for him.

He stroked her cheek with the tips of fingers that he willed not to tremble.

He had to protect her. She was so young. *And pregnant.*

She would never understand the danger. Her careful education at St. Clare's College in Heliopolis had prepared her well for her present life. A perfect hostess. None better.

As for any knowledge of magic, no doubt that was restricted to the Arab galla-galla man, with his baby chicks and sleight-of-hand, hired to entertain at children's parties.

What would she know of the black art of Hakau? Or even understand what it could mean?

She stirred restlessly, sighing.

"Ramsy, are you going to stay up all night? What time is it? It must be very late."

Very late. He stood up quickly, murmuring to her reassuringly as he took off his bathrobe.

Tomorrow he would go and talk to Brenholt. If the American curator had spent any time in the Egyptian desert, he might be made to believe the unbelievable.

His wife's breathing steadied, became deeper, as she drifted into sleep. He would have liked to hold her close, to make love to her, to find something real, something tangible to cling to. A feeling of safety in her generous arms.

"Meena," he whispered. But this time, she really was asleep.

"What did you think of them?" the Mayor of New York asked, as he removed his shoes.

Mrs. Tanner sat at her dressing table, cleaning her face with a sweet-smelling lotion from a pink bottle. "I liked the wife. She's a real doll."

"What about him?"

"Ramsy? Well, it's hard to say." She began to remove the lotion with a wad of Kleenex.

"Try."

She turned around on the satin-topped stool and stared at her husband in surprise. "This sounds important. Don't tell me that little man is more than he seems."

"No, no. Nothing like that. He's the Chief of the Egyptian Mission to the UN, all right. No secret stuff. Except . . ."

"Except what? Come on, you can tell me, Ted."

He got up and began to walk about restlessly in his stockinged feet. "Did you notice how nervous he was? The guy looked as though he had an appointment he didn't want to keep. Like a condemned man." He picked up his shoes, carrying them over to the walk-in closet. "I've seen a couple of those in my time. Condemned men, sweating it out to the chair."

"Oh, I think you're exaggerating." She wiped off the last trace of lotion. "He probably felt nervous entertaining the notorious Mayor of New York."

"Notorious?"

"Darling, I love you dearly," she said, getting up and taking off her negligee. "But you do come on kind of strong."

The belligerent thrust of his jaw seemed to soften as he smiled at her. "I guess you do love me at that."

"Of course I do." She got into bed, holding the covers back invitingly. "Did you ever doubt it?"

FORTY-THREE

A fine miasma of smoke still hung over Central Park. The roaring fire on Fifth Avenue three days earlier had polluted the warm humid air, tainting even the occasional cool breeze that swept up from the river.

The buildings destroyed by the fire left a gaping black hole in the otherwise even smile of the avenue. Small crowds stood around looking at the destruction, still excited by the mystery surrounding the fire, and a cruel sense of satisfaction flavored their morbid curiousity.

Menket lay in his leafy ditch, almost in a state of suspended animation. Almost, but not quite.

Thoughts ripped through his mind with knifelike sharpness, and an inward smile warmed his heart as he remembered the museum.

It had been so easy to slip in just before closing time. So easy to smash the cases, eluding the guards who came running at the sound of alarm.

Like a whirlwind among the splintered glass and defiled relics, he had snatched up the flint ritual knife.

How sweetly it fit his hand.

How cool and familiar the ivory handle, nestled in the curl of his skillful fingers.

Others in the chambers, frightened and confused, had run out awkwardly, careening into further displays, until a shouting, scream-filled pandemonium reigned, spreading like a burst dam throughout the main floor.

Menket's face remained tautly smooth, but a mocking laugh bubbled deep in his throat as he remembered.

The knife rested with him, waiting.

Thieves and defilers all, may they rot in the fiery lake of Amduat, the hell that awaits the enemies of Egypt.

His mouth felt dry, his limbs achingly stiff. He felt the hot, binding pain in his bladder, and yet . . .

And yet it was as if the pain happened to another. A dream without substance, that happened in a place without shape.

He sunk deeper into his trancelike state, his mind lulled by the bittersweet memories of the real time.

Are you traveling onward, O Nefrenofret? Has your spirit reached the stars? Away, away. Far from the greedy hearts that stole your rest.

Their bones are crushed by the fearsome wrath of Re, and I, Menket, am become his chief executioner.

He trembled slightly, nostrils flared.

Then, trembling again, he felt the urge to kill start to overwhelm him with its insidious fury.

FORTY-FOUR

Patrolman Tirelli settled comfortably into the saddle.

Like butter, that leather, he thought appreciatively.

Fine night out. Not much smoke left now. Just a touch of it in the air.

Funny about that fire. Papers hinted at arson. A madman on a bare-assed rampage.

TV coverage too. The redheaded witness had looked like she enjoyed every minute of it. Like to investigate her, one of these days. He could show her police procedure all right.

He rode further into Central Park, keeping an eye out for trouble. *Watch out, trouble. That's my middle name. Better believe it. Anthony T. Tirelli. And the T means trouble.*

Yeah.

He felt good. Pretty good shape for his age.

Everyone wondering about the fire, but the facts weren't known to the general public. Not by a long shot.

Captain said to look out for the suspect. Look out, shit. Son of a bitch was long gone by now. Done what he could and run. But I'd better keep an eye peeled. Lot of crazy people out there. Lunatics. Loony ticks.

He laughed softly, patting his horse Ebony on its broad neck. Beautiful horse, muscles like steel.

Beautiful night. Moon full, just about. Everything lit up like daylight, only softer. Soft moonlight, soft trees, soft shadows. Grass like a silvery carpet under Ebony's hooves.

He began to hum softly. He loved this park.

If I weren't so goddamn busy patrolling, I could write a song about it. Sing it too. Tony Bennett, eat your heart out.

A sudden rustle of leaves caught his attention.

Wait a minute. Wait a goddamned minute. Something moving on the ground over there. By the trees.

He touched Ebony with his heel, and the big black horse cantered up over the grassy knoll.

Probably Old Bleeder, he thought with

disgust. Up to his old tricks, pretending to commit suicide. Well, here we go again.

One of these days the old fart will kick off, and I won't have to drag him kicking and screaming into the station ever again.

That'll be the day, all right. Patrolman Tirelli laughed good-naturedly, leaning forward to avoid a low-hanging branch.

The Captain will throw a party just to celebrate the old guy's departure. Send out for beer and pizza. Pizzerina.

There it is again.

What the hell is it? A shadow?

Ebony is nervous. He sees something too. This old horse is like a human almost. Better, even. Feel safe with him anywhere.

He patted Ebony again, then stroked its neck, murmuring reassuringly, "Easy, easy."

A brisk wind started up, rustling the leaves on the trees. He felt the hair stand up on the back of his neck, a chill caress his spine.

I don't like it. No, sir.

That isn't old Bleeder over there, is it? Is it?

He shifted the reins to his left hand, leaving his right hand free for his revolver.

Well, I'm ready for you, shit-bird.

His mouth felt dry, and a pulse beating a devil's tattoo in his temple echoed the heavy thumping of his heart.

"Easy, boy."

He urged Ebony forward, and the animal

whickered quietly, pricking up its ears, chomping at the bit.

Don't want to call the station. Don't want to look like a jackass if it's only old Bleeder. And it could be. It could be. Sure it is.

But it isn't.

No, sir. Too quiet.

Too . . . careful.

Now where's he gone? Must have doubled around behind.

He opened his mouth to shout out a challenge, surprise stifling the words before they could leave his throat.

The dark form fell heavily from the tree above, knocking him to the ground with the force of its descent.

He felt the knife in his gut with a flash of anger.

Oh shit, he thought in the moment before he lost consciousness. *Oh shit. Now I'll never collect my goddamned pension.*

Inspector Potter replaced the phone receiver in its cradle, and turned to Sara as she stood in the bedroom door.

"That was O'Reilly. Steve attacked a mounted policeman in the park."

Sara's face turned white in the lamplight, and she pulled her robe tightly around herself.

"Did he . . . did he kill him?"

"Well, he tried to. Used a knife, this time. But the policeman will live."

"Thank God!"

"It's not going to make much difference, Sara. Except to the policeman, of course. But Steve's still a murder suspect." The Inspector frowned, his normally smooth forehead deeply furrowed. "He's out there somewhere, dangerous, insane. No one is safe until he's caught. Especially you."

"But he didn't kill the policeman." She sat down heavily at the kitchen table. "What stopped him? I wonder. Perhaps he didn't mean to." She looked up at the Englishman, faint hope lighting her face.

"He meant to, all right. A knife in the abdomen isn't just playing pat-a-cake." He went over to the sink and began to fill up the kettle with water. "It'll be dawn in a couple of hours. I don't suppose you'll be able to go back to sleep. I'll make some tea."

"But . . . I must know if he . . ." An unvoiced question hung quivering in the air.

"No. No cannibalism either," he said hurriedly. "The horse saved the victim. O'Reilly says the ground is churned up like a battlefield." He set the kettle on the stove, turning up the gas. "Funny things, animals. Loyal. And horses are almost human. This one's been with its master for a long time, according to O'Reilly. And hooves!" The Inspector pursed his lips reflectively. "Nasty weapons sometimes. Powerful. And sharp as you please." He stopped talking, suddenly realizing the implications of what he'd just said.

"Ian, how long will this go on? Day after day . . . I never know what will happen next." She placed a hand gently on her abdomen. "I wish I could wake up and have it all turn out to be a nightmare." She put her other hand on the table, and wearily rested her head on her arm.

Ian Potter stood motionless by the stove, looking down at her, filled with pity, and another emotion too powerful to acknowledge. For an instant he wanted to reach out and touch the soft, almost childlike tendrils of hair at the nape of her neck.

Pull yourself together, he told himself firmly.

"Don't worry, Sara. Won't be much longer, you know." His voice sounded gruff with uncontained emotion, and she glanced up at him in surprise.

To cover his confusion, he started to make the tea, getting out the cups and the milk, pretending to look for the sugar.

She accepted the cup of tea he handed her, an uneasy frown drawing her eyebrows together. "Why won't it be much longer? How can you be sure?" Fear lit a sudden spark in her eyes. "What do you know that you're not telling me?"

"I don't *know* anything. It's just something that I suspect."

"You must tell me, Ian. If you think that you know anything, it would be cruel to hide it from me." She looked up at him, her eyes clear with determination. "Don't try to shield me from the truth. I've a right to know. I'm carrying his child, remember?"

"Well." He took a sip of the hot tea. Then he put his cup down on the counter. "Look at the calendar." He unpinned it from the wall and set it down on the table in front of her. "See the eye of Horus?"

"It's just a doodle, isn't it? I mean, Steve was always into Egyptian signs and writing right from the first. Does it mean anything?" She took a long drink of tea. "Can you understand what it means?"

"I think so. It means that he's planning something for tonight. I mean the night that's coming up. The night of the full moon."

"But what, for God's sake?" Her cup clattered back into its saucer, and she pushed it away with a shaking hand.

"Well, I'm only guessing, mind. But that papyrus I borrowed from you contains a detailed formula for a ritual suicide."

"Suicide! Oh, no! We must stop him. Please say that you'll stop him!" She looked up at him fiercely, her face white and strained.

He sighed, uncertain of the strange inner feelings that threatened to shake his mental equilibrium. It didn't make sense, really. He was already near the end of the road. Too late to start over under the best of circumstances.

Still, he couldn't help the way that he felt.

Maybe it was because she was pregnant. Maybe because she had spirit, like Molly. And yet, not like her, really.

He sighed again. No fool like an old fool. One foot in the grave, the other one ready to step in, and here I go getting soft on a girl half my age.

"I don't know how to handle this," he said quietly, speaking more to himself than the girl. "I'll do whatever I can. Can't say more than that, Sara. By all accounts, Steve has displayed enormous strength. Completely unbelievable in some instances, until we remember the old maxim that madmen have the strength of ten."

"He's not a madman! He's just ill. Just . . . very, very ill." Her gentle mouth took on a stubborn slant. Before he could stop her she picked up the calendar and ripped it in half.

"No point in doing that, Sara," he said quietly. "Anyway, whatever he is, he's dangerous. I wish that I could pretend that everything will turn out all right. But I can't. You've just got to face it. One thing I am pretty sure of—tonight is the night of reckoning. He'll be caught, or worse."

"You make it sound so damn final!"

"Maybe that's for the best," he said grimly. "It's gone on long enough."

FORTY-FIVE

A shaft of brilliant light struck suddenly out of the night sky, and Menket threw himself down behind a bush.

Above him he could hear the roar of the rotary blades stirring up the wrath of demons.

"Accursed child of Apep," he muttered. "May the hand of Re strike you from the sky."

Men's voices, calling to one another, sounded far off to his right. Listening carefully, he judged them to be near the scene of his battle with the horse.

Despite his wounds, he had left the place of conflict, forced to leave behind his injured prey. Now weakness enveloped him. And beyond weakness, Death beckoned.

His mouth felt dry, and he turned his

head slightly as a breeze flowed over him, carrying the scent of water.

Water, the bearer of Life. Somewhere nearby.

Soon it would be light, and he would be unable to evade the men who hunted him so ruthlessly. He called on Isis to protect him. As if in answer to his prayer, the shaft of light swooped away. The thundering blades veered off toward the main group of men clustered near the edge of the park, leaving the man in the bushes alone in the dark.

His muscles felt fluid and weak. Turning his head again, he could smell the raw, gamy stink of his own blood souring the torn clothes on his back.

He *must* escape. To die here in this accursed place would be worse than the fiery hell of Amduat. His spirit must survive, travel onward, or end in lifeless dust.

Dredging up untapped reserves of hidden strength, he ran, half-bent over, to where he sensed the water lay. Soon he saw it, green and mystical, promising succor from thirst, from pain, from the raging fever that threatened to encompass his weary body.

Stripping the torn clothes off with a heightened sense of urgency, he slipped into the murky water, a ritual blessing from more than a millennium ago on his lips.

Cool water washed the deep cuts and

bruises on his shoulders, soothing the marks of the horse's hooves.

Breaking off a slender reed, he lay beneath the turbid surface of the green-scummed water, breathing shallowly. He rested.

Still his hunger had not been assuaged. Even now his earthly shell felt weakened by the loss of blood.

And soon another day would start.

He dare not rest for long. Cautiously, he raised his head above the water, gulping in great lungfuls of air.

Suddenly, mouth open, he tasted the heavy, sour stink of human sweat close by, and he quivered in anticipation.

Now come, vessel of life-giving marrow. Let my teeth crush your bones, that my flesh may live, and renew itself.

Crawling quietly out of the water, he listened to the sounds in the night. Green scum dripped from his body as he paused a moment to listen again. Then, with a savage growl of ravening hunger, Menket stalked the old man who staggered down the path towards him.

Clutching a brown paper sack containing a bottle, Old Bleeder muttered irritably to himself.

"Sum'uv a bitch shoulda told me." His toothless mouth drooled saliva as he gummed out his anger. "Sum'uv a bitchin' mutha." He stopped dead, caught in a bone-rattling paroxysm of coughing. Heaving his narrow chest, he hawked and spat richly, laughter bubbling as he ground the thick yellow phlegm into the path with his heel.

He admired the effluvia of his body. Loved and reveled in the oozings and secretions that bore the stamp of his very own being. Relished the smells that clung to him, growing richer and riper with every bathless day, like a lusty stew that seasons with time.

How he hated the showers inflicted on him on his enforced trips to the police station.

Who needed 'em? Even his shit smelled like goddamn roses, goddamnit.

"Sum'uv a bitch," he gummed again, weak-jointed knees giving way as he tried to sit under a bush. Scrabbling back under the low, leafy branches, Old Bleeder clutched his precious brown paper sack to his chest.

"Now try me," he muttered. "Now try. Sum'uv a bitch." Still talking to an unknown, half-forgotten adversary, he unscrewed the lid off the wine bottle.

The sharp smell of cheap port permeated the air, and Menket's nostrils flared in anger.

Pure, pure. The victim must be pure. He hesitated, momentarily uncertain. But the growling hunger drove him on, and he swiftly approached the old drunk under the bush.

"No you don't!" Old Bleeder jerked his bottle back under his ragged overcoat. He peered at the man standing still before him. "God awmighty. What'ud you do?" He bent his head forward under the low branches of the bush. "What'ud you do to your face?" He screwed his eyes, trying to see, trying to make out what was wrong.

The green slime clung like a second skin to the fugitive. Almost full, the moon cast its light through the trees, scattering shadows across Menket's face.

"Here," said Old Bleeder in a sudden burst of generosity. "You better take a swig o' this. Sumpin' happen to you?" He held out the bottle, dressed in its drab brown paper. "Go on, take it. But give it back after. I ain't the fucking Red Cross."

Menket's hand stretched out, clutching at Old Bleeder's arm in an iron grasp, and the old man yelped in surprise as cruel fingers dug into his flesh.

"Turn me loose, you sum'uv a bitch!" Frightened, Old Bleeder felt his bladder release the hot urine into his pants, soaking through the ragged coat into the scrubby ground. "Aw *shit!*"

With a sudden violent twisting jerk of his hand, Menket dragged Old Bleeder out from under the bush. With his other hand he pinched the old drunk's scrawny neck.

"Turn me loose," blubbered the old man, trying to struggle to his feet. "God's sake, mister." His rheumy eyes blurred with fear as he tried to twist his head away from the painful grasp. "I'm shitting my *pants*, for Christsake!" He fell to his knees again as Menket let go of his neck.

Sobbing uncontrollably, gasping for breath, Old Bleeder turned his head up toward the man standing over him. "Don't do it, mister. Don't do it."

But he knew it was over, even before he saw the knife.

Hands of stone, tear the sinews.

Teeth of stone, crush the bones.

How sweet the marrow, giver of life and blood.

Now Re, now Osiris, come. Share with me this feast of nourishment, that we may exult in the day of resurrection.

Old Bleeder's head stared sightlessly from its resting place on a smooth rock. His greasy locks framed his grayish-white face, and a collar of blood spread out around the cleanly severed neck.

His torso, devoid of limbs and genitalia, lay in the moonlight at Menket's feet.

With a frenzied snap, Menket cracked the left thigh bone to reveal the marrow, sucking the velvety red jelly in a rage of hunger.

Then, his voice hoarse with blood, he called on the gods to bring strength to his hand, before crushing the skull on the rock with a hammerlike blow.

Like a split walnut, Old Bleeder's skull cracked apart, shredding the thin flesh, and Menket scooped up the brain as it lay quivering in its shell.

Holding up the massy convoluted matter in both hands, Menket raised it high in symbolic offering, before gorging on Old Bleeder's liquor-soaked brain in an orgy of satiety.

Menket's heart pounded as he felt the sacred nourishment warm his body. Life seemed closer, easier to attain. His hands still trembled slightly with the frenzy of remembered hunger. Finally he licked the blood from his fingers, savoring the coppery tang.

Enough. The sun-god Re prepares to traverse the sky in his golden barque, and the light in the east will herald his coming.

Wrapping Old Bleeder's remains in the ragged overcoat, now stinking with urine and excretia, Menket dragged the bundle to the water. Shoving a jagged rock in with the bloody mess, Menket tightened the sleeves in a knot across the top.

Grunting with the effort, he threw the weighted bundle far into the water.

"I am strong again," he murmured in the ancient tongue. He felt calm, the mortal wounds inflicted by the black horse benumbed and ignored. Hunger had been assuaged once more, and his shattered face twisted in a grotesque smile of victory.

The Day is here. Prepare for the journey.

Moving away from the site of Old Bleeder's slaughter, Menket chose a sheltered hiding place under a bridge.

Above him, the sky paled.

Slipping into the water, he lay under the greenish surface watching the pale gold of daylight sift down beneath the scum. The water rocked him gently as he lay motionless, and curious minnows darted nervously at his wounds.

One of his hands held the breathing reed, the other, the flint knife, glistening once more after its bath of blood.

One more deed must be performed. One more ritual, and then . . . Only the gods know for certain the path that I must tread. For I am Menket, a prince of Egypt, and nothing can forestall my passage through time.

One of his eyes burned with a searing pain. Writhing maggots had begun their eager business in the wounds on his shoulder.

Death beckoned, yet he watched its inexorable approach with disdain.

In a few hours now, none of that would matter. The moon would rise again, and already he had begun to soundlessly repeat the incantation for the holy ritual to come.

Very soon now, he would be beyond reach.

Soon the men would find the shell

discarded and lifeless. Only one other soul would be needed to assist him in his journey onward.

With every breath he mouthed the command that must be obeyed if he were to survive.

"Come to the holy ben-ben. Come to the temple of Re." Menket closed his eyes and summoned all his powers.

"Sara, Sara, come . . ."

FORTY-SIX

Something had happened during the night.

Something violent and horrible.

Ramsy Serafin knew it as soon as he opened his eyes.

It wasn't just the sirens that had screamed out their wailing warning sometime before dawn. Nor even the helicopter overhead, circling, circling, like an angry buzzard cheated out of its share of tainted meat.

No. Just a feeling, drying his mouth, turning his hands to ice.

He sat up in bed, hunched down like a sick bird in the woolen robe his wife had insisted that he wear.

"It must be a virus that you've picked up at the UN," Meena said, bustling about straightening the bedcovers. "God only knows what kind of germs the African delegates bring with them."

"Egypt is in Africa," he said dully. "I'm an African delegate myself."

"You know what I mean," she said petulantly. "It's not the same thing at all." She handed him a cup of coffee. "Drink this down, and I'll go and find some aspirin."

He drank the coffee obediently, waiting for the hot liquid to ease the knot in his stomach. "I've got to get up," he said, putting the cup down on the bedside table.

"They can do without you at the UN for one day," she argued, her dark, luminous eyes suffused with anxiety. "The world's not going to come to an end just because you take the day off."

"I have an appointment . . ." he began, not quite truthfully.

"Break it," she said firmly, then bit her lip, as though surprised at her own temerity.

Despite his agitation, he smiled at her, amused. What a mother she would make. "No, Meena. This is too important. Nothing to do with the UN." He hesitated a moment. "As a matter of fact, I called someone at the Metropolitan Museum last night. Before I came to bed."

She looked hurt. "You didn't tell me."

"I didn't want you to be worried."

"But you *did* worry me. I could hardly sleep all night."

He smiled again, remembering her

steady breathing the night before. "Perhaps you should rest today. Let one of the servants do your errands."

"You just want me to stay home."

"That's true. Will you do that for my sake?" he asked gently.

"Such a fuss over nothing. I don't feel like going out anyway." She left the room to find the aspirin, and he leaned back against the pillows, sighing with relief.

Am I being foolish? he wondered. *After all, this is the twentieth century.*

But not in Egypt. Not in the ancient tombs.

Still. After all the years. After all the thousands and thousands of years that had passed like falling grains of sand in an hourglass.

Still the tombs lived, the colors bright, the hushed interiors filled with an atmosphere that tugged at the sensibilities. Dragged the imagination back through centuries upon centuries to the time when it all began.

Having seen them once, he could never forget. They were his heritage, the blood-line drawn with a steady finger through magnificent history.

He had always known, always felt a kinship with the majestic stylized figures adorning the ancient walls with details of their lives.

Cities and towns rose and fell. Built again and conquered. Raised and razed and raised again.

But the tombs in the desert lived on, eternal.

Even as a child, he had been enveloped in a deep sense of mysticism on seeing the tombs. A feeling that if he shut his eyes tightly enough, and wished hard enough, he would find himself back in ancient Egypt.

A childish fancy. But what if someone had managed to do the opposite?

He threw back the bedcovers, anxiety chilling his hands again, filling his bladder.

He couldn't confide in Meena. She would never understand.

But perhaps, somewhere among the thick foliage of Central Park, hidden, evil beyond any mere imagination, waited someone who would.

The curator of the Egyptian wing at the Metropolitan Museum of Art looked up with ill-concealed impatience at the dark slender man standing in the doorway.

Place was getting to be a regular zoo. How was he expected to take care of the mess in the Egyptian section, when he kept getting interruptions like this?

If people didn't leave him alone to do his job, he'd have to set young Miss What's-Her-Name to guarding the door.

"Can I help you?" His truculent expression belied his offer of assistance.

The man edged into the room. Dr. Brenholt noticed with some surprise that the visitor's face seemed tinged with yellow and bathed in sweat. He looked ill. Or scared to death.

Either alternative could be termed unwelcome at that moment as far as Brenholt was concerned. He just didn't have time to deal with any more visitors. He picked up his phone, but before he could dial his assistant's extension, the visitor spoke.

"I called you last night, Dr. Brenholt. I left a message for you on the machine." Ramsy Serafin pointed at the Duofone on the desk.

"Oh, was that you? I'm sorry, I just didn't realize." He stood up then, holding out his hand. No good alienating someone from the UN. Especially an Egyptian. Who knew what favors might have to be asked of the Egyptian Ministry of Antiquities. So many things to be replaced. "Won't you come in, Mr. Serafin?" What ailed the man? His hands felt like ice. "Would you care for a cup of coffee? Tea?" What the Egyptian really looked in need of was a stiff drink. Maybe two. But perhaps black coffee would do the trick. "Please sit down, and tell me what I can do for you."

"I've come . . ." The Egyptian paused, moistening his dry lips. Before continuing, he looked around at the chair, then sat down. "I must speak with you on an urgent matter."

"Please proceed."

"I've checked up on you, you know,"

began Mr. Serafin quietly, almost as if talking to himself. "I wanted to be sure. A man in my position can't risk ridicule of any kind."

What the hell was the Egyptian diplomat talking about? Dr. Brenholt began to feel uneasy. His visitor didn't look dangerous exactly. But his words did make him sound unbalanced. Perhaps the shock of finding out about the vandalism had caused some kind of a nervous breakdown. After all, the loss of irreplaceable Egyptian artifacts must have seemed like a deliberate insult to his country.

"What do you know of the art of Hakau?" asked Mr. Serafin suddenly. "The formula for rebirth and resurrection in particular."

Brenholt stared at the Egyptian in surprise. "Funny you should mention that. Someone came in only the other day with a most interesting papyrus on that very subject."

Ramsy Serafin's mouth dropped open in surprise. "Who . . . who was it?" he asked.

"Someone from Scotland Yard, strangely enough." Brenholt paused thoughtfully. "Maybe not so strange, after all, eh, Mr. Serafin?" He stared at the Egyptian from under a deeply furrowed brow. "I think you'd better tell me what's on your mind."

Mr. Serafin got into the gray limousine waiting for him at the curb outside the museum. He felt slightly relieved, although the danger wasn't over yet.

Just as he'd expected, Dr. Brenholt hadn't believed that the horror in the park came from ancient Egypt. Perhaps that would be too much to expect, even from someone so knowledgeable about the history of that country.

But at least he had been able to impress upon the curator that an attempt to perform an ancient ritual at the obelisk could take place that very night. If the American chose to believe that the man responsible for the vandalism and murders only imagined himself a priest of Hakau, so be it. At least he had been warned, and would, in turn, warn the police.

Mr. Serafin's eyes caught those of his chauffeur in the rearview mirror.

"Where to, sir?" asked his driver. "The UN building?"

"No." No use going there. He wouldn't be able to concentrate on anything for the next 24 hours.

And Meena might decide to go out, after all.

He stared blankly out of the window as the limousine pulled out into traffic on Fifth Avenue. The once-beautiful stretch of fashionable buildings looked like the aftermath of a holocaust.

"Take me home," he said, his voice barely above a whisper. "And you can take the rest of the day off. I won't be leaving my apartment tonight."

FORTY-SEVEN

Sara stared down at the papyri spread out on the worktable. The colorful hieroglyphics seemed to be dancing across the crisscross grain of the ancient material until she wanted to scream at them to stop.

Shouldn't have come in to work today, she thought. *Not today, of all days.*

She felt lightheaded. *God, don't let me faint. I never faint. But then I've never been through anything like this.*

Pull yourself together. Think of the baby.

No! Don't think of the baby.

Who said that? Was it me?

Now I'm hearing voices. Oh, God, don't let me be crazy too.

She looked down at the papyri angrily. *God, I'd like to tear it up and scatter the pieces out of the window.*

Everything had been great before Steve went to Egypt. Then everything turned to shit.

"Shit!" She spoke the word aloud, her voice harsh with anger. Unshed tears stung her eyes as she remembered all their plans. She had been so proud of Steve. A budding Egyptologist—after all his other jobs, all his other false starts.

But something terrible had happened out there instead. Something powerful enough to shatter all their plans. And rip apart their lives, while it was at it.

She looked at the papyri again. The bright colors took on an evil caste, the painted figures somehow threatening.

A random thought came to mind, and fear clutched at her throat. *Oh, God. Supposing it's some kind of curse? What was that man's name? Howard Carter. And all the others who helped him discover Tutankhamen. Didn't they all die mysteriously?*

Or did that story turn out to be just a figment of someone's sick imagination? Just like Steve imagining that he was being taken over by the spirit of . . . of . . .

She could hardly bring herself to say the name. It hung on her lips like a vicious epithet, until she finally spat it out. "Menket!"

Quick as a flash, she heard her own name whispered softly in the empty room.

"Sara-a-a-a-a."

No! She squeezed her eyes shut and covered her ears with her clenched fists.

"Sara! What's the matter with you?"

"Nothing. Nothing." She ran a hand through her short hair, forcing a smile as she looked up at the woman in the doorway.

"Well, I don't know. You look sick to me. Would you like to go home?" The woman's eyes looked worried behind her thick lenses.

"No. I'm fine, really. I mean it." Sara smiled again, trying to control her trembling lips. "Did you want something?"

"I came to see if you want to come with us."

"Where?"

"Lunch. We're going to the park. Did you bring anything to eat?"

"No." She had left the apartment in a daze. Food had been the furthest thing from her mind. "Damn. I'm hungry too."

"I've got enough, if egg salad is okay."

"If you're sure."

"Of course I am. Come on, don't be long. We'll be waiting downstairs."

How could she be doing this? Eating lunch in the park, talking with friends, just as though nothing were wrong.

Just as though Steve wasn't crazy and deluded enough to try suicide.

Maybe I still don't believe it. Maybe it'll hit me later on and then I'll fall apart.

But I mustn't, for the baby's sake.

What was it Ian Potter said? The baby is my future. Well, it's going to be Steve's future too.

Suddenly she shivered.

Someone's walking on my grave, she thought.

She shivered again.

Lieutenant Patrick O'Reilly put a fork into the boiling pot of water, and scooped out a single strand of spaghetti.

"Well, how is it?" asked the woman setting the table. Small and plump, with fair hair pinned up in a knot, she moved gracefully between the counter and the table in the middle of the kitchen.

"Al dente, what else?" replied her husband.

"That's what I like about you, Pat. So damn predictable." She turned back to the kitchen sink and began to wash the lettuce, smiling to herself. She sliced the cucumbers quickly, sleeves rolled back to show the smooth round curves of her arms. A good-natured, pragmatic woman of 40, she knew that she could be described as plain. But O'Reilly had liked her from the first. Not that he ever said anything. And God knows you couldn't read it in his face.

But Rafaela knew, and was content.

O'Reilly drained the spaghetti and emp-

---

tied it into a bowl. He tasted the Bolognese sauce appreciatively, then poured it over the spaghetti.

"Okay. Let's eat. I don't have much time. I have to get back to the station after supper." He began to uncork the bottle of wine. "I hope you're good and hungry."

"I am." She hesitated a moment, not knowing how to broach the subject on her mind. "You haven't said anything about this case you're on, Pat. Some of the people at work were discussing it."

"Some things are best left unsaid." He poured a glass of wine and handed it to her. "Too many people involved as it is." He tasted the wine in his glass, nodding slightly. "You picked a fine bottle of wine this time, Rafaela."

She blushed warmly. "But still, it's only human to be curious. And that fire on Fifth Avenue. It's not exactly the usual homicide."

Lieutenant O'Reilly allowed himself a slight smile. "No, not the usual." He buttered a roll carefully. "There's even a detective from Scotland Yard on the suspect's trail."

"What! You've got to be kidding. That's the most exciting thing I've heard all day. D'you think he'll catch him?" She glanced at her husband quickly. "Oh, I'm sorry, Pat. I didn't mean—"

"It's all right. Scotland Yard sounds glamorous next to us. But this old guy's a has-been. Came over on his own hook. No authorization of any kind." He paused, a forkful of spaghetti on its way to his mouth. "Still, he *is* tenacious. Like an old hound dog." He chewed the spaghetti reflectively. "You have to admire him, in a way. He followed the suspect here from London."

"He won't hurt the investigation, will he?" Rafaela got up to turn on the coffee-pot.

"No. He's a good detective. Knows his stuff, and always goes by the book. Don't worry, I made some inquiries." O'Reilly took a drink of wine. "The only thing that is going to get hurt is my pride. I can't help thinking that somehow he is way ahead of me. And I can't let that happen, can I?" He finished the wine in his glass. "No. I can't let that happen under any circum-stances."

"So how was it last night? How did you make out with that new broad at the office? The one with the big tits." The foreman sat on a five-thousand-year-old pedestal and picked his teeth with a broken matchstick. Small and wiry, with stringy gray hair, he had small eyes, which added to his overall weasel-like appearance. "What was she like? Any good?"

The younger of the two welders, a dark kid called Al, looked up and grinned. "Why

don't you find out for yourself, old man?
Or won't your old lady let you?"

Joe, the other welder, guffawed loudly,
then hawked and spat on the polished tile.
"His old lady won't let him do nothing," he
said knowingly. "Like she's taken a vow or
something."

The foreman flushed angrily. "Watch
your mouth, asshole." He got down off the
pedestal, his metal heels scraping the
delicate sandstone. He walked over to a
large stone sarcophagus, staring in mood-
ily.

Nothing but a goddamn morgue, he
thought uneasily. He glanced at his watch.
He could almost taste the cold beer waiting for them at Arnie's Bar & Grill. And
Arnie would have the balls racked and
waiting too. He swung around quickly,
walking over to the two welders. The dark
kid was lighting up his torch.

"Let's pack it in, Al," the foreman said
impatiently. "This Egyptian shit gives me
the creeps."

"Just gotta do this frame," Al answered.
His torch flared suddenly, scorching the
wall behind him. "Shit. Did you see that?"
He pushed his mask back and stared at
the wall in surprise, just as another burst
of vivid blue flame shot across the room
to engulf a discarded pile of paint-
spattered drop cloths.

Within seconds, the flames spread to
the ceiling, burning out the lights.

"Move! Move!" yelled the foreman.

"Christsake, the whole fucking museum is going up."

Purple twilight slowly evaporated in the deep canyons of Manhattan, and the long evening shadows lazily stretched their fingers into Polly Winslow's rococo bedroom. She was ensconced for the night in her large ornate bed, but her carefully massaged and moisturized face wore her usual full complement of makeup.

"If I should die before I wake," she was frequently heard to say, "the last thing I want to look like is a goddamn ghost."

Now she rang for her maid, Renée. "For heaven's sake turn on the lamps," she told the aging woman. "It looks like a morgue in here. And if Dulcie's client calls again, tell him I'm out." She frowned peevishly. "No, no. Better not say that. Just think of something clever to say."

As if on cue, the phone rang shrilly. Renée picked up the receiver, listening intently.

"It's him," she mouthed silently.

Polly closed her eyes with exasperation, and leaned back against the lace-trimmed pillows.

"I can't bear any more of this," she said irritably. "I don't know what to say to the man. What on earth did Dulcie do to him anyway?"

The maid stared at her with worry, her hand over the phone's mouthpiece. "Do you want me to put him off? Say that you're too sick to speak to him?"

"God knows that's the truth." Polly sighed. "My head is killing me. No, I'll speak to him. But I can't help him. None of the girls want to go out with that madman still at large. And I don't know *where* Dulcie is. I told Raul that she wasn't trustworthy. Here, give me the phone."

She took the phone from her maid, a conciliatory smile smeared like jam across her painted mouth.

"Hello, *darling* . . ."

About a half a mile away, at the southern end of the park, a quiet clearing had settled into its cloak of darkness.

Soon, now, the moon would rise, full and round, to cast its light on the sepulcher of mud and leaves that sheltered the rotting remains of Dulcie Bennett.

Something had disturbed her shallow grave. Something with claws and sharp, pointed teeth, drawn to the site by a tantalizingly tainted odor, sweet and rotten in the warm night air.

Digging feverishly into the soft dirt until it found the half-crushed bones, the decaying shreds of flesh.

Digging and tearing, until a tattered remnant of white satin fluttered like a ragged flag in the breeze, waiting for the moon to highlight its message of defeat. Of surrender.

Of final, violent death.

FORTY-EIGHT

"Try to eat something, it'll do you good." Inspector Potter stared with concern at Sara's untouched plate of food.

"You sound like an English nanny." She smiled wryly, pushing the plate away. "Isn't that what nannies say? Finish your peas or whatever?"

"I never had one, so I don't know. The closest I got to a nanny was the time one clipped me on the ear for bumping into her little charge. Proper martinet she was. Anyway, I'm just concerned that you're not eating anything. The baby needs food too, doesn't it?"

"Look," she started irritably. "I can't eat, and that's that." She saw the shadow of hurt in his eyes and reached over the table to lightly touch his hand. "I'm more grateful than you'll ever know. If it weren't for you—''

"Well.'' He stood up awkwardly and stacked the plates. "I don't feel like eating either.'' He glanced at his watch. "It's almost time to go.''

"You haven't told me where yet.''

"Not far from here, Sara.'' He turned on the kitchen faucet and filled a glass with water, drinking it down slowly. "You'd better get ready if you're so dead set on going.''

"I've had a weird feeling all day. I know he's thinking of me. Wants me to help him in some way.''

"Could be,'' he agreed cautiously.

"I mean, even when I was in the park with my friends, I thought that I heard him call me. Heard him calling, over and over, Sara, Sara.''

He rinsed out the glass and placed it on the drain board. "I understand how you feel, but I really don't want you to come with me, Sara. I mean it. I just wish you'd let me handle this on my own.''

"No.'' She shook her head stubbornly. "We've gone over this all evening. If you don't take me, I'll only follow you, and then O'Reilly's man will know where you are going too.''

He spoke patiently, trying to make her understand. "Whatever happens, it's not going to be something you'll want to see. This isn't going to be pretty.''

"You're underestimating me again. I saw what his craziness made him do." She swallowed convulsively. "Damn it, I *felt* what it made him do, didn't I? I just want to salvage something of the old Steve, if I can. The one that I love."

The Inspector sighed with resignation. "All right, then. But first we have to lose O'Reilly's man. Go comb your hair or powder your nose or something. We're going out to dinner."

"What?"

"That's what we want them to think, Sara, if we're to get to Steve first. I'm not promising anything, mind. But if I can, I'll talk him out of suicide."

"And if you can't?"

"Then I'll detain him. One way or the other, this will be the end of the road for Steve."

She winced, almost as though he'd struck her. "Don't say that," she pleaded. "You promised to help."

"I shall. But for God's sake look at this realistically. It's not just the murders. He's made you a captive too. You can't get on with your life until he's put away. You can't even go out of your house without someone watching your every move. It's just not good." He stared at her unhappily, hurt by the pain in her eyes. "Go on, Sara. Get ready."

She turned away from him silently and went into the bathroom, fumbling in her purse for the tube of lipstick. She propped up the Inspector's shaving mirror, and began to apply a touch of lipstick to her mouth.

Jesus, what am I doing?

She stared at herself in the mirror with blank eyes. Quickly putting the lipstick back in her purse, she left the bathroom without looking at her reflection again.

I don't feel anything, she thought. *Nothing. Maybe I've OD'd on pain, or I'm in some kind of shock.*

Tonight Steve is going to try to kill himself, and all of a sudden, I can't feel it.

She walked back into the kitchen. "I'm ready," she said quietly.

Something had happened.

Small groups of people stood clustered near the intersection of Columbus Avenue and West 80th. Most of them were looking in the direction of Central Park, an almost tangible feeling of excitement prodding their curiosity, surrounding them with its electricity.

The Inspector recognized the owner of the grocery store on the corner. "What's going on?" he asked her.

"The Metropolitan Museum is on fire," the woman answered. She shrugged slightly. "No one knows too much about it, except that they're keeping everyone out of the park."

The Inspector grabbed Sara's hand and

started to run across the street. He headed for a police car parked near the middle of West 79th.

"What does it mean?" gasped Sara. "It can't be Steve."

"I don't know what it means." The Inspector felt the familiar tightness in his chest. "That's why I'm going to ask someone in the know."

They reached the squad car just as it was going to pull out into traffic. Flagging it down, the Inspector held up his identification. "Scotland Yard," he said hurriedly. "What's happened?"

"Fire at the Metropolitan. Started by a welder's torch"—the car began to pull away—"in the Egyptian wing. No one allowed in the park because of the possibility of looting." The police officer quickly drove off, sirens blaring.

"A welder. Well, at least that's nothing to do with Steve." Sara couldn't hide her relief. "Nothing to do with him."

"Maybe not." The Inspector waited a moment, catching his breath. "Funny, though. I mean the fire being in the Egyptian wing."

"Funny nothing. They had to make repairs and it must have just happened. An accident, that's all."

"You don't think it's strange that tonight of all nights no one is allowed in the park? Pretty convenient fire if you ask me," he said grimly.

"We're not going to find out anything if we stand around here."

"You're right. Come on, then." He slipped a firm hand under her elbow, guiding her through the crowds on the sidewalk.

"What I'd like to know is how he did it," said Lieutenant O'Reilly, his voice dangerously quiet. All hell had broken loose as the fire raged on. "The bastard couldn't have gone for something small, like the craft museum on West 53rd. Oh no. Had to be the goddamn Metropolitan. All or nothing. That's what our boy Harrison is like."

"You can't be sure that it's Harrison," Detective Sergeant Schwartz argued. "Even the welders said that it was some kind of crazy accident."

"Accident my ass. And what about the vandalism? As soon as I heard that the museum guards had reported seeing some guy with a shaven head, I knew. Why wasn't I told about that sooner?"

"Christ, Lieutenant. No one thought Harrison was involved. No one was killed. Only a bunch of cases smashed. Pots, statues broken, stuff like that. And those kids running wild. No one investigating the vandalism saw any reason to bother Homicide. There's no connection, believe me."

"I'll be the judge of that." O'Reilly stared coldly at the younger man. "We had new descriptions of Harrison posted everywhere. If you'd been doing your job, those guards would have been looking at mug shots before the dust settled." He jerked his chin at the front of the museum, where a harried group of officials were packing up the priceless artifacts brought out earlier. "They're not getting anything else out. When this is over, they'll have to start from scratch." He paused gloomily. "And you and I'll be pounding a beat in Brooklyn if Harrison isn't caught."

He started to go back to his car, when a police officer came up accompanied by an official from the museum.

"Just a minute, Lieutenant," said the officer. "This man has some information you ought to hear."

"Lieutenant," said the middle-aged man from the museum. "My name's Brenholt."

"Are you going to tell me where we're going?" Sara asked.

"We're going to take some evasive action to lose the man that's tailing you. It won't be easy. But if you do exactly as I say, I think we'll manage it."

They walked down the avenue for a few blocks, buffeted by the crowds on the sidewalk. The Inspector could sense the other man's presence, but he didn't turn around to make sure. He didn't stop to look in shop windows either. A dead give-away. If he and Sara started window-shopping, their tail would know that the game was up.

He remembered an old maxim taught him years ago when he was just a rookie, full of vigor and hopelessly wet behind the ears.

Always assume the worst.

Well, this *was* the worst. For the first time in his life he felt like a lawbreaker. Everything he planned on doing tonight could be considered to be outside the law. Only the apprehension of Steve Harrison could justify his actions in the end.

But what had happened to going by the book? He smiled grimly to himself. He'd thrown that away long ago. Right after they'd told him to take it easy. Easy be damned. Let *them* try it.

His eyes scanned the restaurants, looking for the one he'd noticed two days before. He'd taken the precaution of going in and getting acquainted with the waiter. The Inspector believed in preparation.

The faroff sound of fire trucks played an eerie accompaniment to the snatches of conversation about the disaster at the museum that was on everyone's lips.

He could feel Sara tremble every time she heard Steve's name. She'd have to get used to that, he thought bleakly.

They began to pass a Thai restaurant.

"Wait a minute, Sara. Let's go in here."

The Inspector pushed open the door to the restaurant and escorted her inside. "Make it look good," he said quietly, after they had been seated. "Take your time, and study the menu."

"I feel so nervous," she whispered.

"Relax. You're not breaking any law. Not yet anyway," he added gruffly.

Outside in the street, lights from the heavy traffic masked the darkness.

"Is O'Reilly's man out there?" Sara didn't want to look. Picking up the menu with trembling hands, she pretended to study it. After a disconcerting moment she realized that she was holding it upside down.

"Don't turn it around," the Inspector murmured hastily. "Just put it down after a while, and then go to the ladies' room."

"But I don't—"

"Don't argue, just do it. But move casually. He's watching us. Wait for a knock on the door. It'll be me."

He half rose politely from his seat as she got up from the table. As he resumed his seat, he pretended to continue to study the menu. Out of the corner of his eye he saw her pause a moment and tell the busboy to fill the water glasses on their table.

Good girl! He watched surreptitiously as she moved unhurriedly to the back of the restaurant.

Okay. Now it's my turn, he thought. Better do this right.

Calling over the waiter, the Inspector ordered two drinks. Slipping the waiter a ten-dollar bill, he gave the man an unusual, specific order, then sat back and waited.

He didn't have long to wait.

The Oriental waiter showed no emotion as he brought two drinks on a small tray back to the table. Placing the drinks on the table, the waiter turned to go back to the bar. As he picked up his tray, he allowed it to knock over Inspector Potter's glass, sending a scotch and soda down the front of the Englishman's pants.

"Oh, terrible, terrible," the Thai said loudly, dabbing at the damp cloth with a napkin.

"It's quite all right. Just tell me where the restroom is." The Inspector got up heavily and went to the back of the restaurant, led by the waiter.

He tapped on the door of the ladies' room, and Sara came out quickly.

"I thought you'd changed your mind—" she began.

"Never mind that. Let's hurry. The waiter will let us out through the back door." He winced as he felt the beginning of tightness squeeze his chest. "Come on."

They half ran past the grinning cooks in the steam-filled kitchen. As the waiter held open the door for them, the Inspector handed him two more tens, pulling Sara by the arm into the alley.

"What about the policeman in front?" asked Sara breathlessly.

"He's good, so it'll only take him a

couple of minutes to figure things out. Maybe less. So we must hurry."

Racing clumsily down a side street, they reached Central Park West in time to see the full moon rising above the trees.

"Oh, God! Are we going to make it?" Sara gasped.

"We'll make it." The Inspector gritted his teeth as the pain in his chest grew stronger. His legs felt heavy, dragged down by weights.

Shouldn't have run, he thought desperately. *You bloody fool. You should have sat back and let O'Reilly handle it. Too late now. The lieutenant is probably at the museum sniffing around for any sign of Steve Harrison. Probably bring out the bloody SWAT team. Shoot a tourist.*

Well let 'em. It'll be over soon enough.

But first Sara's going to get the chance to confront Harrison.

Best thing for her. Get that madman out of her system, once and for all. Then I'll get the bastard.

Oh, God, it hurts, it hurts.

In front of the Thai restaurant, Sergeant Johnson couldn't risk waiting any longer. A sick feeling in his gut told him he'd lost them.

You goddamn asshole, he swore as he ran across the street, *the old limey outsmarted you.*

He collared the waiter just inside the

door. "Where'd the old guy go that was at that table? He had a girl with him."

"They left," said the waiter, shrugging slightly.

"Whad'ya mean, they left?" Johnson glared at the Oriental furiously. "What kinda games you playing?"

"No games." The waiter grinned widely, yellow teeth as square as tombstones. "Business. The big man gave me thirty bucks, cash. Big tipper." He laughed happily, showing his teeth again.

"Which way did they go?" Anxiety made the sweat bead across his forehead. "C'mon, c'mon, I don't have all day."

"You his friend?" asked the waiter shrewdly. "Maybe I shouldn't—"

"Police." Johnson flipped out his badge, glaring at the Thai. "Don't stall, buster, or you'll be in a world of shit."

"I don't know where they went. They run out the back door."

Johnson rushed through the kitchen, dodging a plate-laden busboy and two of the cooks. The back door stood open, letting in a cool breeze from the alleyway. Except for a trash can or two, it was empty.

"Ah, shit," muttered Johnson. They must have slipped out a good five minutes earlier. It had all looked too smooth, he should have guessed it was just a setup. Ten to one they were headed for the park. Well, they wouldn't get very far. How was he going to break the news to O'Reilly?

He'll kill me, he thought gloomily, remembering the lieutenant's icy-green stare.

"Where's the phone?" Better get it over with.

"You got twenty-five cents?" asked the waiter. "No money, no calls."

"Regular little banker, ain't you, pal?" growled Johnson. "But you're out of luck. This is police business, and if you don't quit stalling, I'm gonna book you as an accessory."

"To what?" yelped the waiter, alarmed now.

"I'll think of something," said Johnson, reaching for the phone.

Over to the east, an angry red glare stained the sky, and the air felt heavy with smoke.

The Inspector paused a moment, holding Sara by the arm. This was going to be harder than he'd thought, and God knows he hadn't expected it to be a piece of cake.

"Just a minute," he muttered, breathing carefully. "Got a stitch in my side."

Sara stared at him anxiously, and he nodded at her reassuringly. "Okay. Let's go."

The police had blocked off all entrances to the park, and the Inspector pushed past a crowd of onlookers to get to a barricade.

A police car pulled up alongside them.

"Everything's off limits in this area. Get back on the other side of the street now!"

"That's all right, officer." The Inspector took out his identification. "Scotland Yard, special assignment. Miss Fenster's my assistant. I'm after the arson suspect."

"Well, I don't know." The policeman looked doubtful.

"I've been assigned to Lieutenant O'Reilly, Homicide."

"O'Reilly? Oh, okay. He's at the museum. Need a ride?"

"No, thanks. My driver's coming along in a minute." The Inspector's voice sounded forced. He could barely get the words out. A sharp pain ran along his jaw like an excruciating toothache. "We'll be fine," he managed to gasp.

"Well." The policeman still looked doubtful, but a call from his dispatcher sent him speeding off toward the museum.

A distant explosion from the other side of the park gave the Inspector the chance he'd waited for. Everyone's attention seemed to be focused on the sudden eruption of noise coming from the museum.

"Come on," he muttered, grabbing Sara's arm. "Let's go."

Somehow they made it into the park without any further challenge.

Too easy, thought the Inspector. A crazy thought entered his mind unexpectedly.

Could all this be part of a plan?

He dismissed the thought irritably.

Don't you go believing in supernatural powers, or we'll never make any sense out of it.

"Where are we going?" Sara gasped as they stumbled up a grassy hillock.

"Almost there. Wait a minute." He hurriedly shook out two pills from the bottle he carried in his pocket. Swallowing them with some difficulty, he leaned against a tree and caught his breath.

"You're ill," said Sara anxiously.

"Doesn't matter. Must go on." He glanced up at the sky. How beautiful the moon looked.

We're all crazy, he thought suddenly. *Running around like bloody idiots.*

What does it all mean? The moon keeps on waxing and waning, and we're down here killing each other as fast as we can.

"Just tell me where he is. You stay here if you must, just tell me!" Sara clutched at the lapels of his jacket, standing very close, and his eyes stung at the unexpected contact.

Sentimental old fool. He took a deep, shuddering breath. "Come on, then."

"Where to? Tell me where."

"There." He pointed ahead. She turned, looking in the direction he indicated, and saw the ancient Egyptian obelisk rising as straight and slender as a ladder to the sky.

Dark green bushes, clustered like an uneven barrier, hid the base of the obelisk from view.

Sara hesitated, staring at the monument. "Are you coming? All of a sudden I feel so damned afraid of him."

"With good reason," ground out the Inspector. His heart still thumped erratically in his chest, but he could breath, walk, run if necessary. If that's what she wanted.

Should have brought a gun, he thought wearily. What good am I to her like this?

But he'd never used a gun. Never once in all these years. Never wanted to, never needed to. Not even when the others had started.

Time you retired, copper, he thought with disgust. *You're out of step with the times.*

Sara looked at him pleadingly. "Ian, what's the matter? Can't you make it?"

"I'll make it."

The ground felt slick and wet, as though even the grass was invested with a demonic determination to trip them, slip them up, and send the pair of them sprawling in the shadows.

Low scrubby bushes blocked their way, talonlike twigs catching at their clothes, tearing at their faces.

Evil, thought the Englishman suddenly. *I can smell it, feel it, almost as though it were a tangible being.*

Instinct told him to turn and run. Stop the girl before it was too late, and drag her kicking and screaming away from whatever waited beyond the bushes.

It wasn't too late to call O'Reilly. This called for a younger man anyway. But he couldn't do it. Couldn't back down now. Not when he'd come this far, and the whole sickening mess was about to reach its conclusion.

He had to see the murderer for himself. Come face to face with the man who'd led them all such a merry chase, killing and mutilating on a whim.

And not just killing . . .

Pushing ahead of Sara, the Inspector used his bulk to hold back the bushy branches. Looking across to the base of the obelisk, he felt his heart pounding again.

Where is he? He started to move closer for a better view.

Then he saw him.

"My Christ," muttered the Englishman. "My Christ Almighty."

"What is it, Ian? Can you see him?" Sara had come up close behind. He could hear her gasping as she tried to catch her breath.

"Don't go any further, Sara. Stay back, for God's sake!" He tried to block her view, holding his arms outstretched on either side. "Come away! Something's wrong."

"Steve!" Sara bent over and ducked under the Inspector's arm. She banged her hip against a bench and fell to her knees, crying hysterically. "I want to see him. Oh, God! Don't try to stop me, Ian. I've got to help him!"

She scrambled to her feet, and the Englishman caught her by the elbows, pulling her back against him.

"Wait. For God's sake wait. There's something very wrong."

He stared at the naked form standing with arms raised in transfixed homage to the ancient obelisk.

The muscular body gleamed white in the moonlight, the shaven skull as bleached as bone.

But there was something else.

Something about the head.

A wound. Gaping sickeningly where the horse's hooves had cut into flesh at the neck, sliced into tendons and muscles deep enough to show the ridge of bone.

More raw wounds shredded his shoulders, long, ragged strips of flesh turning a crawling, putrid black in the pale light from the sky.

Suddenly the still figure turned towards them, and they recoiled in horror. The left side of his face had been caved in, and a glistening eyeball dangled loosely on his bloodied cheek.

Sara's agonized scream pierced the silence like a violent blow. Animal-like sounds tore uncontrollably from her throat as she struggled to escape the

Englishman's restraining arms.

"He's hurt! Oh, Ian, he's dying. Let me go to him!" She swung around to face the Inspector, pummeling him with her clenched fists. "Let me go! Let me go!"

"No, wait, Sara," The Englishman said urgently. "For God's sake look at him. Look at his wounds. There's something terribly wrong." The Inspector felt his flesh crawl. The man they stared at was already a corpse. Only a shadow of life separated him from death. "Sara, look at him again. Is it . . . is it Steve?"

Something in the Englishman's voice made her stop fighting him. She searched his face for an instant, then quickly turned back to stare at the man at the base of the obelisk.

With an awkward twisting motion, the naked man jerked backwards, slamming against the edifice. Trying to get up, he fell again, this time sprawling on the stone base and striking his head on the sharp edge.

A blood-curdling shriek exploded from the injured man as fragments of torn flesh fell away, sticking to the ancient stone.

"Oh, God," Sara moaned. She turned back to the Englishman, burying her face in his shoulder. "Oh, Ian, help him. For God's sake help him."

"Sara! Run!" She whirled at the sound of Steve's voice. He took a step in her direction, a look of agonized despair on his tortured face. ''Sara, if you love me, run as far away as you can go!'' He fell to his knees, and in that instant something picked him up like a rag doll, dragging him back to the obelisk.

He twitched convulsively, then lay still.

''Is he dead?'' Sara's voice trembled with fear.

''He's not dead,'' answered the Inspector grimly. ''Look at him. It's the other one.''

The man at the foot of the obelisk raised a shaking hand to the ancient stone, caressing the words of worship. Getting to his feet, Menket stretched both arms towards the girl, a bitter smile like a gash across his face.

''Come Sara,'' he coaxed. ''Come join me at the holy temple of Re.''

His words hung in the air for a long moment.

''Who are you?'' Sara whispered at last. A heavy stink of decay seemed to permeate the night, sweet and rotten, filling their nostrils until they could hardly breath.

She shuddered uncontrollably, pressing back against the Englishman.

''Who are you?'' echoed the Inspector. He stared at the naked man, now standing rigidly, flint knife in hand. ''In God's name. *What are you*?''

''In God's name?'' Menket laughed harshly, the hollow sound mocking the beauty of the night. ''What do you know of gods?'' He gestured at them disdainfully, the knife in his hand a magnet for the moon's silver light. ''You live in a world of wonders that defy imagination. Yet you have nothing. Lost, all is lost. What do you know of the ancient mysteries that enshrouded the beginning of Time with magic and love and beauty?'' His other hand quickly felt for the pulse at his throat. ''I pity you.''

''I don't see much beauty in what you've done,'' the Inspector said grimly. ''And you're the one that's going to die.''

''Who can tell? Does not the buried seed of grain sprout when the time is right?''

Sara opened her mouth to cry out again, but the Inspector pulled her back close to him, covering the scream with his hand. ''Don't try to stop him! He has to go. For Christ's sake, let him go, Sara. Steve doesn't exist anymore.''

The Englishman could feel the girl's heart pounding like a wild animal under his arm. The sound of sirens came nearer. O'Reilly must have figured something out.

The Inspector looked up at the sky. A thin curtain of smoke drifted across from the museum. Beyond it, the moon shone full and calm. What would he tell O'Reilly?

What the bloody hell would he put in his report?

Worry about that later. He was his own man now anyway.

Like a streak of lightning, the knife

flashed quickly, and Menket sank to his knees, dimly outlined in the shadows at the base of the obelisk. The strands of smoke seemed to cover the face of the moon, then evaporate before its cold light.

"He's gone," the Inspector said gruffly, after a moment. "It's done with."

He felt the sobbing girl relax against him. Then stiffen quickly in sudden surprise.

"Sara, what is it? Are you all right?"

She put a hesitant hand on the soft, warm swell beneath her heart.

"The baby," she moaned softly. "Oh, my God, oh, my God. *I felt the baby move!*"

"EVERY TIME I HEAR THAT SOMEONE HAS BEEN UPSET BY SOMETHING I'VE WRITTEN— IT REALLY CHEERS ME UP!"

—SHAUN HUTSON

THE MASTER OF SHOCK HORROR